F
HAL

Hallinan, Timothy.

The bone polisher.

$21.50

DATE			

THE
BONE
POLISHER

TIMOTHY HALLINAN

THE
BONE
POLISHER

WILLIAM MORROW AND COMPANY, INC.

NEW YORK

Library of Congress Cataloging-in-Publication Data
Hallinan, Timothy.
    The bone polisher / Timothy Hallinan.
      p.   cm.
    ISBN 0-688-10345-6
    I. Title.
  PS3558.A3923B66   1995
  813'.54—dc20   94-41316
                                                                  CIP

Printed in the United States of America

First Edition

1   2   3   4   5   6   7   8   9   10

BOOK DESIGN BY CLAUDYNE BIANCO

FOR MUNYIN CHOY, MUSE

ACKNOWLEDGMENTS

Conventional wisdom says that writers work alone, but most of the writers I know have more support systems than the average intensive-care unit. I'm no exception. This time around, I'd like to thank:

Bob Mecoy, for being the editor every writer deserves.

Marvin Klotz, for enlightened criticism at a time when I needed to hear it. It hardly hurt at all, Marvin.

The members of Shonen Knife, for all the good energy.

A whole lot of people in Bangkok, Thailand, including the staff of the Tawana Ramada Hotel and all the folks at the Tip Top Restaurant who wouldn't let me pay for my Diet Cokes.

Nicki Heriton, for the guys in the plaid shirts.

I HAVE NEVER LIKED ANYONE AT FIRST
SIGHT.

—W. SOMERSET MAUGHAM
The Summing Up

ONE

EVERYBODY
LOVED MAX

YOU KNOW THE SHERIFF HAS HIS PROBLEMS, TOO,
AND HE WILL SURELY TAKE THEM OUT ON YOU.

—WARREN ZEVON
"Muhammad's Radio"

PROLOGUE
MAYBE NEBRASKA

THE Farm Boy looked no more than seventeen as he bent over the table. He had hair the color of corn.

Dearest Max, he wrote. Then he leaned back and fished a package of cigarettes out of his shirt pocket and lit one. With the cigarette in his mouth, he looked older.

The room was just a room, one in a series of rooms. If he'd closed his eyes he couldn't have said what color the walls were. The low table, with its stack of white paper, was the only piece of furniture. The Farm Boy was sitting on the floor.

Thank you for writing me such sweet letters. I really can't tell you how much they mean to me, here in this wilderness. Just to know there is someone I can talk to. After all these years, even though I'm only seventeen.

He tapped ash from the cigarette onto the floor and laid

the butt on the table, the coal hanging over the edge. The table was striped with burns, long worms of dark wood. Without thinking, he ran his fingernail down one of them. His nails were long and well kept, and he scraped charred wood beneath the nail.

"Shit," he said, staring at the nail. Then he scrubbed it clean on the carpet and picked up the pen again.

Do you remember Nester in the story of the Trojan War? He guided the young men, gave them his wisdom before

He glanced at the book that lay on the floor beside him and swore softly, then scratched out *Nester* and wrote *Nestor* above it, and continued where he had left off:

they went into battle. That's what I hope you will do for me. Prepare me for the battle to come. I'm not sure I have the strength or wisdom to pre

He closed his eyes for a moment, and then wrote:

vail.

Please, Max, write me again soon. You don't need to send me the photo you promised. Your words tell me all I need to know about you. You are good and kind. It doesn't matter how old you are.

I want to come to you, but first I want you to write me again and tell me what kind of boy you really want. Tell me everything. If I am not right for you, I don't want to push myself into your life. I need your help, but I don't want to hurt you. If I think I can be good for you, I'll call to see if you can send me money for the ticket to Los Angeles you promised me. It costs $650, and cash would be best. I am enclosing the gift I promised so I can recognize you at the airport. It belonged to the uncle I told you about, the only one who understood.

He laid down the pen and picked up two silvery metallic objects, which he clinked in the palm of his hand like small change. He dropped them to the wooden surface, beside the letter. Then he took another puff from the cigarette and put it back on the edge of the desk.

Oh, wait, I had to change my post office box because someone saw me there today and I've told you how people talk here, so I'll have to drive into Kearney to get your next letter. Here is the new box number.

He wrote a nine-digit number quickly, without referring to any of the papers in front of him. Then he signed it:

Hope to see you soon,

Philip

"Oh, boy," he said. He crossed out *Philip* and wrote *Phillip*.

The Farm Boy leaned back and read the letter out loud and then reached for a clean sheet of paper to copy it over. He lifted something, a small white paperweight, from the white rectangular stack before he took a sheet, and then he replaced it, dead-center. The paperweight was a human finger, boiled to the bone.

1
THE BOOK OF LOVE

"**IF** he can see the future," I asked, "why does he need me?"

"He doesn't think he needs anything," the young man on my couch said with exaggerated patience. His calm was a cracked shell he was trying to hold together from the inside. "That's why I'm here."

Beneath the baggy expensive clothes, the young man on my couch, who had identified himself as Christopher Nordine, was the kind of thin you don't want to be. I could have closed my fingers around his wrists, and his knuckles bulged like walnuts beneath the pale, papery skin of his hands.

"I don't understand," I said, giving patience back. "You just want me to talk to him?"

A hand went to his slicked-back brown hair, touched it,

and then left it alone. "Well, he won't listen to *me*. We've been fighting night and day."

"About something he should be able to see in the future."

He made a soft sound, like *"peh,"* dismissing the future.

"Maybe he's right," I said. "Maybe he doesn't need anything."

Nordine lifted his hands slowly, as though the gesture hurt the muscles in his back, and rubbed long bony fingers over his eyelids. "Let's say he is," he said from behind his fingers. "Still, it'll make me feel better."

He'd placed a bottle of Evian water on the table—my table, in my living room—and he took his hands from his face and raised the bottle to drink. The October heat was beating its wings against the uninsulated walls of my little wooden house in Topanga Canyon, and the temperature indoors had to be ninety-five, although Christopher seemed to have cooled it somewhat. The growing stack of very odd mail on the table— mail sent to me by dozens of companies whose computers had inexplicably decided I was about to be married—was curling at the corners. A bright brochure advertising HONEYMOON HEAVEN had slipped limply to the floor, belly-up, and gone flat. Even the rug was hot underfoot.

"Are you sure you don't want to take off your jacket?" I was wearing a T-shirt and running shorts, and I was pouring.

"It's wool," he said, giving it a tug. "It breathes."

"I'd have to hear that from a sheep. It looks hotter than hell to me."

"I haven't been hot in more than a year. I'm too skinny to get hot."

I didn't say anything.

He shook the bottle—only an inch or so left—and looked irritated. "So," he said, gathering his calm around him again, "will you do it? I'll pay you five hundred."

"Money's not the issue. And if it were, it'd be because five hundred is too much."

"You don't know Max," he said. Christopher Nordine looked to be in his middle thirties, with thinning straight coffee-brown hair and odd pale eyes that had heavy rings under them. There was a crustiness over the skin of his eyelids, as though he hadn't washed them when he woke up. His eyes, oddly deep set and restless, skimmed the room, my face, the room again, failing to find anything to hold them. He had a high-ridged, narrow nose and a sharp, wide mouth. He hadn't shaved in a couple of days, and the whiskers had come in patchily, heavy at the tip of his cleft chin and lighter on his cheeks. Some sort of heavy cologne rolled off him in waves. Thirty pounds ago, he would have been handsome.

"No, I don't," I said. "More water?"

His sparse eyebrows went up inquiringly. "Have you got Evian?"

"I've got more Evian than the source," I said. "Someone brought me three cases of it."

"He must be fond of you."

"It's a she," I said, "and the fondness comes and goes."

"Ah." He didn't sound very interested. "And whose fault is that?"

When I don't expect a question, I'm usually stranded with the truth. "Mine."

"I know all about that," Nordine said with sudden bitterness. "I could write the book."

" 'The Book of Love,' maybe. Remember that?" I got up and went to the kitchen, a depressingly short walk, and threw open a cabinet. I had half a loaf of stale bread, two dusty cans of tuna, and thirty-six bottles of Evian, courtesy of my ex-girl-friend, Eleanor Chan, who had recently been trying to get me healthy. Again. " 'Chapter One says you love her, love her with all your heart.' "

" 'Chapter Two, you break up,' " Christopher Nordine sang with perfect pitch, " 'but you give him just one more start.' "

"I don't think that's it," I said, toting a full bottle back into

the living room and trying to stay upwind of myself. I needed
a shower. He took the bottle eagerly.

"I hate oldies anyway. I'm getting to be too much of an
oldie myself." He drank.

"Oh, yeah," I said. "You're what, thirty-three, thirty-
four?"

He took the bottle from his lips and smiled, not a pleasant
smile. "I'm twenty-seven," he said.

As hot as it was, I could still feel my face burn. "Oh," I
said.

"Twenty-seven, going on dead," he said.

It was terrible, and it was probably true, but it was also
self-consciously dramatic, and I realized that one of the reasons
I was resisting Christopher Nordine was that I didn't like him
very much. But it wasn't the only reason.

"I still don't really understand what you want me to do."

His eyes gleamed, and I saw what was wrong with them;
he'd lost the fat that cushioned the eyeballs, and they'd sunk
back into his head, too far back for normal eyes, where they
glittered like water down a well. He was burning his own body
for fuel.

"I live with the man," he said fiercely. "He's seventy-seven
years old, and he's living like a fool. He's going to get himself
hurt or killed."

"Living like a fool," I repeated.

"Picking up street boys and taking them in. Haunting AA
meetings and adopting heroin addicts. Turning the house into
the gay *pound* or something. They get food and clothes and, and
support, and clean sheets, and he doesn't really care if they steal
his stuff. He sleeps with them in the *house,* for God's sake. And
he fights with me when I try to tell him he's going to get hurt
some day."

"Maybe he likes heroin addicts," I said. "You know, they
sit still. They're like furniture most of the time, not much trouble as long as they can—"

"They're trash," he said, and he said it in two syllables: "trayush." It wasn't the first time I'd heard the extrasyllabic extravagance of the South in his speech. "He thinks he can save them. He thinks he can"—he lifted the bottle to his lips again and drank, the knobby Adam's apple bobbing up and down— "save everybody."

What the hell. "And you're jealous."

He threw me a scornful look over the edge of the bottle. "Give me a break," he said. "I'm the only one he loves. He's already told me that I'll inherit everything."

"But he won't listen to you. Why?"

"He's seventy-*seven*. He won't listen to anybody."

"But if he knows it pains you—"

"You bet it pains me. He takes them in, he pours money over their dirty little heads, he tries to get them straight, find them jobs, give them a future. They take his credit cards, they use his ATM cards for booze and drugs. They steal his jewelry, his furniture, and when they've gotten everything they can, they split. They rob him blind. They break his heart."

It was actorish, but the rage behind it was real. I cleared some of my extremely peculiar mail away from the middle of the table to make room for him to put down the bottle and to let a few neutral moments ground the electrical charge in the room. "Hearts aren't that breakable."

"There are hearts and hearts," he said, drinking. He put the bottle on the table and picked up a flyer. INSURE YOUR LOVE, it suggested in magenta letters.

"Seventy-seven's old for you," I said neutrally.

He raised his eyes from the flier, sat back on the couch, and gave me the cave-dwelling stare. The suppressed rage blossomed behind it, like a campfire. "And?"

"And you're the legatee."

"I . . . already . . . told . . . you . . . that," he said, coming to a complete stop at the end of each word. "Twice."

"And they're bleeding the estate."

"You're an asshole," he said. He started to rise.

"Sit down," I said.

He ignored me, working on getting to his feet. He seemed to have to test each joint individually to make sure it still worked. "I don't know what your problem is, but I haven't got time for it. I offered you five hundred dollars—"

"Which is about three hundred too much."

"*Fuck* the money," he snapped, standing. "I came here because I'm frightened. I'm scared for him. And you think—"

"So convince me otherwise." I was still in my chair.

He started to pace. "What do you think I'm going to do? Take the money and live happily ever after? Finance a new career? Start *over* somewhere?" He waved an arm, and the flyer skittered out of his hand like an aeronautically challenged paper plane and crash-landed on my dreadful carpet. "Who do you think you're talking to, Methuselah?"

"Okay, then tell me what you're afraid of."

"I'm afraid one of them is going to *kill* him, that's what I'm afraid of."

"But," I said, just trying it on, "he can see the future."

"Yeah, sure. About everyone but himself. The first time he saw me, he knew I was sick. He knew it before I did, but about him, he doesn't know whether the paper will come in the morning."

"And he took you in," I said, "knowing."

He started to say something and then he blinked rapidly and turned it into a long exhalation. "He took me in," he said.

"And you."

"I love him." There was nothing dramatic about it.

I loved somebody, too, but Christopher was apparently better at it than I was. "I don't know what you think I can do," I said, "but I'll go see him."

2
BLUE SKY

"YOU'RE the boy Christy sent." Max Grover looked down at me through the screen door.

"That's me," I said, junking my mental image of the man Christy wanted to protect. I hadn't figured he'd be six feet six or something, nor had I expected the trimmed, cloud-white beard and sky-blue eyes, a color scheme he was keeping intact by wearing a loose, long blue shirt with the sleeves rolled up and creased, spotless white trousers. He was tanned, broad-shouldered, and barefoot, and he had one long brown hand wrapped around a large lemon.

"I must say, you don't look very dangerous." The eyes were not a fool's eyes. They were, if anything, amused.

"Yeah, well you're not what I imagined, either."

"A psychic should be more . . . elfin," he suggested, watching me. "Small-boned and bigheaded, like the aliens people keep showing pictures of to Robert Stack." He snapped the screen with his forefinger, making a little cloud of dust. "Are you disappointed?"

"I'm not much of anything," I said.

He closed his eyelids for a moment and then reopened them and peered at me a little more closely. The amusement had dipped beneath the blue surface. "The danger is there, though," he said. "It runs through your veins, like a heavier blood. I wonder what brings it to the surface."

This was not going as I'd planned.

He must have seen something in my face, because he said, "Control is an illusion. You must know that by now."

"I gave up on control years ago. Now I settle for not being bewildered."

"Can I help?" It was a serious question.

A car passed behind me on the street, Flores Street in West Hollywood, dragging a wake of heat behind it. "Well, you can tell me why you have a lemon in your hand."

He looked down at it and then showed me a row of straight teeth that looked white even in the white beard. "Come in," he said. "Have some lemonade."

He led me through a perfectly restored craftsman's bungalow, circa 1918—high ceilings, white walls, bleached oak floors, and broad arches leading from one room to another. I'd once heard a real-estate agent say that a house had "flow." Max Grover's house flowed like the Mississippi.

I waited in a small book-lined room while he squeezed lemons in the kitchen. He'd never laid eyes on me before, but he trusted me alone in his house. A cut-crystal bowl filled with antique roses scented the room, Mozart's concerto for flute and harpsichord cooled the air, and I indulged a private vice: I absolutely cannot be left in someone's library without checking out the titles. Max Grover had assembled a serious trove of religion and metaphysics: three biographies of the Buddha, a translation of the Dead Sea Scrolls, the Book of Urantia, whatever that was, the *complete guesses of Edgar Cayce*, several feet of baseless speculation on the pyramids, Robin Lane Fox debunking the Bible, a well-thumbed copy of the Book of Mormon, and at least two thousand more. I was leafing through Doré's illustrations of Dante, hunting for the popes in hell, when Max said: "Here we are, then. Find anything you like?"

I turned. "Robin Lane Fox, in a pinch."

"A cynic. But you'd have to be, wouldn't you? With your job." He was carrying a white wicker tray with two tall glasses of lemonade on it.

"But which came first?" I asked. "The cynicism or the job?" I didn't get many chances to talk to psychics. Especially not for free.

"Our primary characteristics preexist us," he said, as matter-of-factly as someone else might have said, "Hot, isn't it?" and lowered the tray on a small wooden table. "But you're the kind of cynic who develops it late in life, who grows—or rather, shrinks—into it. The *better* kind of cynic."

"Which is?"

"A disappointed romantic, of course. You knew the answer to that. Have a seat. Take the soft one, the one nearer the window. At my age, it's wise to keep the back straight."

I sat on, or partway through, an old leather armchair that threatened briefly to let me sink all the way to the floor. Max Grover lowered himself precisely onto a wooden chair with a high, slatted back and combed clean fingers through his beard. Closer up, the skin around his eyes was deeply lined, slices of white cut into the tan of his face. He wore three ornate rings on his right hand: two turquoise in silver and a snake's-eye agate.

"Christy is excitable," he offered, putting an end to the preliminaries. "It goes with youth."

"He feels you're in danger."

"We're all in danger."

"I had something a little less cosmic in mind." The lemonade was tart and heart-clutchingly cold.

He shrugged and turned the sky-blue eyes on me. "While there are homosexuals—and heterosexuals, too, of course—who derive sexual excitement from danger, I'm not one of them. I don't think it matters *how* we die, do you?"

"For a couple of minutes, it might."

"After seventy-seven years on this earth, I'm not going to worry about a couple of minutes. Old age, according to Charles de Gaulle, is a shipwreck. After you've been through a shipwreck it's hard to hang on to your worries."

I thought about all the intensely worried old people I knew, people who tiptoed from room to room behind locked doors and lowered blinds, people afraid to go to the supermarket, worried about the young strong ones who might snatch their empty purses and break their brittle arms. Tall, lithe, ramrod-straight, and trusting, Max Grover wasn't much of a fit.

I sipped my lemonade. "He says you're picking up trash."

"Trash." He laughed. "A vivid word, but just a word, and it means whatever Christy wants it to mean. Words are so useless when things matter, as I'm sure you've discovered in your investigations. We've debased them so. The plumbing in my bathroom is called *Ideal Standard*. Now surely that's an oxymoron. Unless it's a tautology. Meaninglessness isn't one of my fields. And anyway, trash is such a *southern* notion, don't you think? Christy brought it with him from Arkansas. Remember 'white trash'? And he's forgetting that he was trash himself not so long ago."

"Was he?"

"Christy was not above the occasional sugar daddy, and he stole from them in exactly the way he accuses my young visitors of doing. Did it twice, in fact."

"And you knew that when you—" Something moved somewhere in the house. "When you, um . . ."

Grover was looking straight at me, but part of his attention was directed toward the noise. "Brought him home. Certainly. Christy's previous, ah, flame introduced him to me, right after he bailed him out."

"Doesn't sound like much of a favor."

He shrugged, and a long loop of steel chain—a necklace of some kind—worked its way between the open buttons of his shirt. He glanced down at it and tugged it back inside. He also wore two delicate gold chains, and the heavy steel looked odd and out of place. "Christy's had a difficult life. He grew up gay in a wretched little southern town without another homosexual in sight, although I'm sure there were plenty hiding behind their big cracker faces and their Rural Delivery plaid shirts. The pressure in that sort of situation is terrific. He had a kind of breakdown in his second year of junior college and just took off for New Orleans." He gave me a beatific smile and reached up to slip a finger through the steel chain and lift it free of his neck for a second, as though he wasn't yet used to the weight of it.

"New Orleans must have been more congenial."

"I should say so. He landed a job in the Mardi Gras industry. Worked for a man who owned a float and costume business." Max's voice was as deep and sonorous as a Gregorian chant. "They struck up a relationship, and Christy became the man's accountant. That's what he'd studied in college, accounting, until he suddenly couldn't make anything add up. Numbers, life, sex, anything at *all*. When things went sour with the man in New Orleans, he embezzled eighteen thousand dollars, bought an airline ticket for Chicago, and took the bus to Los Angeles."

"That shows a certain flair."

"He'd seen it in a movie. He's a hopeless criminal."

I remembered belatedly that we were supposed to be talking about Max. "And when he got here, he did it again, and you—"

"Well, actually, he lost all his money first. He got—do people still say 'ripped off'?"

"I guess."

"Well, that's what happened, so I suppose it was a sort of poetic justice."

"How?"

"He wanted to be a movie star. He and every other young faggot with a dimple in his chin." He smiled broadly, watching me trying not to react. "It's all right. Gays can say 'faggot,' but I wouldn't sling the term around if I were you. He got an agent, got some pictures taken, and—are you ready for this?—got the lead in a movie."

He was looking terrifically amused. "It sounds way too easy."

"Well, of course, it was." He drank deeply and then gave a faint shudder. "I take it without sugar. It's more intense that way. The older I get, the more intensity I desire. Since one only has so much time left, it might as well be intense. There's not much that one can do about the length of time remaining, but the *depth* can be adjusted. But about Christy. Of course it was too easy. It was a sucker trap, and he was the sucker. They had a script, a director, a star. All they needed was the completion bond."

"Which cost?"

He leaned toward me. "Guess."

"Eighteen thousand dollars."

"Every dollar, and the wallet it was in. Then they closed the office and disappeared. Christy found out later that the script was a translation of a cheap Mexican vampire movie called *Sangre de Muerto*. We saw it on television one night, right here in my living room, in fact. He was *furious*." He laughed again.

"And he couldn't go to the cops."

"Certainly not about *that* money." The laughter deepened, and I heard someone move, possibly in the kitchen.

"Are you alone here?"

"Except for you," Max said serenely. "Old houses make meaningless noise, just as old men do." He toasted me with the lemonade. "So Christy was stranded in the big city, with nothing. And an older man, not as old as I am, but old enough, as they used to say, to know better—"

I had an eye on the door into the hallway. "They still say it."

"Thank you. They say 'There's no fool like an old fool,' too, and they're absolutely right. Anyway, the older man took him under his wing, and Christy decided to go into the antique business. With the older man's antiques. And went to jail."

"And with this curriculum vitae, you took him in."

He looked down at his glass and rubbed his index finger around its rim. "One doesn't choose whom one will love."

"No," I said, "but one can avoid stepping into a hole, can't one?"

"Are we talking about Christy or the new boys?"

"Chris is worried about the new boys. And now I see why."

He looked at me. "Did you choose whom you love?"

This was not on my agenda. "Not very well, apparently."

"She'll come back to you," Max Grover said.

"I know," I said impatiently. "Nostradamus predicted it."

He gave me a little chug of a laugh. "Disappointed romantics."

I felt stung. "And you're a satisfied romantic."

"I do what I can. I've been fortunate, you see, and so many haven't. Sometimes I help one way, sometimes I help another. I like to think that the ones who steal from me are helped, too."

"I'm sure you do."

He refused to take offense. "You think it's self-delusion, and you're probably right. At my age, no one else is going to take the trouble to delude me—at least, not romantically—so I have to do it for myself. Besides, I derive a certain almost sensual pleasure—nothing to start a war over—from doing favors for people. And, since I am Not As Other Men, I tend to do my favors for young men. How can they hurt me? I don't own much. This house, which I bought thirty-five years ago, a few books—"

"They can hurt you," I said. "For example, one of them could decide to cut you open."

"And steal what? A year or two, after I've lived seventy-seven of them? Small change. And anyway, that's not going to happen." He gave me a benevolent smile. "Why did she leave you?"

"I screwed around. I'm a jerk sometimes. Listen, Max—can I call you Max?"

"I can't think of a better name. And believe me, I've tried."

"Your desire for intensity can get you killed."

"I'm safe," he said. "But you're in peril."

I ignored it. "Whatever you get from these kids can't be worth the risk."

"What I *get*?" He pointed a finger at himself. "You think I sleep with them?"

"I don't know," I said. Of *course* I thought he slept with them.

He laced his fingers together over one crossed knee and sat back a good half-inch. There were long ropes of muscle in the tan forearms. "Well, I do. But that's all. Two heads on the pillow, maybe a little buddy talk before the light goes off, someone to squeeze an orange for in the morning. But sex, never. I just want to help. I thought you understood. I'm in love with Christy."

I started to reply, and he said, "That was tactless of me."

I'd missed something. "I beg your pardon?"

"Your relationship. You were in love, but that didn't keep you faithful."

"It takes all kinds," I said. I was suddenly as hot as the day pressing itself against the windows.

"You were unfaithful because you were afraid of being in

love," he said. He looked past me, at the rows of books, and grinned. "Love is nothing to be afraid of, you know."

"We're not talking about—"

The grin broadened. "Most men your age don't blush so easily."

"Yeah, well, I've got a lot to blush about."

"A blush is just the higher nature showing through."

"Poking its big fat nose in," I said.

"The higher nature is always with you. All of you is always with you, the little dirty secret things and the big grand ones, too. Whatever snapshot you think you're posing for at the moment, it's all with you."

"Max," I said, "if you want to keep all of you with you, stop picking up street kids."

"I'm safe," he repeated.

"Christopher doesn't think so."

Max drained his unsweetened lemonade and gave me an encouraging look. "Maybe Christy knows more about what kind of danger I'm in than he told you."

It wasn't the first time he'd surprised me. "I considered that."

"A cynic like you, I'm sure you did."

"And I didn't know then that he had a lifetime habit of ripping off older men."

"Well, now you do."

I replayed my conversation with Christopher Nordine. "I think he cares about you," I said.

"And so do I, about him. But a sociopath—you know about sociopaths?"

"I've met a few."

He beamed at me. "Interesting, aren't they? They can hold two completely conflicting views simultaneously. Like politicians. Or saints."

"The multiple murderer Emil Kemper," I said. "Talking to the psychiatrists, he said, 'When I meet a pretty girl, part of me is saying what an interesting girl. I'd really like to get to know her. And part of me is wondering how her head would look on a stick.' "

"I don't think Christy wants to see my head on a stick," Max Grover said seriously.

"Probably not. Emil Kemper was a special guy."

"But still, let's say Christy wants to kill me. Let's say part of him says, 'Oh, I love Max. He's been so good to me.' And another part of him is saying, 'That disgusting old man, there's nothing but his rotting body between me and his money.' "

"You don't believe that."

"Of course not. But think about it. First he hires a detective to tell me that my life could be in danger, and then he kills me. A self-fulfilling prophecy. Like most prophecies, actually; prophecies are no big deal. Makes him look good, wouldn't you say?"

"Especially since he'd be the obvious suspect."

"The will," Max Grover said. "He told you about the will?"

"First thing."

"Very prompt of him. A bit Victorian, the will. Still, people have killed for less."

"But, as I said, you don't believe it."

Grover rattled the ice cubes in his glass and pressed its sweating surface against his cheek. "Not at all."

"Then why bring it up?"

He wiped the moisture from his cheek and dried his hand on his blue shirt and smiled at me again. "I'm just having fun," he said. Then he reached out the bejeweled hand and tapped me on the knee. "I see a wedding in your future."

I fingered the ring in my pocket. "You certainly do," I said.

3
POINT-BLANK
LOHENGRIN

WEDDINGS seemed to be the theme of the day.

I'd grabbed the latest batch of mail on my way down the driveway to the car, and I thumbed through it as I sat outside Max Grover's house, waiting for a breath of relatively cool air to bumble into the car through the open windows. It came as no surprise that marriage was a profitable enterprise for what economists like to call service industries—travel agents, department stores, florists, insurance companies—but I'd never realized what a boon it was for paper manufacturers and four-color printers.

YOU TIE THE KNOT, WE'LL GIVE THE BASH, prodded a group of professional merrymakers based in Santa Monica, couching their message in words of one syllable, thoughtfully printed in type big enough to read through cement. People of many ethnic backgrounds and several religions celebrated with decorous abandon in the accompanying color photographs. In one shot, the female guests were wearing saris: market research at work. YOUR MARRIAGE WILL LAST FOREVER, predicted another brochure optimistically; SHOULDN'T YOUR PHOTOS? This one was hawking a sort of stainless-steel album that would preserve the visual record of your nuptials against fire, flood, earthquake, and, by implication, atomic attack. A third, less romantically, urged me to give thought to a prenuptial agreement. "All of us at Schindler & Spink share your joy at having found love," it began before getting down to business. "In California, the land of community property . . ." Beneath that, on a loftier plane, was a fanfold with an idealized drawing of a lamb on it, exhorting me to bring Christ into my new home: MAKE YOUR RELATIONSHIP COMPLETE.

Beneath the brochures was what I'd been looking for, my one and only tie, fresh from the cleaner. The last time I'd seen it, it had looked like the entire Mafia had used it for a tablecloth. When I unwrapped it and put it on, sweating uselessly against the dry heat, I was pleased to note that most of the spaghetti stains had vanished. Blooming yellow in the rearview mirror and knotted in a single Windsor, it almost made me look respectable.

Okay, I thought, starting the car, I'd done what I was asked. It had turned out exactly as I'd thought it would, and I was pleased that I hadn't taken any of Nordine's money. Max Grover's house had been on my way to the real business of the day.

Max had been a surprise, though. From Christy's description, I'd expected a gay version of the pathetic sixty-five-year-old movie executives who rent themselves a new eighteen-year-old every week. Instead, Max had revealed himself to be much more complicated. Cheerful, confident, and manipulative, he lived more dangerously than his insurance company probably would have liked, but he seemed to do it because he actually believed he could help people. I had once believed the same thing.

Both Max and the junk-mail hucksters had seen a wedding in my future, but I was certain none of them had seen anything even remotely resembling the wedding I was going to.

I parked in a public lot downtown, near Parker Center, and hiked to the lobby, where I was issued the standard crack-and-peel badge, the kind that leaves stickum on your lapel. Since I could wash my face more easily than I could wash my lapel, I stuck the badge on my forehead. I thought it made me look festive.

"You must be for the wedding," said the weary-looking female cop at the desk.

"I'm the best man," I said proudly.

"Yeah?" she asked. "In what group?" She made a note and waved me past. "Elevator to your left, down three stories, get off at *P*."

A pistol range was an odd place for a pair of cops to get married, but Al Hammond and Sonia de Anza were an odd pair of cops, and the LAPD pistol range was where they'd met. He was the cop I'd picked for a friend when I decided to ignore my various postgraduate degrees and become a private detective, and she was a distractingly beautiful Hispanic whom Al had discovered while his divorce from wife number one, Hazel, was cranking its way slowly through the courts, a marital version of *Jarndyce* v. *Jarndyce*. Hazel had taken everything, including their child, Al, Jr., but Al had gotten Sonia. I'd met Al, Jr., the kind of child antiabortion activists never mention, and I thought Hammond had gotten the better deal.

The elevator doors opened onto a wave of noise and a sea of LAPD blue. Across the room was a tight huddle of Latinos in civilian clothes, whom I recognized as the bride's family. They looked as abandoned as the Last Platoon, surrounded by Saracens. The sea parted before my brown suit as though the color might be contagious, and I saw the groom sweating aggressively in my direction.

"Get *over* here," he bellowed, waving a Gold's Gym arm.

I did as I was told, proud of not breaking into a laugh. Hammond, now a lieutenant of detectives, hadn't been in uniform for years, and he obviously didn't have a tailor. The blues fit him like a sausage skin, just before it splits in the frying pan. Hammond was big in a way that turned defendants' best friends into prosecution witnesses in moments, but I'd never realized that he had love handles. Now I saw that he had love handles so pronounced that they formed blue parentheses around his middle.

He followed my gaze down to his midsection and turned even redder. "Uniform shrunk."

"Congratulations, Al," I said, hugging him in the approved New Age fashion. He backed away from the hug, an Old Age cop, and I resisted the urge to kiss him on both cheeks. "Where's the bride?"

His red face creased into a topography of previously unsuspected fault lines. "In hiding, like some federal fugitive. You know, I'm not supposed to see what she's—"

"Al," I said, "we both know what an LAPD uniform looks like."

The faults crinkled and threatened to collapse inward. "Do I know anything about women?"

"This is a swell time to ask."

"You're not doing so great, either. I think you guys have met."

He stepped aside to reveal my ex-girlfriend, Eleanor Chan, migraine-inducingly beautiful in cream-white silk and an antique necklace of garnets that I'd given her back when we were still giving things to one another. "Hike," I blurted, something suddenly closing my throat. I cleared it and said, "Hi."

"Hi, yourself," she said coolly. Eleanor was getting a lot of practice speaking coolly these days. "Nice to see the stripe in your tie again."

The hope that had momentarily taken flight at the sight of the garnets made a bumpy landing. "How's Horace?" I asked. Horace was her brother and the father of the three-year-old twins she worshipped.

"Who cares?" she said shortly. "How are you?"

"I'm fike. Fine, I mean. You look, you look . . ."

"I should," she said. "It took long enough. How's whatshername?"

"Who?" I asked hopelessly. I actually couldn't think of her name.

"If you don't know, why should I? And you've got something on your forehead."

"Take that fucking thing off," Hammond contributed. "You look like a Chinese ghost."

"Lord, Al, how do you know about Chinese ghosts?" Eleanor asked as I peeled the badge away from my skin. It took a handful of hair with it.

"Hong Kong movies," he said. "Orlando loves them." Orlando was the bride's significantly precocious younger brother, winding up a four-year career at UCLA at the irritating age of eighteen.

"Her name is Wayde," I said, "and she's nothing to worry about. I told you she's just—"

"Wayde?" Hammond demanded. "My best man's turned faggot?"

"Wayde is a girl," Eleanor said, "and a very young girl, at that."

"Oh, well," Hammond said relievedly, waving off statutory rape.

"She's seventeen," I said to Eleanor, "and she just likes to use my deck to sunbathe."

"Geez," Hammond said, one man to another, "can't you think of anything better than—"

"He'll have to think of something that explains her being stark naked in his living room." She turned to Al. "I'd really thought I was over being upset by things like this," she said as though I weren't present. "God knows I've had enough practice."

"I wasn't even there," I said.

"Better and better," Eleanor snapped, the garnets around her neck throwing off mad red glints. "You let this nude *child* into your house, and you're not even there."

Max Grover came to mind. Christy's phrase had been *living like a fool.* "I've known her since she was eight," I said defensively. "She's got time-retarded sixties parents who tell her it's okay to walk around naked. Her real name is *Freedom*, for Christ's sake."

"Freedom," Eleanor said, rolling her eyes. " 'License' would be more like it."

An invisible orchestra struck up the wedding march from *Lohengrin.*

"Mother of God," Hammond muttered, soaking wet. "Have you got the ring?"

"The ring?" I asked, looking blank.

He reached out a hand and grabbed my newly clean tie. "The *ring*," he said feverishly.

"Got it," I croaked.

"And you two," he barked, releasing me as the cops divided into two groups to create an aisle, his cops and her cops, "No bullshit. I'm getting married here."

"So's she," Eleanor said, gesturing toward a double door at the far end of the pistol range. Hammond turned to look, and his mouth fell open.

Here came the bride. Sonia de Anza was in uniform, but the sharply pressed blues were topped with a bridal veil of gossamer or tulle or something flimsy and ethereal that fell almost to her waist. Walking with her, in the position of the man who gives the bride away, was her brother Orlando. Orlando had always been a good-looking kid, but in a tuxedo he was resplendent.

"He's beautiful," Eleanor whispered.

I couldn't see Sonia's face beneath the veil, but I could see Orlando's. He didn't look left or right as they marched forward: His eyes were fixed proudly on his sister.

"Here's the deal," Hammond said hurriedly. "We walk toward the targets." Twelve paper men with black circles drawn around their pulpy vitals dangled at one end of the room. "When I stop, you stop."

"Then what?"

"Then you just stand there until Sergeant God calls for the ring."

A police chaplain in full uniform, plus collar, had emerged from between the targets. He stood there a bit nervously, as though awaiting a hail of bullets from the agnostics in the crowd.

I scratched my head, looking puzzled. "And then?"

"And then you give me the ring, asshole." Hammond was redder than the bulb of a thermometer.

"Al," Eleanor said, "relax. If there's anything Simeon knows about, it's other people's weddings."

"Yeah," Al said, not listening. "Isn't she gorgeous?" He couldn't see her face through the veil any better than I could. Then he drew a long, profoundly shaky breath. "Let's get it over with."

We followed Sonia and Orlando down the improvised aisle toward the targets. I suddenly realized I was nervous. *Lohengrin* was bouncing back and forth between the walls of the pistol range, and someone, probably Sonia's mother, was weeping copiously—possibly over the choice of venue—while cops looked embarrassed. Cops see mayhem and mutilation every day of their lives, but the tender emotions embarrass them. Well, they embarrass me, too.

I could feel Eleanor walking behind me, feel the pull of her emotions. Eleanor has a vast capacity for emotion. She's capable of entertaining eight or nine simultaneously, wearing every single one of them on her sleeve. The last time I'd glanced at her, I'd seen anticipation, happiness, regret, and anger, at least two of which were directed at me. Since I was walking with Al, I couldn't turn to face her, but I reached my left hand behind me, and after a moment she brushed my palm with warm fingertips and then gave my wrist a fierce little pinch. The woman was an emotional mosaic. Something inside me uncoiled and relaxed, leaving me free to focus on the ceremony.

The chaplain, a wispy-looking man in his fifties with damaged skin that suggested a teenage addiction to chocolate, gave Sonia a smile that was probably meant to be reassuring. The smile revealed about six teeth up top, each separated by a gap he could have put his little finger through, teeth that seemed to have fought for territorial imperative, the kind of teeth I usually associate with British National Health.

"Sonia and Al have written their own ceremony," he said, and something like a muted groan went up from the cops massed behind me. "But before we proceed, I'd like to say a few words."

"Only a few?" somebody whispered, and Hammond jerked his head around with a glare that could have knocked down a building.

"When I was told that Sonia and Al wanted to be married here, I have to admit that it threw me for a loop. A big loop. What do love and weapons have in common? But then I thought about it. Sonia and Al trained here to gain the skills that keep them alive in the field. Alive on the job. What could be more important to each of them than that their partner should remain among the well and, um, the living, able to give the love and support each deserves? They have chosen this job, our job, for society's sake, a job that will take them out of the home they will create together and into the streets of madness. For each of them there will be many long and frightening nights and days when they can only hope that their partner's survival skills will prove adequate to the danger of the hour. The bride and groom whose love we have come here to celebrate are veterans. Veterans who know how hard it can be to survive. Now they have, together, a new reason to live. Here is where they trained to live."

"Fuckin' A," a cop said softly from behind us.

"And then I also thought about marksmanship. Cupid's weapon was a bow and arrow. If Cupid were a modern-day mythical figure, his weapon would probably be a service revolver. The metaphor would remain the same: Love must take accurate aim. It must not only strike the heart, it must strike the *right* heart. Love wrongly given, wrongly received, has no place at this altar."

Hammond shuffled, probably thinking about Hazel.

"And so I say to Sonia and Al, paraphrasing the pop songwriter Elvis Costello, 'May your aim be true.' "

Sonia sniffled, and I thought, *Elvis Costello?*

"Sonia," the chaplain said, "Do you have something to say?"

"I have come—" she began, in little more than a breath.

"Can you please speak up?" the chaplain asked. "I'm sure everybody here would like to hear you."

"I have come," Sonia repeated more boldly, "to give to one man something no other man can ever have. I know it is precious, but it can only be given freely, and only once. There are people here today who love me, and whom I love, and they know that the love I give today to Al can only make me love them more."

The woman I guessed was Mrs. de Anza gave out a teary little whoop, and Orlando put a finger to his eye.

"A woman is a river," Sonia said. "Love flows through her. But unless love flows in, no love can flow forth. I look to Al as the source of the love that will flow through me, to my family and friends, and ultimately to my child. Nothing is sadder than the woman in whom the source of love has dried up. I trust Al to keep the love flowing."

I looked at Al, the source of love. Al looked at his feet.

"From now on, I say to Al Hammond, you are the source of my love. And you are the basin into which it will flow. I will make this promise only once in my life, Al, and I make it to you. I am honored to wed you."

Al made a sound like someone swallowing his tie.

"*Querido mío,*" Sonia said, her voice quivering. "*Yo te amo, para toda mi vida. Tu es mi corazón y mi esperanza. Por favor, dame tuyo amor siempre.*" She lowered her head, the veil brushing against the blue trousers.

"And Al?" the chaplain prompted.

"Huh?" Hammond said, staring at Sonia as though she'd just emerged naked and pearly from the sea.

"You have something to say to us, don't you, Al?"

"Yeah," Hammond said, blinking heavily. "Yeah, I do."

"You may begin," the chaplain intoned, tossing Al the territorial teeth in a fatherly grin.

"Sonia," Hammond bellowed, and then started at the sound of his own voice. "Sonia," he repeated more softly, "I am here today to make you my partner for life. I ask you to partner with me, even when I'm working solo. I promise that our home together will always be my heart's home. As partners, we will share equally, good or bad, and I promise to bring as much good as I can home with me. We both know how hard that can be." He paused, and then added: "In this job." He looked around the pistol range, and opened his mouth for a breath.

"I haven't always been a good man, but I promise to try to be the kind of man you deserve. Sonia, I promise to love you and honor you, the same way you've honored me by promising to be my partner. I'm not much good at anything but the job, but I promise to work on our marriage harder than I work at the job."

Suddenly the room went watery, and I had to blink. Hammond had lost his first wife because of his total absorption in the job.

"And I forget the rest," he said belligerently, "but I love you all to hell, and I want to marry you."

Some cops clapped.

"The ring, please," the chaplain said, looking at me.

"Right here," I said, handing it to Hammond.

"Repeat after me, please, Al. 'With this ring, I thee wed.' "

"With this ring, I thee wed," Hammond said, taking Sonia's hand and slipping the ring over a slender finger.

"For better and for poorer, in safety and in danger—"

Hammond repeated the words.

"To love and to honor, to cherish and obey, until death us do part."

"You bet," Hammond said, nodding.

"Say the words, Al," Sonia urged, and Hammond said the words.

The chaplain beamed at him. "You may kiss the bride."

"God, I'd love to," Hammond said. Orlando helped him lift the veil, and Sonia, dazzling and tear-streaked, gazed up at Hammond and tilted her face to his. Orlando looked at me and grinned, but it was pure show: His cheeks were as wet as mine. A couple of stolid macho jerks, we avoided each other's eyes as the new man and wife kissed.

"By the power invested in me," the chaplain announced, a beat behind the course of events, "I now pronounce you man and wife."

There was a general readjustment of feet, and a moment later we were headed back up the aisle. I caught a glimpse of Eleanor, sympathetic water all over her silk, before a woman pushed herself into our way, a woman not in uniform. At the moment I recognized her as Hazel, I heard my name being called over a loudspeaker.

Hammond stopped dead in his tracks, bringing all of us to a halt like a railroad collision, people piling into each other's backsides.

Hazel stared balefully at Sonia and then at Hammond. She was wearing a sweatshirt and blue jeans, and her hair had been haphazardly bleached by the chlorine in the modest pool behind the house Hammond's alimony was paying for. She glared at them like the harpy at the banquet, the uninvited fairy at the christening.

The loudspeaker blared my name again.

"Just wanted to see her," Hazel called to Hammond. "Is she going to be nice to my kids?"

Hammond said, "What the fuck?"

Sonia put out a hand to silence him. "Al says you're a wonderful mother. I hope we can be friends."

"Well, hope again, honey," Hazel said. "But don't give my kids any trouble, hear?"

"I have my own child," Sonia said, touching her stomach, "to worry about."

From Hazel's expression, as blank and astonished as the paper targets at the far end of the room, this was the first she'd heard about it.

"That call's for me," I said to the nearest cop, taking the coward's way out. "I left the number on my answering machine."

Hazel's voice rose behind me as the cop led me to a phone mounted on one of the white walls. "Yeah?" I said into the mouthpiece.

"This is Christy," the voice said. It coughed, and the cough turned into a choke and then a sob. "Max is dead."

I looked around the room. Hazel was still yelling at Sonia and Hammond. "Where? How?"

"Home. Be . . . ah . . . beaten to death. Where are you?"

"Doesn't matter. Have you called the cops?"

"And give them a voiceprint?" he asked. Then he laughed,

and something lassoed the laugh and choked it off, and he coughed again. "Are you crazy?"

"What am I supposed to do?"

"Call the cops," he said, and hung up.

I turned to the nearest cop, the cop who had led me to the phone.

"I want to report a murder," I said.

4
SPURRIER

"**DAMN** it, Al, I think the guy who did him was in the house. When I was *there*." I swung out into the fast lane on Fountain to pass someone who was carrying on an animated conversation in an otherwise empty automobile, and the limousine trailing us followed suit. Hammond, sitting next to me in the passenger seat, was absorbed in a bright yellow brochure that offered a staggering variety of "His & Hers" items.

"Washcloths I can see," he said. "But matching golf shirts?"

"You couldn't know," Sonia said to me from the backseat, where she and Orlando had been murmuring conspiratorially to each other for miles. "There's no point in kicking yourself."

She and Hammond wore flower leis given them to speed

their way to Hawaii. The cops who hung the tiny pink orchids around Hammond's neck had managed to keep straight faces, but just barely.

"How about some nice pillowcases?" Hammond asked. "Blue for me, pink for you. Christ, it'd be enough to keep you awake, lying there in the dark and wondering if you've got the right pillow."

They'd volunteered to drive to Max's house with me on their way to the airport, but Sonia's remark was the first either of them had addressed to me. Hammond had been too busy going through my morning's mail, and Sonia and Orlando apparently had pressing business to whisper about.

"You'll have to tell the sheriff's deputy about what you heard," Sonia said as though Al hadn't spoken. "All we can do is hand you off to them. It's their territory."

"We'll put you right with them, though," Hammond offered. "All you got to do is tell them what happened, tell them about the little doily who hired you, and go home."

"*Al,*" Sonia complained, sounding like a wife.

"Yeah," Hammond said. "Sorry." Then he chuckled, deep in his chest. "How about old Hazel, huh?"

"Don't go thinking she's still in love with you," Orlando volunteered maliciously. "It's just the loss of power she's worried about."

I turned left from Fountain onto Flores as Hammond maintained a ponderous silence. I could practically hear him counting to ten.

At about eight, Sonia observed, "Nice area."

"If you like fruitcake," Hammond said automatically. "Sorry, sorry, sorry. But you know, even though there may not be a lot of real good reasons to work for the LAPD, one of them is that the Sheriffs got Boys' Town."

"West Hollywood, you bigot," Sonia snapped.

"The city government leases them," I said, trying to avert

a prehoneymoon separation. After all, they'd only been married half an hour. "It's a private contract. But they're thinking of setting up their own force."

"I can see the uniforms," Hammond said. "Like Singapore Girls, only packing."

"That's enough, Al," Sonia said sharply.

"What're we, on *60 Minutes?*" Hammond grumbled. Then he caught his bride's eyes in the rearview mirror. "Sorry, darling."

"What a piece of raw material," Sonia said, softening. "Absolutely everything needs to be changed."

"Over there," I said, looking at the cluster of Sheriffs' cars and the yellow crime-scene tape.

As I pulled Alice toward the curb, a deputy stepped forward. He had the standard-issue mustache, mirrored sunglasses, and tight khaki uniform. In his early thirties, he had no love handles to speak of. I braked, and he came around to the driver's side and tapped on the window.

"Help you, sir?" he said as I rolled the windows down.

I looked up into two convex versions of my face, reflected in his shades. "I'm the one who called it in."

"And how did you—" he started, and then peered into the car, seeing Hammond in his LAPD blues and the orchid lei, Orlando in his tux, Sonia in full uniform with a bridal veil in her lap, and, behind us, the black stretch limo. It was enough to make him take off his sunglasses.

"He got a phone call, sonny," Hammond growled. The LAPD and the Sheriffs had a long and stormy history. "And he was here just before the old queen got killed. And he's volunteered to come all the way here—"

"Fine, sir." The deputy looked at me. "I'm sure Sergeant Spurrier will want to talk to you."

"I'm sure he will, too, stupid," Hammond muttered, setting me right with the Sheriffs.

Two minutes later Hammond and Sonia were Honolulubound, and Orlando and I were following the deputy up the steps to Max Grover's front porch. I'd promised to run him back to Parker Center to pick up his car, and the deputy had looked at him when he didn't get into the limousine, and then looked back at me. Then he'd shaken his head.

On the other side of the screen door, flashbulbs popped and someone laughed. The laugh ripped a little hole in the waning daylight and let in an early piece of the night: It was a nasty little laugh, the laugh of someone who's just seen a silent-movie actor slip on a banana peel and thinks it's funny because he doesn't know the man wasn't really hurt.

"Fasten your seat belt," I said to Orlando. "This is going to be a bumpy flight."

The deputy swiveled to face us. "Was he here with you?" he demanded, referring to Orlando.

"No."

"So who is he?"

"A friend."

The deputy thought about it. His face took on the expression of someone jogging dutifully uphill, suggesting that thinking was something he did infrequently and reluctantly, and only when there was no alternative. Then he pointed his chin at Orlando. "He stays here."

"Your *tuchis*," I said pleasantly.

He slid the mirrored shades back up the slope of his nose so that his eyes were concealed. "Beg pardon?"

"He comes in. With me."

"The kid stays here," he said, going for tough. The tag on his chest read KLEINDIENST.

"Get your superior, Deputy Kleindienst," I said. "Surely you have many."

"Kleindienst," someone called through the screen door, "who you jacking around out there?"

Kleindienst seemed inclined to give the question some thought, so I said, "I'm the one who called you on this."

"And he brought a little friend along," Kleindienst said scornfully.

"That so," said the man behind the door. He pushed it open and looked out at me. "Ike Spurrier," he said. He was short and compact and broad through the chest, with coloring that made him look as though he was dissolving slowly in a glass of water: almost albino, with white-blond hair and a spiky little white-blond mustache and melancholy eyes the color of wet sand. Beneath the mustache was a plump, shiny red lower lip, as wet and sharply articulated as an earthworm. He wore street clothes: a rumpled off-yellow tweed sport coat with a red polo shirt beneath it, and pressed blue jeans.

"Simeon Grist." We didn't shake hands.

"Thanks for calling us." Spurrier's sad-looking eyes drifted beyond me and found Orlando. "How'd you know he was dead?"

"Someone phoned me and told me so."

"That so," he said again. He shifted his gaze back to me and pushed the screen door open. "Whyn't you come in here and tell me about it."

"Let's go, Orlando," I said.

"He's not going to want to come in." Spurrier leaned toward me and raised his eyebrows like someone sharing a confidence. "He's *really* not going to want to come in."

"I can handle it," Orlando said.

"I don't give a shit," Spurrier said tranquilly. "This is a crime scene, and I don't need you in it."

I didn't like the way this was going at all.

"He comes with me," I said.

Spurrier looked directly into my eyes for two or three long seconds. "Or?"

"Up to you. I can either tell you what I have to say, or I can go to the West Hollywood station and tell them."

Spurrier tucked a portion of his lower lip between his teeth and gave the street a thorough survey before allowing his eyes to settle on Orlando again. "If you faint, sonny, don't hit any furniture. We're not through printing." He held the door all the way open, and I went in with Orlando following and Ike Spurrier taking the rear. Spurrier let the door bang shut behind us.

The house seemed dark after the slanting afternoon light on the street, and I had time to make out a group of four or five men huddled around something on the floor before a flashbulb went off and blinded me completely. Orlando must have been looking away when it popped, because a second later I heard him gasp, and then I felt his fingers on my arm.

"Told you," Spurrier said, sounding satisfied, and my vision cleared and one of the men in front of me stepped aside and I saw Max Grover.

He lay on his right side in a shallow lake of blood that surrounded him completely, head to foot. The little white pebbles were teeth. Bloody footprints, many sets of them, went toward him and away from him. His knees were pulled up self-protectively, and his right arm was beneath him, twisted somehow, so that it extended behind his back. His shirt, dark with blood, had been ripped open, baring one of his shoulders. The thing on the floor was a discard, the carelessly mutilated remains of some animal traditionally eaten on a holiday, the way a turkey carcass might look to a turkey. Nothing that had been Max was left.

"Boots," Spurrier said conversationally. "And a knife, of course, there." He pointed with his toe at the blood on the front of Max's shirt. "Oh, and over here, too, unless he used a bolt cutter or something. You'll have to come around to get a look."

I took three steps around the carcass and saw what he meant. Max's right arm ended at the wrist.

A mosquito began to whine in my ears, and it whined more loudly until it turned into a dentist's drill, and then I was sitting on the floor with my head between my knees.

"I thought it'd be *him*," Spurrier said to someone. Orlando was still standing, but his face was as white as though his blood had been drained. "You never can tell."

"He had three rings on that hand," I said when I'd located my voice.

"That so," Spurrier said. "Well, our boy worked like hell to get them, considering he left about twenty more in the bedroom. Didn't take his necklaces, either." I forced myself to look at Max's throat and saw the two gold chains I'd noticed earlier.

"He was wearing a steel necklace, too," I said.

"It'll turn up here somewhere." Spurrier turned to Orlando. "What's your name?"

"Orlando de Anza."

"That's not a name," Spurrier said, "it's a living-room set. Hey, Orlando, I'm going to ask you to go into the kitchen with Stephen here, and he's going to ask you a few questions, nothing much, just where you've been and so forth, while I talk to Simeon out here. Okay with you?"

"Sure," Orlando said. He sounded lost.

"You ready to get up?" Spurrier asked me.

"I knew him," I said, feeling vaguely ashamed of myself. "I talked to him for the better part of an hour."

Spurrier nodded and then extended a hand to help me up. I ignored it and pulled myself to my feet, and Spurrier put his hand into his jacket pocket. "How about we go into the book room?"

"Fine," I said.

"You know where it is," Spurrier said, not asking a question.

"It's where I talked to him."

"He give you anything to drink?"

"Lemonade."

"Just the two of you, right?"

"Right. I also touched a table in there and a few books."

"And now you've touched the floor in here," he said.

"That's right," I said, feeling myself flush. "With both hands."

"Your prints on file?"

"Yes. I'm a licensed private detective."

"Ah," Spurrier sighed. "Shit."

In the library, still fragrant from Max's bowl of roses, he waved me to the wooden chair, and I watched him sink into the leather one. "Jesus," he exclaimed. "Quicksand." He took a pack of cigarettes from his pocket and held them out. "Smoke?"

"Thanks anyway."

He put them away without taking one and looked around the room. "What I'd like you to do, I'd like you to tell me what you know about this, straight on through. I'll ask questions when I need to. Okay?"

I told him about Nordine and the job he'd asked me to do. I downplayed the fights they'd been having because it was inconceivable to me that someone as frail as Christopher could have found the strength to do the violence that had been done to Max. I told him about the other men Max had been picking up, about the talk I'd had with Max, about the sense I had that there'd been someone else in the house when I was there, and about Max's certainty that he'd been in no danger.

"Psychics," Spurrier said disgustedly. "So you saw Nordine yesterday afternoon and came here about two this afternoon, and you were here about an hour."

"Right."

"You must have been the last person to see him alive."

"Obviously not," I said.

"And from here you went where?"

"Parker Center. A wedding, a big one. I got there about three-forty-five, and Christopher called me about four-thirty."

"A cop got married?"

"Two of them."

He rubbed the space between his eyebrows with a fat index

finger. "So your alibi is a few hundred cops. That's a new one."

"I don't need an alibi," I said.

"We've got a very narrow window here. You say he was alive when you left at—"

"Three," I said, ignoring the implication.

"And Nordine calls you at four-thirty. I'd say that's a pretty narrow window." He worked his way out of the chair and went to the bookcase. "Of course, he wasn't necessarily alive at three, was he?"

"No," I said. "You've broken me. I killed him, took a shower in his bathroom to get the blood off, burned my clothes in the fireplace, put on a suit, and went straight to LAPD headquarters, having arranged the wedding in advance to give me an alibi."

He was looking at me intently, his mouth very tight. "Took a shower in his bathroom, huh?"

"Oh, Jesus," I said.

"Sure did," he said. "Didn't burn the clothes, though. Took them with him, apparently. You got your car keys, smartass?"

I tossed them to him, and he handed them to a cop outside the door. "It's the old blue Buick," I said.

"What route did you take to Parker Center?"

"Flores to Santa Monica, Santa Monica to La Brea, La Brea to Beverly, and Beverly downtown."

"All surface streets."

"My car doesn't like freeways."

"I don't like snappy answers. How'd Nordine know where to reach you?"

"I left the number on my answering machine."

"What's your phone number?"

I told him, and he wrote it down. "What's that," he asked, looking at it, "Santa Monica?"

"Topanga."

"We're your neighborhood cops, then," he said, sounding

pleased. He held up the phone number. "You mind if I have somebody call this?"

"Would it matter if I did?"

"Wouldn't slow us down a second. Dial this," he said to a cop I hadn't seen before, who had taken up the station outside the door. "Write down the message and bring it to me."

"My tax dollars at work," I said.

He picked up a snapshot that had been facedown on the table and showed it to me. Christopher Nordine, a healthy Christopher Nordine, squinted happily into the sun. "Is this your buddy Nordine?"

"He's a lot thinner now."

He looked at me through the wet-sand eyes. I guess it was supposed to be frightening. "That's not what I asked you."

I hesitated. "It's the guy who told me he was Nordine."

He nodded: I was learning. "Why'd he call you instead of us?"

"How would I know?" I wasn't about to tell him what Christopher had said about a voiceprint.

"Okay. Why'd Nordine choose you to talk to the old man?"

"He went to someone else for advice, and that someone recommended me."

He waited a moment, making a show of being patient, and then asked, "And who would that someone be?"

"William Williams. Also known as Wyl Will." I spelled it for him.

"Cute," he said, writing. "He a hink, too?"

"Is he gay? Yes. He runs a bookstore on Hollywood Boulevard."

"That so. What kind of bookstore?"

"Hollywood memorabilia. It's called Fan Fare."

"Joan Crawford posters?" he asked, reaching into the pocket of his jacket. "Bette Davis's old scripts, Judy Garland concert programs, that sort of thing?"

"He's got some of that."

"I'll bet he does. You a collector?"

"No."

"How do you know him?" I paused, organizing an answer, and he snapped his fingers. "Williams, how do you know him?"

I was disliking Spurrier more with every passing minute. "It's a small world," I said.

"And where in your small world is Nordine?"

"I haven't got any idea."

He dropped his notebook to the table. "Try harder."

"You want me to make something up?"

Spurrier pulled a latex glove out of his pocket and slipped it over his left hand, snapping the opening over his wrist, and started to put on the right. "Get up," he said.

"I'm comfortable," I said, watching him. His neck and cheeks were flushed, and I saw rage in the tight set of his shoulders.

"So what're you?" he asked when he had the second glove on. "Sherlock Homo? The Gay Detective? You investigate a lot of police brutality?"

"I don't think there is a lot of police brutality." My throat was very dry.

"Think again," Spurrier said, and he stepped up to me and hit me with the heel of his right hand, just below the heart.

The chair went over beneath me and splintered on the hardwood floor, and I curled reflexively into a ball, trying to find some air somewhere in the world and fighting down a hot, poison-green wave of nausea. Spurrier's shiny black shoes were inches from my face.

"Not a mark," he said. "Not even a red spot." His fingers curled around my arms and pulled me to my feet, but I couldn't straighten up, so I was leaning forward when he turned me around and brought a fist down on my kidney.

I went to my knees. "Why didn't Nordine call us?" he said quietly.

"Because he didn't want to talk to an asshole," I gasped. I barely had enough breath to get to the end of the sentence.

"Well, I suppose he's an expert on assholes." Spurrier sounded meditative. "You know what my big question is?"

"Which shoe to take off first at night?"

He brought a cupped hand around and slammed it over my left ear. It sounded as though someone had fired a pistol inside my skull, and the pain skittered like foxfire through the bones of my jaw and straight down my throat to my heart. "Can you hear me?" he asked. The hand came up again.

"I can hear you," I said.

"Nothing in his car, Sergeant," said a cop at the door. Behind him, I saw Orlando gazing at me with wide eyes.

"Give the gentleman his keys," Spurrier said, and the cop tossed them at me. They hit my shoulder and clattered to the floor. I tried to pick them up, but my fingers wouldn't do anything I wanted them to.

"My big question is what a faggot P.I. was doing at a cop's wedding."

"I was a bridesmaid," I said through jaws that felt like they'd been wired together.

He laughed, and I heard the snap of latex as he peeled a glove from his hand. "Who was calling that phone number?" he yelled.

"I was, Sarge," said a very young cop. "I had to call a couple times to get it all down."

"Give it here." He looked at the paper the cop had handed him and said, "What's this number?"

"Parker Center pistol range," the cop said. My fingers finally managed to wrap themselves around my keys.

"They have a wedding there today?"

The young cop shifted nervously. "I didn't ask."

"Ask," he said, giving the piece of paper back and turning to face me. He ran his tongue over the plump red lip. "I believe you, of course. You're just a good citizen who did his civic duty.

Wish we had more like you. Well, maybe not exactly like you. Get up and sit in the other chair. You seem to have broken this one."

I did as I was told, trying to sort out the various sources of pain and rank them by intensity. The ear was the worst.

"You are completely unbruised," Spurrier said, stuffing the gloves into his pocket. "Nothing happened here, and a lot more nothing will happen if you stick your nose into this affair. I've got your address and I've got units in the neighborhood twenty-four hours a day. If you don't want to develop undiagnosable internal injuries, you stay miles away from all this. Am I communicating?"

"Very unambiguously."

"Just so we're straight. Sorry, wrong term. Just so you're clear on it. Are you? Clear on it?"

"Yes," I said through a spasm of hatred that threatened to close my throat completely.

"Good," he said. "Stephen, the pretty boy check out?"

"He's a cop's little brother, the bride's. He was at the wedding, went there with her. With her all day, he says."

"Where's she?"

"On her way to Honolulu."

Spurrier screwed up his face in frustration. "How long?"

"Two weeks."

"You get a number?"

"Yeah. Maui."

"How nice for her."

"There was a wedding there today," the young cop said, coming into the room. "At Parker Center, I mean."

"My, my," Spurrier said admiringly. "It all checks out."

"You primitive piece of shit," I said.

"I can understand your frustration, sir," Spurrier said. "Wasting so much of your day this way. But I'd like to thank you for coming forward and assisting us with our inquiries.

"You'll be wanting to get along now." Spurrier backed

away from the chair, his face tight, as though he hoped I was going to come out of it and try to rip his heart out. "I'm sure you two have a big evening planned."

I got up more painfully than Christopher Nordine had. "I'll be seeing you," I said.

"I'll be looking forward to it," he said. "But not on this case."

As we went down the porch steps, I heard the laugh again, and recognized it as Spurrier's.

"Is that what they're like, the Sheriffs?" Orlando asked twenty minutes later. It was the first thing he'd said since we left Grover's house.

"It's what some of them are like. Not many. There used to be more like Spurrier. Now the problem is that the better cops don't do anything when a bad one gets out of line. White people don't generally see too much of it, though."

"White heterosexual people, you mean."

"Yeah. Spurrier's a little twisted on the subject of gays. I wonder what his analyst has to say about it."

"He thought you were gay." He turned on the radio and gave the indicator a skid across the dial.

"He thought we both were."

Orlando found a station playing heavy metal, something that sounded like a head-on collision between San Diego and Tijuana, listened for a second, and turned it down. "I am," he said.

"Oh," I said, nonplussed. The first time I'd met him, he'd been hondling Eleanor to introduce him to a girl.

He fiddled with the tuning knob on the radio, giving it all his attention. "I know what you're thinking," he said. "About Eleanor and that Chinese girl."

"That's what I was thinking."

"I was fooling myself. Telling myself I couldn't get dates

with girls because I was too young for the ones at UCLA, telling myself I was too shy to talk to women, when what was really happening was that I didn't want to." He threw me a quick evaluative glance. "I was in denial."

Denial. "*You're* seeing a therapist," I said.

"At school. She's helped a lot. It's hard for a Latino guy, especially when he comes from a family of cops."

"Therapists like to tell people they're suppressing homosexual feelings," I said cautiously. "It gives them something to do."

"In my case, though, it's true." He gave up on the radio and began to gnaw on the nail of his right index finger.

"Don't bite your nails," I said automatically.

He laughed. Then I started to laugh, too, and he leaned back and made hooting noises, laughing off some of the tension from Max Grover's house.

"Was your cop okay to you?" I asked, braking to avoid rear-ending someone who was apparently multiplying addresses in his head as he drove. The laughter had hurt in several places.

"Stephen? No, he was very nice, really sympathetic. In fact, I think he might be gay. He was good-looking enough to be gay, anyway. Has anybody told *you* you have repressed homosexual feelings?"

"Lots of people. All therapists."

He hesitated. "But it isn't true."

"If it is, they're *very* repressed. I mean, I think men are interesting people, and some of them are good-looking, but there's nothing sexual about it."

"I think I've known forever," Orlando said dreamily. "Since I was eight or nine or something."

"Does Sonia know?"

"Of course." He sounded affronted. "That's why she got so mad at Al in the car."

"Then Al doesn't—"

"Not yet," he said quietly. "He's got a surprise coming."

"It'll raise his consciousness," I said. "Something has to."

"Al's all right," Orlando said, surprising me a second time. "He's probably not ready for me to bring anybody over to spend the night, though."

"No. Probably not."

"If it was a girl he'd be all ho-ho-ho and hearty and nudgy, winking at me across the room and thumping me on the back whenever we were alone. But a guy—no way."

"Not yet."

"I've got a boyfriend," Orlando said with pride. "My first."

"Well," I said banally, "good for you."

He caught my tone and pulled away slightly. "Does it bother you?"

"No," I said. "I just don't know what I'm supposed to say. I'm not very good at intimacy."

"And I'm not good at anything else. Eleanor's the same way. That must be a problem between you."

I was beginning to feel like our relationship was on CNN; everybody knew everything. "You could say that."

"You never told that sergeant you weren't gay."

"It wasn't any of his business," I said. "Anyway, you know, it's just one thing about you. Whether you like guys or girls or Eskimos or Arabian horses. It's just one thing out of thousands, like who you voted for or whether you shave before you shower or after. It doesn't have much to do with who you are."

"It does when you can't admit it," Orlando said.

"I guess it would."

"Here we are," he said. "The next lot." We negotiated the parking lane, deserted at this hour, and I braked at the curb when he told me to. He started to get out of the car, and then stopped and looked at me. "You're okay," he said. "Al is always talking about you being somebody unusual, but I never knew what he meant. You took everything that stunted little clown could dish out, and you never lost your dignity. I don't know if I could have done that."

"I got beaten up," I pointed out.

"What you said about his shoes," Orlando said, and then he laughed again. He extended a hand, and I shook it and watched him slide out of the car and angle across the parking lot, a slender teenager in a tuxedo, heading toward God only knew what. Then I drove home through the ragtag remnants of the rush hour, climbed the driveway to my house, and took a pistol away from Christopher Nordine, who was waiting in my living room.

5
REQUIEM FOR MAX

"**WOULD** you like to tell me what you think you're doing?"

The couch had broken Nordine's fall. He sat there and rocked back and forth, flexing the fingers of his right hand, the hand that had held the gun. I had the gun now, and it was pointed at his solar plexus.

"I don't know. I don't know *anything*. Only that Max is—"

"You saw him," I said, wondering whether it had been smart not to tell Spurrier everything, swine though he was.

"Oh, my *God*," Nordine said, blinking back tears. "It was, it was like *Friday the Thirteenth* or something. Poor Max, poor sweet old Max. And I thought, I guess I just went crazy, I thought, well, you'd been there—"

"So had you," I said.

"But *after* he was dead," Nordine said. He raised both hands, as though I'd put the gun to his head. "Wait, wait, you don't think that—"

"The cops do."

"Well, of course *they* do," Nordine snapped. "What would you expect? Why do you think I called you instead of them?" He was wearing the same clothes he'd worn the day before, and I couldn't see anything wrong with them.

"Listen, Christopher, they're going to be hard-nosed about this. There are guys with guns looking for you. You had means, motive, and opportunity. And don't tell me about how much you loved him. I'm tired of hearing about people loving each other. Open your coat."

"What?"

"Open your coat. I want to see your shirt."

"Oh," he said flatly. "How thorough of you." He unbuttoned the jacket and held it wide. The shirt was damp with sweat but unstained. I gestured for him to button up.

"How'd you do that?" he asked sulkily.

"Do what?"

"You were supposed to come in over there." He waved a hand in the direction of my front door.

"I smelled your cologne," I said. "So I went around the side of the house and climbed up onto the sun deck, and threw a folding chair over the roof toward the front door. When you got up and faced the door, I came in behind you."

"You threw a chair over the *roof*?"

"It's not a very big house."

"No," he said, giving it an unaffectionate eye, "it isn't. It's not very nice, either."

"Did you kill him, Christopher?"

"Do you honestly think I could kill Max?"

"I don't know. That's why I asked."

"Max was the best human being I ever met." He sounded like he was about to cry.

"So somebody else killed him."

"Well, of course they did. One of those walking trash heaps he was always picking up on the street."

"Okay," I said, popping the clip out of the gun and emptying it: seven rounds. I pocketed the bullets and held the gun out to him. "Get out of here."

He gazed at the gun without taking it. "But *wait*. You have to help me."

"Why do I have to do that?"

"Because they're looking for me."

"You should have called them in the first place."

"No," he said. "I couldn't." He shook his head, and the joints in his neck popped. "Absolutely not."

"It's just made it worse for you."

"That means you told them about me."

"Christopher," I said, as though to a five-year-old, "I had to explain why I was there."

He stared up at me, white completely surrounding the irises of his sunken eyes. "You told them *everything?*"

"I didn't tell them about the will. I didn't tell them what you said about the voiceprint."

"Thanks for nothing," he said. "They'll find out about the will in fifteen minutes, and that'll be it. Do you know what those guys are like? About gay people, I mean? They'll treat me like I'm Typhoid Mary. Gloves and masks and I don't know what all."

The kidney Spurrier had slammed sent off a little skyrocket of pain. With the pain came a sudden, overpowering conviction that I was sick and tired of other people's lives. "I've got to sit down," I said.

"It's your house." He was back to a sulk.

"Do you want some water?"

"I already took some." He leaned over the edge of the couch, and I started fumbling in my pocket for the bullets, but all he came up with was a half-drained bottle of Evian.

"Good," I said, sitting in the only other chair in the room. "But don't do that again."

"Do what?"

"Bend over and pick up anything I can't see."

He put a hand to his chest. "Oh, my God, you still think it was me."

"I." It was involuntary.

"You? Oh, I see. You're correcting my grammar. How—"

"Old-fashioned," I suggested.

"I was going to say how anal-retentive."

"I'm almost as tired of that," I said, "as I am about hearing people talk about love."

"You really must be hurting," he said, unscrewing the cap on the bottle of Evian. "Oh, I remember. 'The fondness comes and goes.' Gone at the moment?"

I was tired, and my left kidney was sending out painful little pulses, blasts of cold air aimed at my back. "Leave me alone. When I want analysis, I'll pay for it."

He drank. "Sure," he said. "It's a *lot* easier to be detached when you're peeling off the bucks to a shrink. That's half the problem with psychiatry, the money."

"What's the other half?"

"It doesn't work."

"There's that," I acknowledged.

He sat back, wedging the bottle between his legs. "I had analysts all over the South. Max was the only one who ever helped me, even a little."

"Throw me the water." He tightened the cap and tossed it to me underhand, like a softball, and I drank half of what was left. It tasted like warm plastic. "Okay," I said. "Tell me how Max helped you."

He grimaced. "Is this necessary?"

"No. You could just leave."

The deep eyes fastened on mine and then cruised the room,

settling on one of the darkened windows, and he sighed. "We always want to be the hero," he said.

"We want a lot of things," I said.

He gathered his lips together and let out another sigh, one with a big *P* at the beginning of it. "I was just a total waste," he said. "A mess. I hurt people and stole from them. I told lies day and night. I lied about who I was and what I'd done and when I'd gone to the bathroom last and how tall I was. It didn't matter what, I lied about it."

Outside a coyote yowled protest at the heat, and Christopher Nordine sat bolt upright at the sound. "Why?" I asked.

His eyes remained fixed on the window. "Why does anybody lie? Because the truth isn't good enough. *I* wasn't good enough. I was a nobody. I hadn't done anything, and I didn't think I ever would. I was a little ball of fear with legs and arms, so I lied to everybody. Some of them believed me, or wanted to, so I despised them for believing me, and that made it all right to steal from them. And when they caught me stealing, I lied some more, and they believed me again."

The nakedness of it unsettled me, and I got up and opened the door to the deck. The moon hung white and remote across the canyon, cold and alone and proud of it. "They were lonely," I suggested.

He shrugged. "They were old."

I turned to face him. "Max was old, too."

"Max has been the same age all his life. Max is ageless." He stopped and put the pale fingers to his eyelids. They shook. "Was. Was ageless."

"Did you lie to Max?"

"Of course I did. I gave him all the best stuff, right off the bat. He laughed at me. He said it was up to me, I could tell him lies and he could pretend to believe me if I wanted him to, or he could help me lose the fear. Up to me."

"And you?"

He crossed a leg and then uncrossed it. "You have to understand, this was in the first fifteen minutes we knew each other. We were at some stupid party in the hills, and there we were, standing in a corner, and he's saying all this stuff to me. So I hesitated, really just trying to think of something plausible, and he laughed and said he'd pretend to believe me on Monday, Wednesday, and Friday, and on Tuesdays and Thursdays we'd work on the fear."

I caught myself starting to grin: "What about weekends?"

He saw my smile and the corners of his mouth went down, but then he relaxed and smiled back. It was a sweet smile, a slightly awkward smile that didn't look like it had gotten much use. "I asked the same question. He said he read on weekends, and I could go lie to someone else if I liked. To keep in practice."

"And did he? Read a lot?"

"All weekend long, fourteen hours a day. He'd get up around five and meditate for an hour, and then drink some tea, and the books would come out. Max learned to meditate in India. He went in the early sixties, years before anyone else did."

"And you decided to let Max work on the fear."

"No." He looked around the room, not really seeing it. "I decided to *pretend* to work on the fear, to let him think I was—" He cleared his throat, and I threw him the bottle of water. He caught it with both hands but didn't open it. "I said something like when do we start, and he said, 'Right now.' And then he whispered in my ear, 'This is the worst thing I've ever done. I killed a man. Do you want to come home with me?' "

For some reason, Max Grover's long slender hand, clutching a lemon, popped into my mind's eye. "Max killed someone?"

"In India. It was self-defense, a French guy who was going to murder him and take his money. Max had a lot of money in those days. He got away with it, he literally got away with murder. And he told me about it, fifteen minutes after we met. A stranger, and he told me. So we went home, and we talked until two the next afternoon. Except for crying breaks. At the end, I couldn't stop crying long enough to breathe, and he put his arms around me and held me until I went to sleep. I slept until it was dark again, and when I woke up he was still awake, still holding me. 'Good start, Christy,' he said. By then it was almost nine, I mean nine the next evening, and he went into the kitchen and made dinner." His voice hadn't changed, but tears were rolling down his cheeks. "And before we went to sleep again, he told me he'd take me in the morning to get an HIV test."

"And you tested positive."

"He knew I would. He'd felt it inside me." He pushed himself to his feet slowly, putting a hand against the wall for support, and started toward the front door. "When I got the results, I went wild, just totally insane. I thought I'd be dead in days or something." He got to the door, opened it, and closed it again, moving just to move. "Max drove me to the clinic to get the report. He took me back to his place—I'll never forget that car ride, all those people on the streets who were going to live forever—and when we got home I started screaming and breaking things. He just handed me new things to throw until there wasn't anything left in the living room small enough for me to break, and then he took me by the hand and led me into the kitchen so I could start on the dishes. I guess I broke a few, and then I passed out." He turned toward the open door. "Did you say that was a deck?"

"Good idea," I said. "Let's go out."

We climbed out onto the deck. Christopher's eyes went to the moon, four-fifths full, hanging over the mountains to the west with a high thin line of cloud above it. Below us in the canyon people's lights were on.

"This is why you live here," he said, taking it in.

"It's one reason."

"Did your girlfriend live here with you?"

"She found it."

"So that's another reason." He looked around the deck and spotted the remaining canvas chair. "I guess the other chair's out near the front door."

"Sit. I usually let my legs hang over the edge anyway."

"Long way down."

"Somebody once injected me with vodka so he could throw me off it and it'd look like I'd been drunk."

"That'd do the job," he said, easing himself into the chair. "What happened?"

"I killed him."

"My, my." He leaned back and stared up at the moon. "All those pockmarks," he said. "I never thought the moon was romantic."

"It's okay at a distance."

He started to move his feet, preparing to get up. "I forgot the water."

"It's almost gone anyway. I'll get a new bottle."

In the kitchen, I realized he was talking.

". . . after I'd burned out on the terror, Max started talking to me about what I should do with the rest of my life. Nothing was different, he said, except now we had a deadline. I don't think I'd ever really *heard* that word before. And I, I was just amazed. Because, you see, I'd assumed he'd throw me out."

I stayed where I was, holding the bottle of water like a chalice of some kind.

"So he said we had to start making time count. We had to build my strength and work on my spirit. My spirit, Jesus, no one ever talked to me about my spirit before. I figured I had a spirit like some people have lint in their pockets, no more important than that, and I tuned him out and interrupted him with something I thought was *really* important, like whether he was actually going to let me stay. And he said to me, 'Where else would you go?'

"And then he put his hand in the center of my chest, his

palm to my chest, and held it there, and I felt a kind of warmth come into me, and the warmth turned into a tingle and flowed into my arms and legs. 'What *is* that?' I asked him, and he said, 'That's your spirit.' " He stopped talking for a long time, but I didn't move. "So we went to work on my spirit," he said at last.

I waited a moment and then took the water out onto the deck. Christopher was slumped in the chair, his head down and his hands folded in his lap. I unscrewed the top on the water and sat next to him. "Two days later," he said without moving, "Max told me about the house, that he'd willed it to me." He reached over, and I gave him the bottle. "I didn't kill him," he said. Then he drank.

"Okay," I said.

"And I have maybe two years left, if that, and I am not going to spend even one day in a jail cell."

"Okay," I said again, thinking about how Spurrier would treat him, remembering the latex gloves he'd put on before he hit me.

Christopher coughed, then cleared his throat of something with a sound that reached all the way down into his midsection.

"I'll need information," I said.

He put his hand on my shoulder. It was very light.

"You'll have to move fast," he said. "When the publicity hits, there's going to be a lot of pressure on the cops to find someone, and I'm the one they're going to try to find."

"I don't think there'll be that much publicity," I said. "They'll keep quiet about most of, um, what was done to Max. They always do. And anyway, it's just another gay murder as far as they're concerned."

He turned to me and gave me the smile again. "There'll be tons of publicity," he said. "All over the country. Max used to be famous."

6
TARNISHED STAR

"**HE** was *Rick Hawke*," Wyl Will exclaimed, wide-eyed. A couple of years ago, after his mother died, he'd had his eyelids tattooed to spare himself the necessity of putting on makeup every day, and the combination of the heavily lined eyelids and the wide eyes made him look something like the latter-day Bette Davis.

"Humor me," I said. "I'm a little young for Rick Hawke."

It was ten A.M., and busloads of tourists in short sleeves were already sweltering up and down Hollywood Boulevard, reading the names in the brass and terrazzo stars on the sidewalks and stepping over the bums who keep the stars company on the concrete. Only in Hollywood can a penniless wino sleep on top of a star.

"I knew you'd say that," Wyl said peevishly. He'd gotten

to the point where he took youth as a personal insult. "But there's *cable*, you know. *Everything*'s on cable now. I flipped on the set last night and saw *I Married Joan*, of all things. Do you remember how *she* died?"

"Who?" I was facing the window, watching a sleek, well-dressed Arab shepherd a flock of heavily robed women up the sidewalk. They may have been wrapped to their eyebrows, but the heat didn't seem to be bothering them. The other tourists, the ones in shorts and T-shirts, were red and wet.

"Joan *Davis*." He blinked fast, either tears or something in his blue contacts. "Burned to death, poor thing. Just like Gene Tierney."

"Who?" I said again. "Oh, yeah. Gene Tierney."

"Played a Chinese in one movie." Wyl clasped his hands prayerfully in front of his chest. "Lord, she was beautiful."

The Arabs passed from view, followed by two heavyset *cholos* in plaid wool shirts and wide black pants who looked very interested in them. The ear Spurrier had slapped had been ringing all morning, and my lower back hurt. "Rick Hawke, Wyl."

"Well, he was beautiful, too. I saw him on TV in 1957 and thought, Well, *California*, don't you know. We were about the same age, but he looked younger. I wrote him a fan letter and got a signed photo back, not that he signed it himself, I'm sure, but they did things right in those days. Imagine getting a reply to a fan letter to Madonna."

"And then you came out here and met him." I was the only customer in Wyl's store, and he was seated behind the counter that ran along the left-hand side of the shop. Between me and the window, shelves housed thousands of books about show business, and tables and glass cabinets offered up boxes full of old posters and glossy studio stills.

"Decades later," Wyl said. "The early eighties, I guess. Have you had coffee?"

"If I hadn't, I wouldn't be standing up. How did you meet him?"

"Circles," Wyl said airily, making a vaguely circular gesture with his right hand.

I massaged my bruised kidney. "That must have been nice, traveling in the same circles as one of your favorite stars."

"Oh, I had no idea who he was. He'd stopped being Rick Hawke twenty-five years before that. He'd operated a charter yacht service in Hawaii and gone to India to wash some holy man's feet or something, and he'd grown that beard and let it go all white, and he never ever talked about his career in television. No, he was just this courtly gentleman who wore too many rings and always seemed to have some odd boy in tow."

"Odd in what way?"

Wyl dipped a finger into a mug of coffee to test its temperature, licked off the drops, and drank. "Glum," he said eventually. "They were all glum. Monosyllabic, like two syllables might prove to be unbearable. And knobbly, not smooth and symmetrical. Some of them didn't smell very good. Either cheap cologne or no baths, it was hard to say which was worse. They didn't seem to have pasts."

"A lot like Christopher," I ventured.

Wyl blushed crimson. "Christopher is good-looking. And he can talk."

I tried not to grin. "How many of your antiques did he take?"

"Scads," Wyl said, his color deepening. "But, you know, they were all old."

"Antiques generally are."

He gave me a sharp glance with the heavily lined eyes. "You're very clever this morning. You might at least have waited until I finished my coffee, so I could be clever back."

"You introduced him to Max."

He sipped again and put the cup down. "By then I knew that Max wasn't just chasing rough trade. He saw himself as the stairway out of the gutter. Christopher seemed to be headed for the gutter, so I referred him to Max. I would have tried to help him myself, but I was running out of antiques."

The grin won, and I turned and looked out the window to hide it. "Tell me about Rick Hawke."

Wyl sighed: This was easier ground. "I've got an eight-by-ten on table five." He rose from his stool, a slender man in his youthful seventies with silver-blue hair and a dancer's narrow waist, set off by pleated trousers into which he'd tucked a yellow silk shirt. As I followed him to table five, the bell over the door rang and about seventeen Japanese came in, all dressed formally, as though they were about to have their photos taken, which I supposed they were.

"*Konnichiwa,*" Wyl said without breaking stride.

"*Konnichiwa,*" all seventeen said politely. They waited for the next step in the conversation.

"Look, look," Wyl called, giving up on Japanese and waving his hands in the general direction of the books. "Number one store, *ichiban* in Hollywood."

"*Hai,*" said the oldest of the Japanese. "Famous store."

"*Domo arigato gozaimashta,*" Wyl pronounced. He sounded as though he'd learned it through Hooked on Phonics. "Look around. Buy something." He turned to me. "If we're going to be conquered, it might as well be by somebody polite. God, imagine if it were the French. Rick's in here." He started rifling through a box full of glossies, each encased in a transparent sleeve. Faces I hadn't seen or thought of in years flipped past: Bob Cummings, Dennis Day, Red Skelton, Robert Horton, Hugh O'Brian, Faye Emerson, Ida Lupino.

"Wait," I said.

"It's further back."

"Just a second. I like Ida Lupino."

"You *do* have a frame of reference," he said. Ida Lupino gazed up at us, tough and broken at the same time, wearing the face of someone too intelligent for the game she'd allowed herself to be trapped in.

"I'll take this," I said, pulling Ida out.

"You're a romantic," Wyl said, suppressing a smile.

"That's what Max told me. A disillusioned one."

"Poor Max." Wyl used a single fingernail to separate the photos and then withdrew one. "Here."

Rick Hawke had been splendidly handsome. All the conventions of the photo—the dramatic lighting, the pancake makeup, the too-slick hair—couldn't mute the individuality of the human being peering out through the angular face, the person sporting the silly western-style shirt and the kerchief tied around his neck. He looked faintly ill at ease, but he also seemed privately to be enjoying the joke. My memory stirred, and I realized that I recognized Max's younger face from my childhood.

"That's a good one," Wyl said, eyeing it critically. "That's what made him a star. That sense that he was laughing at himself. That bodybuilder with the impossible name has the same quality."

I picked up the photo. "What's this from?"

"His show," Wyl said, masking astonishment at my ignorance. "*Tarnished Star.* He played a sheriff who was really an escaped murderer. Self-defense, of course."

"Slow down," I said. "That was the story?"

"Imagine the conflict." Wyl closed his eyes, looking dreamy. "There he is in this dusty little husk of a town with a badge on his shirt and this *vast* secret in his past, and *every week* someone came into town who knew who he really was. Everybody in the *world* came through that town. Sometimes good guys, sometimes bad guys. Once it was Oscar Wilde, if you can believe that, and Oscar *Wilde* knew. And, of course, he can't just kill them, because he's not a murderer at heart, so he has to—"

"Excuse?" the oldest Japanese said.

"Yes?" Wyl said, shaking his head free of memories. "I mean, *Hai?*"

"Dirty book about Madonna?" the Japanese man said.

"Over there," Wyl said dismissively. "With the soft porn."

"Excuse?" The Japanese man looked confused.

"*Poruno*," Wyl said impatiently. "*Pinkku.* There."

"*Hai, arigato,*" the man said, trundling off in the direction Wyl had indicated.

I was examining Rick Hawke's two-dimensional face. "I remember him," I said. "It was a pretty good show." I'd seen it in reruns as a little kid.

"It was a smash." Wyl stared over my shoulder at the street. "Could have run for years."

"And you say he quit."

"In the middle of the third season." He looked up at the ceiling. "Maybe 1957, '58. Went to Hawaii, as I told you, and then to India."

"Why?"

"Why'd he quit?" He drew in the corners of his mouth, sorting out his answer. It gave him a judicial air. "None of this is from the horse's mouth, you understand."

"He never talked to you about it."

"Exactly. The trades said at the time it was a salary dispute. Later, people told me that it was because of the Black Widow."

He seemed disinclined to go further, so I said, "The Black Widow."

"You know," he said reluctantly, "like the spider. His agent. He had the same agent as all those fifties actors whose names sounded like laundry detergents. Zip and Punch and Coit, and, oh, I don't know, Tweak. The agent's name was Ferris Hanks. He was a *very* bad man."

"How was he bad?" A cluster of Japanese had formed around a large book that bore the bald title *SEX*.

"Manipulative, power-hungry, sick." Wyl blinked the lined eyelids and opened his mouth to draw air. "Power and pain."

"Ah," I said. "And he made Max quit?"

Wyl shook his head. "No. He wanted Max to continue, I'm

sure. Max—Rick—was a big star then. But the contracts back then were ironclad. If Max wanted to keep working, he had to keep working for Ferris. And Max wasn't willing to have ten percent of his salary go for whips and bludgeons and star-struck boys for Ferris. So he quit. Heavens, but Ferris was mad."

"I'll bet he was."

He seemed to get taller. "Are you going to continue making pointless interjections, or are you going to let me tell the story?"

I thought about it. "Should I say something?"

"A polite expression of interest wouldn't be unwelcome."

"Please, Wyl," I said, "oh, please tell me the rest of the story."

"Ferris went after him publicly." His eyebrows chased each other toward his hairline. "*Publicly*, can you imagine? In the fifties?"

"I'm not sure I follow you."

"Perhaps that's because you're trying to lead," he said. "Six months after Max quit, a story appeared in one of the scandal magazines of the day, implying quite clearly that Max—Rick— was gay. They didn't say *gay*, of course. No one said 'gay' in the fifties. They simply suggested, quite openly in kind of a sneaking way, that Max preferred men to women, which was quite enough back then. Some of us, of course, were thrilled. I'm sure champagne corks popped all over the country. But a story like that would have finished Max, if he hadn't been finished already. Everyone said later that Ferris had planted the story, even though it would have been suicide for him to do it." He wound down, putting a hand over his heart as if to slow his breathing.

"Why suicide?"

"Because *all* of Ferris's clients were gay. He was playing with fire, so to speak. The bad apple and all that. *Contagion.* Hollywood was absolutely gripped with paranoia at the time. The House Un-American Activities Committee, the Hollywood Ten and all."

"That was communism."

"That was rampant stupidity," Wyl corrected, "seasoned with the most pernicious kind of cowardice. But if they can investigate one thing, they can investigate another. It was very dangerous for Ferris to have leaked that story. He must have been beside himself."

"Why would he have done it?"

Wyl gave me a sidelong glance, Bette Davis at her most mysterious. "Wounded pride, perhaps. Hell hath no fury, and so forth."

"Is Ferris still alive?" A boisterous laugh went up from the group of Japanese, crowded around the book.

"He couldn't be," Wyl said, glancing at his customers. "He'd be in his nineties."

"I'll let you get to them in a second. Wyl, do you know anything about Max having a new boy, just before he died?"

Wyl gave me the age-old gaze of the innocent. "How could he have? He loved Christy."

The newspapers had taken note of Max's death, but just barely. WEST HOLLYWOOD MAN KILLED read the headline on the third page of the Metro section of the *Times*. So they hadn't yet figured out who Max had been, not too surprising when the call reporting his death came in so late. As I'd assumed they would, the cops had sat on the details of the mutilation.

I had a notebook page full of names and numbers from Christopher, and I used Wyl's phone to call the first on the list, Marta Aguirre, his housekeeper, an illegal from San Salvador whom Christopher loathed with unconcealed intensity. A snoop and an eavesdropper and a petty thief, he called her. Everything stuck to her fingers. She sounded like just what I needed.

Unfortunately, she wasn't home. I got an older woman who told me, in Spanish, that she was tired of people calling up and asking for Marta. I asked what time she'd be back and got hung up on.

Wyl was seated at the cash register, ringing up his entire stock of Madonna memorabilia—which included an aluminum brassiere of dubious provenance—as I tried the second number. "Shaw, Barron, and Jenks," a woman said brightly, as though she'd thought of it herself.

"Mr. Jenks, please." Holding the phone between ear and shoulder, I put both hands in the small of my back and arched backward. The ache in my kidney eased slightly.

"Who shall I say is calling?"

I bent forward, provoking a dry chuckle from Wyl, who enjoys seeing the aging process at work in other people. "Lysander Atwill, regarding Max Grover."

I listened to two verses of "Under My Thumb" played pizzicato on what sounded like a pocket comb. The revolution was definitely over.

"Jenks," said a man with an ersatz deep voice, sort of a near-beer bass. I had a feeling Mr. Jenks was a very small man.

"Lysander Atwill here," I said, "calling from Boulder?"

"Yes?"

"I'm a partner in Atwill, Grey, and Gorgonzola. We handle affairs for Mr. Grover's sister, Helen." According to Christopher, Helen was the sole surviving member of Max's family, the last Grover left back in Boulder.

"Terrible thing," Mr. Jenks said, letting his voice ease up half an octave.

"We're all shocked here in Boulder, of course."

A lawyer's pause. "How can I help you, Mr. Atwill?"

"Well, I know this sounds a bit quick off the mark, but I have a question about Mr. Grover's will, which I understand you prepared."

"I can't discuss the terms—"

"Of course not. We know them anyway. We know that, um, Christopher Nordine is the primary legatee and that Miss

Grover stands to inherit only certain memorabilia of a senti-mental nature, plus twelve acres of undeveloped land outside of Boulder."

"And the question, Mr. Atwill?"

"My client was just wondering whether the will had been altered in any way in the last year. There's no need to discuss specifics."

"I should hope not," he said primly.

"Please understand, Mr. Jenks. My client is an elderly woman of uncertain means who is devastated by her brother's death. She's seizing on this issue because she doesn't want to confront her loss. She's not, if you understand me, being reasonable."

"I see." He made mouth noises into the phone, mulling it over. Finally, he said, "Negative."

"Negative what?"

"Negative to the question you asked me. Nothing of the kind."

"All provisions remain intact?"

"I just told you that the answer to the question you asked was negative." No one was going to trick Mr. Jenks into speak-ing English.

"Are you positive?" I asked. I couldn't help it.

"Good-bye, Mr. Atwill." He hung up.

"People do hang up on one," I said to Wyl, who was count-ing a wad of gaily colored Japanese traveler's checks.

"The world's rife with it, Mr. Atwill," Wyl said blithely. "Full of people who don't give their right names, too."

"It's a scourge," I said, getting up.

"Be careful with that back," Wyl called after me. "A man your age can't take his spine for granted."

Max Grover's dry cleaner was a large, fierce-looking Ko-rean man in a little shop dead center in a minimall on Sunset Boulevard, just east of Sunset Plaza, a mall he shared with an Arab yogurt parlor, a Vietnamese nail salon, and a Thai restaurant. He regarded me darkly, as though he were wondering whether it would be simpler to comply with my request, or just fold me into equal threes and throw me through the window. "Mr. Grover not come himself?" he asked suspiciously.

So he didn't read the English-language newspapers. Or maybe, like so many Koreans, he started work before they were delivered.

"Mr. Grover died," I said. He was going to learn about it sooner or later, and I didn't want him to call the cops when he did.

"Hah?" he said, blinking at me.

"He's dead," I said. "Somebody killed him."

He was taken aback. Literally. A full step. "Mr. *Grover?* He dead?"

"I'm afraid so. Mr. Nordine sent me to pick up his things."

"Oh, no," he said. "Oh, nononono." His voice was shaking.

"I can pay the bill," I said stupidly.

"Bill? I don't care bill." He balled up a fist and brought it down on top of the Formica counter. The entire shop shook. "You think I care bill? Bill, hell to it. Mr. Grover good man."

"He was," I said. "He was a very good—"

"He give me money my sister," the Korean said. His face was scarlet. "Money bring her from Korea." He wiped a callused palm roughly across his eyes. "She problem," he said, "he pay bring her from Korea."

"Well," I said, seeing Max in an ocean of blood, seeing Max's chopped right wrist.

"I pay back." The man was crying openly now. "One year, pay everything back. Try pay interest, Mr. Grover say no, no interest. Want my sister make him one dinner, *bulgogi.* Mr. Grover love *bulgogi.* Mr. Grover love everybody."

"I'm sorry," I said.

"Ayyyyyy," he said, a prolonged Asian syllable of unadulterated grief. "You wait." He shuffled toward the back of the shop. "We make *bulgogi,*" he said without looking back. "We make *bulgogi* enough for one year." He went into a room at the back of the shop and slammed the door. A moment later I heard him blow his nose with a sound like a tuba tuning up, and he reemerged. He'd washed his face, and his hair was spiky and wet.

"Mr. Grover cleaning," he said, gathering plastic-wrapped clothes from the track that snaked around the ceiling of the shop. He bundled them against his chest like he was afraid someone might snatch them from him. "And for Mr. Nordine, too." He lowered them to the counter and wiped his nose.

My antenna went up. "When did Mr. Nordine bring these in?"

He looked at the tag, blinking rapidly to clear his eyes. "Two days. Mr. Grover bring."

I looked down at the pile, mostly long, loose-fitting shirts on hangers, shirts like the one I'd seen Max wearing. "Nothing else?"

"*Eigo*," he said. "Yes. Always. Mr. Grover never empty pockets."

"Most people don't." I hoped I sounded calm.

"Not same Mr. Grover." He fished around below the counter and came up with a package wrapped in blue paper. "Key, money, papers, rings, everything."

I picked up the blue package and began to grapple with the things on hangers. He put out a hand to stop me.

"I carry clothes," he demanded fiercely.

"That's not necessary." I didn't want him to get a look at my car.

"I do, I do."

"I'm parked a block away," I said, which was true. "You can't leave the shop that long."

"I close anyway," he insisted. "Today I go drink for Mr. Grover. Make remember for Mr. Grover."

"Never mind," I said, scooping up the clothes. "Have a drink for me."

"Remember for you, too."

"That's great," I said. "How much do I owe you?"

"Go now," he said, blinking again. "Say hello Mr. Nordine. Tell him sorry, very sorry. Tell him I make farewell service for Mr. Grover."

"I will."

"Good-bye." He turned his back on me and started banging things around: a clothes press, a big trashcan full of hangers. I left.

In the car, I opened the blue package. It contained thirty-two well-laundered dollars—two tens, two fives, and two ones—a heavy turquoise ring with white tape wrapped around it to make it smaller, a credit card receipt for a restaurant called The Fig Tree, dated three days ago, and a piece of newsprint, tightly folded. When I had it open, I was looking at perhaps a quarter of a page from a tabloid, carefully scissored around a block of four ads.

It was evidently a specialty paper. The advertisements were for a gay dating service called First-Class Male, an "adult" telephone line that identified itself as the Long John Connection, a bookstore named A Different Slant, and a bar called The Zipper. The other side was taken up with part of a classified section, maybe forty short notices, mostly along the lines of *hard jock seeks same.* Max had paid no attention to the borders of the classifieds; the ones at the borders were cut into fragments. Written in the bottom margin on the classified side, in pencil, was a string of digits: 237/10/21/6:2.

I wrote down the numbers on a pad I keep on Alice's dashboard and turned the page over again. There was no way I could check forty classifieds. It was only eleven-thirty, and The Fig Tree probably hadn't opened yet. I drew and then let out a long breath and headed for The Zipper.

7
CEREAL KILLER

THE Zipper—I'm sorry—was open.

I'd never been in a darker room. Heavy, wide strips of black plastic, like the ones used to keep warmth out of a supermarket meat locker, hung in the front door to hold October at bay. When they flapped shut behind me, I found myself completely blind. Since my eyes weren't doing me any good anyway, I closed them.

When I reopened them, a world appeared. A bar, lighted by seven or eight flickering Christmas bulbs, was to my immediate right. The man standing behind it wore a motorcycle jacket and an LAPD cap, complete with badge. He regarded me as though he was afraid I'd come in to sell him a vacuum cleaner. "You're new."

"I was a few minutes ago," I said, sliding my shoes over the floor in case there was a step up.

I sat down on a squeaky stool, and the man behind the bar studied my face while I glanced around at nothing in particular and tried not to look like someone whose face was being studied. "About thirty," he finally announced, with the muted pride of someone pulling a playing card out of his ear. "I'm Stan."

"It's dark in here, Stan," I said, "and you're being nice."

"Been years since I saw anybody in the light," he said. "Complimentary bullshot?"

"Why not?" After all the water with Christopher, I would have drunk Mogen David from a workboot.

"Interesting clothes," he said, setting the drink down in a glass that looked uncomfortably like an erect penis on a flat, circular base.

"I thought so when I bought them."

"Thirty-four?" he asked, squinting at me.

"Thirty-seven." The bullshot was vile and wonderful at the same time. The glass felt silly in my hand. Somebody laughed roughly behind me, and I turned to see two men entwined in a booth.

"You're taking care of your skin," the bartender said, pursuing his theme, "but you want to watch the bullshots."

I tapped the glass with a forefinger. "I'm keeping my eye on this one."

"You know," the bartender said, watching me carefully, "there are other bars up the street." He mopped the surface of the bar with a rag that might have been Veronica's Veil two thousand years ago. "Straight bars, you know? If that's where you'd rather be."

"Is it as obvious as that?" In some unweeded corner of my soul, I was dismayed.

"About two blocks up. Like I said, this one's on the house."

Everyone was offering me freebies today. "But I like it here."

"You're being asked to leave," a new voice said, and I turned to see one of the men in the booth standing up with evident hostile intent. He was bigger than Godzilla and he was wearing most of Argentina's annual export of black leather. "And you're being asked real nice. Stan's a lot sweeter than I am."

The situation was slipping away from me, a familiar sensation lately. "You know Max Grover?" I asked the giant.

He paused for a count of five. "Max?" he said. "Everybody knew Max."

"What's Max to you?" Stan the bartender asked.

"Christy hired me," I said. "The cops want Christy, and I'm his, um, his guy to, um, keep them away from him."

"Prove it." That was Stan.

I swiveled on my squeaky stool. "Oh, sure. Prove it. There's no way I can prove it. I mean, I've got a card, but—"

"Let's see it."

I decided not to finish the sentence, which had been something to the effect that anyone could print a card, and pried one of my detective cards out of my wallet. I handed it to Stan, and he held it under one of the Christmas lights, reading it during blinks. This was obviously an acquired skill.

"Simon Grist," he read aloud. "Private investigator."

"*Simeon*," I corrected him. "As in 'Simeon.' "

"Apelike," the giant supplied into the conversational void.

"As in Simeon Stylites," I said, stung. "A saint who spent most of his life standing on a pillar in the desert. My parents are interested in—"

"He's a private eye," Stan said. He sounded impressed; maybe I was the first one he'd met. If so, there was disillusionment in his future.

"And Christy hired me," I said.

There was a long pause.

Then the man still seated in the booth stirred and raised his face to mine. It was a memorable face, the face of a prizefighter who'd gone fifteen rounds with a 747. "Poor Max," he said in a voice softer than a fresh diaper.

"Everybody loved Max," Stan the bartender said, nodding. "Max was a hundred per cent."

"A thousand per cent," said Mr. Leather. "Oh, Jeez, Max."

"So he was in here?" I asked, breathing again.

"In and out with his caseload," Stan said. He touched his index finger to his forehead. "You know, his lost souls."

"The kids he was helping," I suggested.

"There's never been anyone like Max," the leather giant said tenderly. "Easiest touch in the world. Money for nothing, you know? And too old to expect anything for it."

"And now the cops want Christy," I said.

"Christy." Stan sounded reflective. "Harmless plus."

"But they *were* fighting," said the man sitting at the table.

"Jealous, Christy," Stan offered, immediately revising his opinion.

"Didn't mean anything, though," the giant tendered fondly. "Those guys had a karmic link."

"Ancient souls," Stan said, nodding. Agreeing with everyone was apparently part of his job description.

"Took a swing at Max, he did," the sitting man said, "at Dante's a couple of weeks ago."

"He always had a violent streak," Stan agreed.

"But he couldn't have *hurt* Max," said the giant.

"Absolutely not," Stan said.

This could go on all day. "There's a guy with the Sheriff's Department who thinks he did," I said.

"Name?" asked the giant.

"Spurrier."

"Spiky Ikey," the man sitting at the table said, surprising me. "Ike Spurrier couldn't find his asshole in a shitstorm."

The pivot beneath my seat squealed as I turned. "You know him?"

"Everybody knows Spurrier." The man at the table emitted a choked sound like a muzzled dog barking. A laugh. "The Sheriffs' Department's number one closet case."

It was mildly interesting. "You think so?"

"This is a guy in deep denial," Stan said.

I considered it for a moment and then stopped considering it. "So who killed Max?"

"Somebody," said the giant, who had taken the hand of the soft-voiced man at the table, "who should have his skin stripped off inch by inch."

Realizing I had the bullshot in my hand, I drank some. "Did Max bring any new kids in here in the last month or so?"

"Other than the caseload?" That was the bartender.

"How would you know who wasn't part of the caseload?"

"Street kids," the bartender said. "You can smell them in the dark."

"There was the pretty one," said the man still seated at the table.

"Shhhh," the giant said.

"Whenever anyone says 'shhhh,' I get real interested," I said. "Maybe I should have told you that before."

"Skip it," said the giant apologetically.

"The hell I'll skip it. Max is dead, and you're hushing people because, um, because—"

"Because he thought the kid was cute," the man at the table said, drawing the word "cute" into three heavily sugared syllables: *kee-yee-ute.*

"He *was* cute," Stan the bartender said.

"The boy was nice," the giant said defensively. "Everybody liked him. You," he said to the man at the table, "have a mind like a third-world latrine."

"Just that one boy," said the man at the table to me. "Very young, very pretty. Hair like corn."

"Like wheat," the giant said.

The man at the table looked up at him. "When was the last time you saw wheat? When was the last time you were *outdoors?*"

The giant opened his mouth, then closed it again. "I get outside," he said, sounding hurt. "Wheat, corn. Some kind of cereal. Rice puffs, maybe."

"Hair the color of corn," the man at the table said dreamily. "Scared eyes. Looked maybe seventeen, eighteen, but he had I.D."

"I.D." I swiveled around to regard Stan. "Was there a name on the I.D.?"

"Sure," Stan said. "But who remembers? Danny? David?"

"Something with a *D*," the giant said. "I remember a *D*."

"What kind of I.D.?"

Stan thought about it. "Driver's license. Out-of-state, kind of funny-looking. No, I don't remember which state."

"Someplace where they grow them big and blond," the man at the table said. "Like a farm state. He was, I don't know, a farm boy. Hair like corn."

"Wheat," the giant murmured rebelliously.

"When were they here?"

"A couple of days ago."

"Sunday?"

Stan the bartender looked at the wall opposite. "I guess so. It was pretty quiet. Could have been Sunday."

"How were they getting along?"

"Max treated him like he was a piece of candy," said the man at the table. "The kid was staring like a tourist who'd never been to town before, afraid to talk to anyone."

"Everybody liked him," the giant in leather repeated defiantly. "There was something really sweet about him. Not just the way he looked, either. I've seen lots of great-looking kids who gave off negative vibes, but this kid was really . . ."

"Sweet," offered the man at the table. He nodded his head. "I guess he was."

"Okay," I said, "he was sweet."

"You ever like anyone on first sight?" the man at the table asked me.

"My job doesn't really lend itself to snap opinions."

"Well, everybody here liked him on first sight." He lifted a broad hand and massaged a scar on his cheek. "Funny thing, charm."

"It certainly is," I said. "How tall?"

"Stand up." That was Stan again. I did. "Same as you," he said. "Six feet or so."

"What color eyes?"

Stan lifted a hand. "Who could see?"

"Blue," said the man at the table.

"Ho, ho," the giant said softly.

The man at the table blinked up at him. "Same color as mine."

"Blond hair, blue eyes, six feet, seventeen or eighteen. Build?"

"Strong," the man at the table said. "I told you. Like a farm boy."

"Anything else?" I asked the room at large. No one spoke. I turned to face the bartender. "How much do I owe you?"

"On Max," he said mournfully.

So, everybody loved Max, I thought outside, squinting against the glare. So, a farm boy.

Twenty-five cents in a pay phone bought me two messages on my answering machine. Christy, sounding brisker than he had last night, said he'd found a place to stash himself for the meantime, and he'd call later, he didn't want to leave the number on a machine. I was commending him for his discretion when the machine beeped and my mother's distinctive cigarette rasp asked if I was there. When I wasn't, she snorted impatiently and ordered me to call. If I still remembered the number.

I dropped another quarter into the phone and dialed, inhaling the reek of ammonia and remembering a time when phone booths didn't double as public urinals. Phone booths probably thought of it as the golden age.

"This is your son," I said when my mother answered. She wore her hearing aid in the ear she didn't put the handset against, and lately she sometimes failed to recognize my voice.

"Oh," she said. "Hold on." The phone clattered to the surface of her kitchen counter. I used the idle moment to watch a young businessman in a Heineken-green Mazda Miata gently rear-end a large truck on Santa Monica Boulevard. The truckdriver climbed deliberately down from his cab, an unusually wide man with a Marine buzz cut, wearing camouflage combat fatigues and seven-league boots, and stalked slowly back toward the Miata. The yuppie in the Miata took one horrified look, reversed out from under the truck, and backed away rapidly, cutting the wheel sharply and bumping up into the parking lot of a minimall.

"Had to turn off the stove," my mother said.

"I don't know how you can cook in this heat," I said, just to be polite.

"And you don't much care, either. Are you sitting down?"

"No. Why?"

"I just wondered. I thought perhaps you were ill or something."

"No, I'm fine." The man in the Miata threw the car into first and squealed off down Santa Monica Boulevard.

"Or had broken your leg."

"Both legs in working order, thanks."

"Or your dialing finger."

"Here I am, Mom," I said. "Standing on a sweltering corner in West Hollywood, up to my ankles in urine, calling my dear old mother."

"I want to see you." Mom didn't waste a lot of time on chat.

"Fine. When?"

"Whenever you can spare a moment for your only mother."

"Anytime that's good for you."

"Well, as you know, we have a very crowded social schedule, your father and I. Channel nine is showing back-to-back reruns of *M*A*S*H*.*"

The truckdriver had run out of profanity after unleashing a long and inspiringly original stream of invective. "Just say when."

"Three," she said. "*M*A*S*H* starts at four-thirty."

I check my watch: one-forty. "Fine," I said.

"Three sharp," she said. "You know how your father feels about Alan Alda."

The man who answered the line at the Long John Connection was even less chatty than my mother. A shrill chorus of phones rang insistently in the background.

"Yeah, I heard about Max," he said. "Awful, just awful."

"I need to talk to the owner."

"That's me. I'm a little short on help here."

"It won't take much time."

"I doubt that. Look, I can't keep this line tied up. It's costing money. Can you come over here?"

"Where's 'here'?"

"Kings Road. Just north of the Boulevard."

"Which boulevard?"

There was a pause. "Santa Monica," he said patiently. "The *Boulevard.*"

"Sorry, I'm a little addled today. See you in five minutes."

Addled was an understatement. The bullshot had cooked up in the sunshine, sending its fumes directly to my frontal lobe, by the time the door to apartment 8 opened to reveal a man who looked like Grizzly Adams's more poorly groomed younger brother: maybe forty-five, beard to midchest over an Alvin Ailey T-shirt, thinning hair pulled back into a ponytail, tinted aviator-style glasses over odd gold-colored eyes.

"You're the pay phone?" The gold-brown eyes flicked over my shoulder, making sure I was alone.

"About Max," I said.

He ran the name through his frontal lobe while he looked at me. It was a speculative look. Finally he nodded. "I'm Jack." He put out a hand and mauled mine with it. "Come on in, air-conditioning's expensive. I can give you ten minutes."

Four men sat on couches and director's chairs, talking on phones. "Oooh, I'd *like* that," one of them said in a seductive voice. "Do you think you could do it twice?"

I closed the door behind me. "You knew Max?"

Jack straightened his glasses, which were already as straight as a plumbline. "Everybody knew Max." It was beginning to sound like a litany. "The saint of the sidewalks. What's your connection?"

I told him. He never took the gold-brown eyes from my face. No polite nods, no reflexive sounds of agreement. When I was finished, he said, "Christy," in a noncommittal tone.

"That seems to be the general opinion."

Jack turned toward the kitchen, and I followed. "He's a Jonah. You a sailing man?"

"I know what a Jonah is. Bad luck."

"More than that." He reached back and pulled fingers through his ponytail. "Bad luck for other people, too. Some people trail clouds of it, like scent." The kitchen was white and spotless, with three electric coffee makers on the tile counter. Labels on the pots read CINNAMON, DECAF, and ECSTASY BLEND. At the far end of the kitchen was one of those little greenhouse windows people are so fond of these days, jammed full of terra-cotta pots sprouting foliage. Jack pulled up a stool at the counter and indicated another for me.

I eyed the coffee. "Who had it in for Max?"

He shrugged. "Nobody. What was there to hate? He was generous, good-hearted, and stupid. The perfect mark."

"He didn't strike me as stupid."

"About himself. He was brilliant about everybody else."

"You know that personally?"

He looked puzzled. "What's that supposed to mean?"

"Was he brilliant about you?"

Jack chewed the inside of his lip, looking dubious, and followed my gaze toward the coffeepots. "You're confusing me. You want some coffee?"

"I'd love some. I'm recovering from a bullshot."

"Lady Ecstasy for you," he said, getting up to pour.

"So what about Max?"

"I'm not sure why you're here." He held out a heavy white mug.

"I told you." I took the mug and wandered toward the greenhouse window.

"Max," he said, weighing his words, "Max just had to help people. There weren't enough hours in the day, you know?"

"So I gather." The plants in the little pots were herbs: rosemary, basil, mint, and a couple I couldn't identify. They gave the air near the sink a pungency that clashed pleasantly with the coffee.

Jack's stool shifted behind me. "What do you know about us?"

I turned to look at him. "Who's 'us'?"

He made a circling motion, index finger down, as though stirring the air in the apartment. "Us."

"You're a, what, a hot line."

"Safe sex," he said. "Through the ear, like the Holy Ghost's words to Mary. Did you know that Mary was impregnated through the ear?"

I pressed a leaf between thumb and forefinger and inhaled the dark, sweet green-clove scent of basil. "Sounds uncomfortable."

"We're more than a hot line. We're also a dating service.

Not-so-safe sex, but people are people. They've got to take their own precautions."

"You're First-Class Male, too?" I asked.

He nodded. "And we're a computer bulletin board. Something Fine Online." He looked dissatisfied. "Got to work on that name," he said.

"So tell me about this," I said. I licked the basil from my fingertips and pulled the folded newspaper from my pocket. Jack peered across the kitchen at it.

"Our ads," he said, sounding satisfied. He got up and held out a hand, and I passed the page to him. "Designed them myself on the computer. That's the *Nite Line*. Comes out once a week, on Monday. It's a bar rag. Lots of little ads." He turned the page over and ran a thumb over the classifieds. "Like these. All these beautiful, sensitive, lonely young men, desperately seeking a soulmate. Preferably a soulmate with many credit cards."

"Not on the level," I said.

"About as much as the sex ads in the straight papers. Hustlers, mostly, or old fatties pretending to be twenty-four and buffed up. Sad stuff. Where'd you get this?"

"It was Max's. It's what brought me here."

Jack's eyes widened briefly. "Max? Max had this?"

"Not what you'd expect?"

"Not bloody hardly. Max found his kids on the street, where he could see they were desperation cases. Plenty of kids on the pavement these days. One side of the economy the *Times* rarely sees fit to cover."

"So why would he have the paper?"

He refolded it along the sharp creases, looking at me. "God knows. He had his hands full as it was, between his lost kids, Christy, and the service."

I was getting confused. "Which service?"

"The computer service. Something Fine Online. I thought that's why you were here."

"I'm just blundering around," I said, "chasing lines in the *Nite Line*."

Jack jerked his head over his shoulder. "Come on. So your day shouldn't be a complete loss. I'll show you a new side of Max."

We went through the living room, where angel's flight seemed to have struck: All the phones were silent, and the young men sat staring into the middle distance, gathering their energies for the next erotically charged encounter. One of them was doing a crossword puzzle. Jack led me down a hallway hung with a few small and unconvincing Dali lithographs, mostly watches that seemed to have collided with pizzas, and into a bedroom where a tower-model desktop computer hummed away on a huge desk made from two tables placed end to end. The setup covered an entire wall. Multiple-tiered in and out baskets screwed to the wall held stacks of modems, their red lights blinking like the eyes of animals in a Disney forest. Four screens were filled with flying text, scrolling almost too rapidly to be read.

"About thirty online at the moment," Jack said, eyeing the modems. "What do you know about how this works?"

I'd come up against a bulletin board before, a particularly vile heterosexual meat market where children were the merchandise. "People call in on their computers and talk to each other in real time, using their keyboards, or leave messages for each other." It didn't sound very expert. "I guess all boards are different, though."

"All boards are exactly the same, at least as far as the hardware and software go," Jack said. "It's the wetware that makes them different."

"Wetware."

"The people." He gestured at the screen, at the ribbon of words. "Boards are neutral, just like a TV set or a telephone line, until you add in the human factor. This is a gay board. Most everybody on it is gay, they live in the local calling area, and they give it its distinguishing characteristics, which is to say they make it a West Hollywood gay board, lots of jokes, lots of industry talk, lots of jokey, horny e-mail. And, naturally, a psychic flavor, since this is probably the only city in America where psychics outnumber real people."

"And that's where Max—"

"Not entirely. Close, though." He seated himself at the computer and did something fast and practiced. "Look here," he said.

TALK TO THE THERAPIST glowed in the middle of the largest screen.

"I'll be damned," I said. "Max?"

"Therapist and psychic," Jack said. "All-around emotional handyman. Some of the strangest questions you ever read. That was one of the things I loved about him: Nothing struck him as weird. If someone said to him that he needed his aura fluffed, Max would have figured out a way to fluff the man's aura. He dealt with some pretty disgusting stuff here, too, but Max never got disgusted."

"Nothing human disgusts me," I said.

Jack gave me a skeptical glance. "Or Max."

"That's a Tennessee Williams line," I said. "Actually, I disgust fairly easily."

On the screen, I read:

I'm thirty-eight years old, and lately I've been fantasizing sex with women. My dreams are totally peculiar, but I wake up with a big woody anyway. My lover is beginning to suspect something is wrong. Do you think you can help?

Beneath it was the Therapist's—Max's—reply:

You lucky boy. It's a new world. Don't be afraid of facing it. Look at it this way: It doubles the number of possibles. Anyway, it may only be a phase. I'd suggest that you talk to your lover about it. He might actually like it if you suggested he run down to Victoria's Secret and buy a little—

Beside me, Jack gave a kind of gasp, like someone exhaling a knot.

—peignoir or something. Of course—

"Holy Jesus," Jack said, and I swiveled to look at the screen in front of him. Words were scrolling past, black on the white display. Jack turned wide eyes to me and put a hand over the screen as though it were emitting heat.

"It's from Max," he said.

8
EAT AT MOM'S

THERE'S a lot of money in Boys' Town.

The recently incorporated city of West Hollywood nestles up against the southern base of the Hollywood Hills, where tidy little hillside châteaus begin around $750,000 and climb into the double-digit millions. Lots of people from the entertainment industry—agents, directors, actors, writers, producers, poseurs, parasites, Picassos of the pitch—drive down the hills in the morning and up them again in the evening, where they join their new Iranian neighbors in worrying about fire all summer and mudslides all winter.

The north-south streets, streets like Miller Drive and Sunset Plaza Drive, empty into the Sunset Strip. If you think of Boys' Town as a sort of cultural toupee planted cosmetically onto the map of Los Angeles, the Strip would be the part in the hair, dividing the hills from the flatland. It's the thoroughfare the white people from Beverly Hills use to go east in the morning in their Rolls-Royces and Mercedes, passing the brown people from Central America going west on the bus to clean houses and tend other people's children.

The shops along this section of Sunset are small and precious, selling imported flowers, new furniture that's been artfully slammed with chains to make it look old, designer outfits with exotic sequins, designer shoes, designer sound equipment, and designer everything else. Alternating with the shops are a great many sidewalk cafés that cater to young, slender, aggressively attractive types who toss their hair back a lot. People who spend several hundred dollars a month on their hair want it to *glimmer*, and it's hard to make hair glimmer when the sunlight striking it seems to have passed through an ocean of iced tea. So they sit there in the beige sunshine and toy with their Caesar salads and toss their hair back whenever they sense a stray sunbeam. Or, at night, a headlight.

Below Sunset, in the apartment complexes and small houses that stretch south on the flats to Santa Monica Boulevard and beyond, is the workaday Boys' Town. The classic old apartments, high-ceilinged and spacious, that housed the stars of the thirties and forties, and the postmodern concrete steamships disguised as condominiums house a politically significant community of gays and lesbians who haul themselves out of bed every day to face the same kinds of jobs that wear people out in Dubuque, Medicine Hat, and Little Rock. They count other people's change in stores, cash other people's checks in banks, sell ugly shoes for other people's feet, deal in second trust deeds on other people's property, fix watches, clean teeth, and dispense medicine. And when the day is done, many of them go home and dispense care and love to people who need them. People who are sick or dying.

In the past I'd attended community meetings here, I'd hauled friends to Alcoholics Anonymous and Cocaine Anonymous meetings here. I'd seen gatherings delayed for moments of silence in remembrance of the just dead. I'd seen guys who looked like the Masters of the Universe come into rooms supporting men who were almost transparent with illness. I'd seen those transparent men rise to give love and support to the healthy-looking ones as they wrestled with their addictions, and I'd come back months later to see the healthy ones weep over the transparent ones who were no longer there. I'd seen courage and heroism.

To the casual glance, West Hollywood looked prosperous and happy, and it *was* happy, most of the time, for most of the men who lived there. They'd fled communities in the heartland, in the wheat belt, in the Bible Belt, in other belts less appealing than the thirty-one-inch variety that seemed to circle most of the waists in Boys' Town. They'd established the City of Gratified Desire, a place where they could lead the lives they wanted to lead. Like everyone else did.

The Fig Tree fronted on Sunset, looking out onto the street through plate-glass windows etched with trailing branches and leaves. The clientele, visible through the frosty foliage, was almost exclusively male, almost exclusively young.

Two days ago—the day Christopher Nordine had first come to my house—Max had taken the Farm Boy into The Zipper. The receipt from The Fig Tree was dated two days ago. The kid had been described as a "tourist," and I was willing to bet that Max had been giving him a guided tour of West Hollywood's hot spots.

As much as I wanted to go into The Fig Tree, it wasn't a sound idea. Spurrier's men would have accessed Max's credit-card records first thing, and if the Sheriffs hadn't already been here, they would be soon. Spurrier had been very convincing about not wanting me anywhere near the case.

So I sat at the curb, letting Alice idle for fifteen minutes or so, pushing my sore back into the upholstery and thinking about Christy. Spurrier again, and thanks for the thought, Ike.

He'd chosen Christy as the Boy Most Likely, and it would have made a lot of sense to someone who hadn't met him. The heir threatened by a new affection, the long-term planner hiring someone to establish in advance his fear that Max's life was in danger. He'd shown up at my house with a gun in his hand the night following Max's death: second thoughts? Panic? Get rid of a potential witness?

Against all that, I had my conviction that his grief for Max had been real.

But there was also the fact that someone had been in Max's house when I was there, someone Max hadn't wanted me to see. Not Christy: He wouldn't have been there when I was coming, not if he was afraid to talk to Max about the Farm Boy himself. He would have waited a few hours to give Max some time to absorb it all.

Since there was a reasonably hygienic phone booth on the corner, I left Alice to the mercies of the parking patrol and called Marta Aguirre, the housekeeper, again. I got the same indignant lady, with the same indignant mix of Spanish and English. Marta wasn't around and wasn't ever likely to be around, and why didn't I get a job or something and stop bothering people in the middle of the day?

Max's message—another therapist's column, sent over the phone lines to Jack's computer more than twenty-four hours after his death—needed attention, but that would be better left until dark. Ike Spurrier was the type who might get touchy about people wandering around in sealed crime scenes.

That left Mom.

I don't know when my parents got old. It seems to me that they'd been vital and vigorous, kicking and carping their way through advanced middle age, until one Saturday morning when the light slanted just wrong through their living-room windows and I found myself staring, almost openmouthed, at two senior citizens. Since then I'd listened to the commonplace complaints, watched the hearing aids appear, picked up prescriptions, chafed impatiently as my father drove more and more slowly, until the car began to go unused for months at a time, and come to realize for the first time in a largely optimistic life that things don't always get better. The houses—we'd lived in what seemed like dozens—had dwindled to a small apartment in Santa Monica, and the luggage they'd hauled all around the world had become furniture, stacked in the living room with a thick piece of glass over it to serve as a coffee table.

My mother was sitting in the chair in which she's spent much of her adult life, a high-backed, regal affair that is continually being reupholstered in a shade of blue indistinguishable to me from any of the previous blues. My mother, though, is capable of distinguishing among blues in much the same way Eskimos are said to be able to do with snow, and the current shade, she assures all who ask, is the most pleasing yet. Since it was early in the day by her standards—only three-fifteen— she had the *Los Angeles Times* spread out at her feet and about twenty of her daily sixty cigarettes pronged down and lipsticked in the cut-glass ashtray at her side.

"You're late," she said, leaning forward and scanning the obituaries. "Cripes, but people are dying young these days."

"I made a few stops," I said, "trying to squeeze in as much life as I can before the ax falls."

"You lack focus." She peered down at a particularly large obituary, ornamented by a photograph of a woman who had probably planted a great many fringed geraniums in her all-too-brief day. "You run around like a chicken with its head cut off. It's the family curse."

"I thought the family curse was drink." She obviously wasn't going to slip into maternal mode anytime soon, so I took the initiative and kissed her cheek. Bending over brought both the bullshot and the sore back into play. "Coffee on?"

"I made an upside-down cake." She flicked the newspaper noisily with her index finger and made a clucking noise. "Only sixty-three."

I crossed the small living room to the kitchen. "What the hell is this, hot water?"

"Caffeine's bad for you," she said complacently. "Especially if you lack focus. The Chinese drink lots of hot water. Ask Eleanor."

"I'm going to close my eyes and name the presidents, and when I get to Madison there'll be real coffee in this pot."

She heaved a sigh, preparatory to getting up. "I spoiled you," she said.

"It was the piano lessons," I said, sticking my finger into the upside-down cake.

"I never gave you piano lessons. Take your finger out of there this minute."

"That's what I mean." My finger was sticky, brown, and sweet with caramelized sugar, a taste that took me back to a time when I had barely been able to reach the counter. "If you'd forced me to take piano lessons, I might have developed some character."

"Actually, I *wanted* you to take lessons. Your father said no. Said the scales would drive him stark staring mad."

"And then there was the piano." I put my finger back into the cake as she ladled a tablespoon of instant expresso into a cup and then added some more, direct from the jar. My mother's coffee was a cardiologist's nightmare.

"What piano?" She sloshed water into the cup, getting most of it on the counter. "Hell's bells," she said.

"The one we didn't have."

"That was your father, too," my mother said. She leaned against the sink and took an absentminded sip of my coffee. " 'If the boy wants to play something,' he said, 'get him a harmonica. At least we'll have someplace to put it.' "

I took the cup from her hand. "You could have talked him into it."

"He's a stubborn man. I tried. Got him up to a ukelele before he dug his heels in. Is that strong enough?"

"It'd raise the dead."

"Sweet words from my sweet son." She patted me on the cheek in a brisk, businesslike fashion and scanned the counter. "Did I have a cigarette?"

"Since I came in, you mean?"

"I've taken to putting them down and walking away. It worries your father."

"And so it might. Where is he?"

"At the golf course."

"Dad doesn't play golf."

"He likes to laugh at their trousers. Why is it that old men become such fools?"

"Ask me in a few years."

She started to roll her eyes, thought better of it, and blinked. "You have to mature before you get old."

"Ah. We're getting to it, are we?"

She sat in her chair and pushed the newspaper aside with her foot. "Of course," she said, putting a cigarette to her lips and lighting it, "you may have matured since I saw you last."

"I was here last week."

"I sometimes ask myself what I did wrong. Other women don't need to make an appointment to see their sons." She reached out and folded the paper, signaling that I had her full attention. "Do you still see that nice Peggy whatshername?"

I sat on the couch and blew on my coffee. "The last time I saw Peggy, I was sixteen."

"Such a pretty girl."

"As I recall, you said she reminded you of Secretariat."

She didn't even blink. "Horsy women," she said, "breed well."

There was absolutely no point in trying to hurry her, so I took a sip of coffee and felt my throat close involuntarily against the strength of it.

"And Eleanor. Is she still putting up with you?"

The coffee was as bitter as aloes, whatever they are. "Not very well."

My mother shook her head. "We're not a very communicative family, are we? And most Irish talk so."

"So what about Eleanor?"

She blew smoke at me. "Such a pretty girl."

"I thought that was Peggy."

"Peggy looked like a horse," she said. "And not a very attractive horse, at that."

"I'll just bet," I said, "that you sent Dad to the golf course."

She tapped ash into the crystal. "Why don't you marry Eleanor?"

I lifted the lethal cup from the saucer, but it didn't get to my lips. "I'll be damned," I said. "It's you."

My mother examined her cigarette as though she suspected it might have a tear in it. "Don't swear. What's me?"

"My mail. All that junk aimed at people who are tying the knot, as you usually say. All those phone calls."

"You're confusing me. Are we talking about mail, or—"

"You know perfectly well what we're talking about. How did you do it?" I didn't have much hope of getting a straight answer; my mother regards the truth as something you tell when you can't think of anything more entertaining, but she surprised me.

"I went to Bullock's." she said. "I registered you for china and silver. They sell their mailing lists, you know."

"What in the world motivated—"

She squinted at me through the smoke. "You're not as young as you used to be, you know."

I made the cup clatter against the saucer. "My God. That had never occurred to me."

"Good Lord, if anyone had told me twenty years ago that I'd be asking my son to marry a Chinese girl, I'd have slit my throat and danced in my own blood."

"Not on the carpet," I said.

"I'm serious, young man."

"Has anyone ever told you that you have a highly sanguinary turn of phrase?"

She tilted her head back and looked down her nose at me. "I'm *serious*."

"I know you are." I was touched. Like most Wasps born in the thirties, my parents were garden-variety racists, and their desire for a daughter-in-law of "good family" had been a frequent theme when I was growing up. The equine Peggy, I recalled, had come from my parents' idea of a good family. "Still, I don't think the bells are going to ring real soon."

"Well, I tried," she said. "But you're going to die a disappointed man if you don't marry that girl."

"It's not a unilateral decision, you know."

"Bah. She'd marry you in a minute, if you stopped acting like such a simpleton."

"I wish it were that easy."

"Your generation," she said impatiently, "complicates everything. Sometimes I think it has to do with physics. In the old days, in my days, I mean, things moved in a straight line unless something bent them. Now you've got all kinds of particles and whatnot, and something called the law of uncertainty. Well, I ask you. How can a law be a law if it's uncertain? How can you be certain you're obeying it? It's like the speed limit, if the sign said 'fifty-five or thereabouts.' What's 'thereabouts'? It's no wonder you've got, oh, punks and homosexuals everywhere."

"What do you think about homosexuals these days?"

She put a hand over her heart. "Are you trying to tell me something?"

"Give me a break. Just because I haven't married—"

"Well, it would be a relief if you did. Whenever I tell people my son is single, I always wonder what they're thinking. There's that little pause."

"Gay people," I prompted.

"I liked it better when they were all decorators and actors. They were so good with flowers. Now you just never know. They're even in the army."

"I guess they've finally been given the right to die for their country."

"I'm sure they're as brave as the next man."

"Or woman."

"Please." She pursed her lips and closed her eyes briefly. "If you're suggesting that women . . . That's something I *can't* get used to. I mean, men, we all know they'll sleep with anything, your father excepted, but women are supposed to have some sense."

I had memories of very loud late-night discussions between my parents when I was small, and the name *Betty* had figured prominently in many of them, but there had never been an appropriate time to bring it up. As my mother said, we weren't a very communicative family. Still . . .

"I guess old Dad always behaved himself."

She gave me a severe look. "He didn't sleep with infants," she said briskly.

It took me a moment to realize we'd taken up the next item on my mother's agenda. "You called Eleanor."

"Perhaps," she said airily.

"Or Eleanor called you."

"If you had an ounce of tact, you'd know I don't intend to—"

"It's flattering to be discussed by two attractive women, but that's hooey and you should know it. Infants indeed."

"At first I thought she was a boy. That peculiar name."

"This seems to be the theme of the day. Your Deviant Son."

"It gave me a turn, I can tell you."

"She's not an infant, and what's more important, we're not sleeping together."

"I think you should tell that to Eleanor."

"I did. She didn't believe me."

"I don't blame her," she said promptly. "Your life is entirely too irregular. You spread yourself all over the landscape. That was all right when you were a boy, but the time has come to steady yourself. Focus. Settle down. Have some cake."

"In that order?"

She got up to cut the cake. "You're a trying child. And you're going to miss the best bet of your life. Eleanor, I mean."

"She's too good for me." I was only half kidding.

"You're my son," my mother said, plopping a slice of cake onto a paper plate. "She loves you," she told the plate.

"Hell is almost getting what you want."

"That's fatuous. You behave as though your life had nothing to do with you."

"I don't feel as though I've got very much control over it," I said, and Max flashed into my mind: *Control is an illusion.*

"I'm an old woman," my mother said with surprising bitterness. "Things are ceasing to work. *That's* something that can't be controlled. There's nothing wrong with your life that couldn't be fixed with a little common sense. Eleanor is a good, steady girl. Your children would be perfectly beautiful. Sometimes I wish I could just choke a little sense into you."

"Yeah, well, I love you, too."

She put the cake firmly on the sink, went to her chair, and leaned down and opened the paper. The audience was over. "I'll say hello to your father for you."

The moon had risen earlier and brighter than I would have liked. It hung fat and full and pasty in the sky, skipping over a thin wisp of low-hanging clouds like a stone on ocean foam.

Eight o'clock, and not a parking space in sight. The night was still hot. Alice's windows admitted a stream of dry air as I circled the block, passing Max's house, making a right onto Santa Monica and then another right—north again—on the next street. While Max's street, Flores, was still slumbering peacefully in the 1920s, with rows of craftsmen's bungalows lighted up on either side, apartment houses had taken root on the parallel street. Many of them had broken out in almost dermatological eruptions of architectural whimsy: portholes and ship's railings, abstract neon compositions wired to the stucco, free-standing sculptures planted on the grass. Others rose blank and austere, Art Deco reincarnated.

Max's house, of course, was dark. I could make out the yellow crime-scene tape across the porch and the seals pasted to the door. A driveway, lined with bougainvillea, ran alongside the bungalow, and a row of Max's roses gleamed healthily in the moonlight on the far side. He had dozens more, Christy had told me, in back.

I didn't want to park near the house anyway. Alice was far too distinctive. I might be ignoring Spurrier's command, but that didn't mean I didn't take it seriously.

Four blocks away, on the other side of the Boulevard, I eased Alice into a space and climbed out, my joints stiff and cranky from sitting still for so long. I loosened up as I hit the sidewalk, and by the time I'd reached the lights of the main street I was walking like a more or less upright primate. A pair of latex gloves, pulled from a box of fifty I'd bought on the way, bulged uncomfortably in my pocket.

The restaurants and bars were full, men in jeans or shorts and T-shirts standing in line in front of the more popular ones. I flowed with the current on the sidewalk, feeling anonymous and even confident. This was sheriff's territory, though, and it took an effort not to glance at the occasional black-and-white, idling slowly by in the traffic. Some of the deputies, I noticed, wore their shades even at night. Never a good sign.

Flores Street was dark and relatively deserted. Walking quickly, like someone who knew exactly where he was going, I turned up Max's driveway and past the house, my heartbeat accelerating and the taste of my mother's coffee sharp and sour in the back of my throat. I found the gate in the center of the shoulder-high chain-link fence, wincing as it squealed open. This was not something I would be able to explain if a patrol car spotted me.

Roses lifted pale faces to the moon, and the breeze, a real fire breeze blown down from the desert, stirred the tendrils of the pepper tree that arched high above the yard. The tree soaked up the moon's light, and I had to grapple in my pockets for the little medical flashlight, the size of a ballpoint pen, I'd taken from Alice's dash compartment. Then I slipped into the latex gloves.

The key to the back door, one of several Christy said Max had stowed around the property, was where he'd told me it would be, under the center cushion of a small vinyl-upholstered couch shoved up against the side of the sagging wooden garage. It faced a dry birdbath that contained a pyramid of spherical Christmas ornaments, a decorative touch that seemed uncharacteristically tacky for Max. Maybe it was meant to be funny.

Out of curiosity I first tried the keys I'd gotten from Max's dry cleaner, but none of them could be fitted into the lock. The one from the couch slipped in easily. I gave it a full turn and pushed against the door, but it didn't budge.

It took me longer to figure it out than it should have. I turned the key farther and pushed against the door again, and then I backed away from it as though it were red-hot.

I hadn't unlocked the door. I'd locked it.

My shirt was suddenly wet beneath the arms. Leaving the key in the lock, I stepped away from the house, still walking backwards, until a rosebush poked its thorns into my back. I sidestepped and kept going backward, my eyes on the house, until I was pressed up against the rough trunk of the pepper tree.

No lights showed in the house, no signs of movement. The pepper tree sighed and whispered, bumping against my back in time with the pounding in my chest.

To the right, the fence joined the corner of the house. To the left, the driveway stretched on its way to the street, past more windows than I liked to think about. Behind me, on the other side of the pepper tree, loomed the blank wall of an apartment building, at least three stories high. My rosy bower was a cul-de-sac, as they like to call dead ends these days.

The darkest part of the shade was just next to the pepper tree. I sat there in the warm dirt, my back against the apartment building, and waited.

When the moonlight began to spill over me, maybe two hours later, I shifted to the other side of the tree. Nothing had stirred in the house, and although the breeze kept making a racket in the tree above me, I hadn't heard anything else. When the light reached me a second time, the moon far to the west now, I got up and shook the kinks from my legs, my back creaking petulantly, turned away from the house, and shone the little penlight at my watch. I'd been there for more than four hours.

The key was right where I'd left it. I turned it, to the left this time, listening to the tumblers' reluctant click and fall, and slowly pushed the door open. Max's kitchen lay in front of me, illuminated by a milky patch of moonlight on the littered linoleum floor. It wasn't much light, but it was enough to show me the place had been ransacked. Drawers had been ripped from their housings, cupboards emptied. Silverware skittered away from my feet as I moved forward toward the pile of food in front of the refrigerator. I smelled sour milk and onions.

The idea of leaving presented itself with some force. I was not looking at the aftermath of a police search.

The kitchen opened into a small breakfast area, rounded and windowed to my left, and I remembered I'd passed a bay window in the driveway. This was a part of the house I hadn't seen, so I paused a moment to get my bearings, trying to reconcile the rooms through which Max had led me and the side of the house as I'd seen it from outside. More data: Christy had said Max sometimes slept in his room and sometimes in his own, so there were at least two bedrooms. After a few minutes of silent visualization, I had a hypothetical floor plan: Behind me, the kitchen; the small dining room would be in front of me, opening into the living room, and beyond that, the front door. To the right would be the library where I'd talked to Max, a hallway, and the bedrooms.

The moonlight through the bay windows showed me a wilderness of broken dishes and torn cookbooks, ripped open and flung to the floor. The cookbooks I could understand—lots of things can be hidden in books—but the dishes were frightening. They bespoke rage, pure and simple, rage so powerful that its owner hadn't been able to contain it even though the sound of the shattering dishes must have been deafening in the small room. He would have known the neighbors might have heard them, but he had thrown and trampled them anyway.

A more reassuring idea: He'd obviously come in through the back door and probably left the same way. I didn't think he'd have risked going out through the front. Maybe he'd started his search at the far end of the house and worked his way backward, his fury mounting with every fruitless room until, with only the kitchen and the breakfast room left, he'd felt secure that he would be out of the house and blocks away before the sheriffs responded to a neighbor's call. He'd been gone before I arrived.

Maybe.

Whatever he'd wanted had been small enough to hide in a book. What I wanted was Max's computer, so I could move fast. It was a great relief to move fast.

I barely glanced into the living room and the library. I'd seen them the day before—it seemed like a week ago—and I couldn't have missed a computer. Both rooms had been tossed violently. Max's books had been torn from their shelves, flung into piles that spilled into the hallway. Paintings had been slashed, their frames snapped. Stuffing bled out of the incisions in the deep chair.

The hallway was completely interior, so no moonlight reached it. My penlight picked out details of destruction: a rug sliced into parallel strips three inches wide, the bright shards of a broken mirror scattering light on the walls as I passed.

A small bedroom that opened to the left, toward the front of the house, was in total confusion, the mattress standing against the wall, the frame upended, and the box spring slit open from head to foot. The glass shower door in the adjoining bathroom had been shattered. It was not so much a search as an evisceration.

The door at the far end of the bathroom was ajar, and I pushed it open with an extended hand, harder than I'd intended, and waited as it banged against the wall of a larger bedroom, Max's bedroom, I guessed. The human bomb had gone off in here, too, but on a small desk across the room I saw a compact computer, intact.

I'm not familiar with Macintoshes, but I expected at least to be able to turn one on. I found a switch that seemed to be in the right place and flipped it up. Nothing. Running my hands around the frame, I located no other switches, and I got down on my hands and knees, feeling the room yawning wide behind my unprotected back, and pointed my penlight along the power cord until I came to the socket into which it was plugged. Scratch the first hypothesis, always presented so helpfully in the manuals as a panacea when trouble is encountered: Make sure the system is plugged in.

That left the unwelcome possibility that the outlet was controlled by a switch, probably just inside the door. Craftsmen's bungalows, for all their strong points, are generally underwired, with few outlets. I guess people in the twenties just didn't have so much stuff to plug in.

There were only two lights in the room, one a lamp next to the bed and the other a ceiling fixture in the center of the room. I hauled the chair on which I'd been sitting across the floor until it was beneath the fixture and climbed up. The milk-glass covering pulled away with a shower of dust and a couple of dead moths, revealing a small bulb, touchingly pink. It unscrewed easily, and I tossed it into the center of the bed. Then I clambered down, yanked the plug on the bedside lamp, crossed to the door, and threw the switch.

The Macintosh came to life with a startlingly loud whir. The screen glowed and then snapped alight to reveal the fabled user-friendly interface, full of little bugs, pictures that presumably launched programs. There we were: a tiny telephone icon and the legend *modem*. I highlighted it with the mouse and pushed the *enter* key, and the screen flickered again and came up with a dialogue box, full of buttons. One of them said *Timed Send*. It sounded right, so I pushed down on the mouse and the button on-screen turned into a box containing the words *Timed Send: 10/26 14:00*.

At two o'clock I'd been sitting in Jack's computer room, watching the text fly by: Max's ghost message, dispatched by the clock in a machine.

As long as I had the computer on, I figured, I might as well search Max's hard drive. I kicked out of the communications program, located MacWord, and booted it. It only took a few seconds to figure out how to access the list of document directories, and when I did I found that Max had obligingly named one of them *Correspondence*.

There was quite a lot of correspondence, and absolutely none of it was personal. I found dozens of drafts of his "Therapist" replies and some stuff to his lawyers in Boulder, as well as a few hopeful notes to a publisher to whom Max had apparently submitted a book called *The Map Within*. Nothing else.

"Damn," I said aloud. Max was being secretive.

I was trying another directory when someone said behind me, in a pleasant voice, "I couldn't find anything, either," and then the computer went dark and took the room with it.

9
CARPET CUTTER

THE chair I'd thrown clattered harmlessly against the opposite wall, and the noise reverberated in the room as I stood stock-still and waited, willing my breath to slow. The moon was on the far side of the house now, leaving the bedroom harmfully dark. A small part of my mind, the only part not clinging to the immediate issue of survival, asked a question: How long had he been standing there?

A quick scuffling sound, and the chair struck me in the chest and knocked me back against the desk. The keyboard of the computer pitched forward, striking the back of my legs, and I jumped forward and picked up the chair, holding it with the legs pointed away from me, lion-tamer style. "Gotcha," the voice said, and chuckled.

"You made quite a mess," I said, willing him to reply.

I heard the door to the hall close, heard the lock snap shut.

"I got a little irritated," he said, and I held the chair at arm's length and launched myself toward the voice, hearing him bump up against the wall as he shifted left, and I compensated and felt the chair strike something yielding, flesh, and he grunted, and something either very cold or very hot punched against the bare skin of my left forearm, backing me away. My hand was immediately wet and warm.

"Carpet cutter," he said. "Very sharp." He wasn't even winded.

I hoisted the chair and advanced, swinging it down hard in front of me, and one leg caught him, on the shoulder, maybe, and I heard him go down. A vision of the carpet cutter slicing from below, its hook pointed up to tear, pushed me away like a cold current, and I backed up again, lowering the chair as I went so its legs pointed at where I thought he might be.

I still couldn't see much of anything; the afterimage of the computer screen floated in front of my eyes, pale and blue and opaque. I took another step away from him, rifling my memory of the room for something that might serve as a weapon, and the chair came to life in my hands, bucking once, and he pulled it free by the legs, bringing its back up under my chin.

The phantom computer screen shivered into a million tiny lights: an exploding Christmas tree. I felt myself fall backward, onto something soft, and let myself go the rest of the way down, twisting and rolling away, toward the far side of the bed. The mattress heaved and jumped, and something tore through layers of cloth in a long, rending arc. I went for the arm above the carpet cutter with both hands, missed, and landed on my stomach on the bed again with a hard lump beneath me.

The tearing sound had traveled toward the foot of the bed. I scrambled toward its head, grabbing at the lump as I went, and came up on my knees, holding the light bulb I'd taken from the ceiling fixture. It was slippery in my gloved hand, and I realized the front of my shirt was soaked. I'd been bleeding the whole while.

"Come to Papa," he said from the foot of the bed.

I went to Papa, grabbing at the blankets with my free hand and throwing them in front of me like a gladiator's net. He made a surprised sound as they swept over him, and I tightened my hand on the base of the light bulb and brought it around, side-arm, with all the strength I had. It exploded in my hand as it struck him, and I dragged the ragged edges down along his arm until they snagged on cloth and the bulb pulled free from my grasp, and now he was the one backing away.

"You cut me," he said, sounding amazed.

With the bedroom door locked, there was only the one leading to the bathroom, and he was between me and it. I side-stepped around the bed, feeling light-headed and almost exhilarated. He couldn't have been more than eight feet from me; I could cover it in a leap, get the hand with the carpet cutter in it, and . . .

Get killed. I was losing blood more quickly than I'd thought, getting giddy. I reached behind me, felt the computer desk, and knocked over a can of pencils.

He was on me faster than I would have believed, the full weight of him, all hard surfaces: chin and shoulders and elbows and knees, and the edge of the cutter against my shoulder as his arm came up, trying to pull the point across my throat. I twisted right, away from the blade, a sharp, hot sting at the top of my arm, and I dropped to my knees and brought both fists up, together, between his legs. He jumped back with a strangled sound, far enough to allow me to stand, and I picked up the computer display, yanked it free of the system unit, and threw it through the window. Glass splintered into the front yard, and he positively screamed in rage, the scream following me as I hurled myself after the computer display, feeling the broken edges of the windowpanes rake my legs, brush tearing at my face and hands. The ground came up under me hard and fast, and I was lying on my stomach in Max's front yard, gasping for breath and looking at Flores Street.

I covered the distance to the sidewalk on hands and knees and sat on the pavement, looking at the broken window. White curtains stirred peacefully in the breeze.

Some soprano was singing in my ears, thin and high as a far-off violin. The porch light came on in front of the house to the left of Max's, and at the sight a wave of delayed panic rose in me, a swarm of gnats in the muscles and veins, and I got up and ran, bleeding back and front, toward the lights of Santa Monica Boulevard.

I was on the Pacific Coast Highway before the fear subsided. I pulled the car over to the dirt shoulder and rested my forehead against the steering wheel. My shirt was stiff and scratchy with dried blood, and my shoulder and forearm burned as though coals had been slipped beneath the skin. The air seemed almost solid. I drew it in and let it go in great shuddering gulps until one caught in my throat and I opened the door and leaned out and vomited coffee and hot bile onto the road. My stomach kept heaving long after the coffee was gone.

It was cooler here, the air chilly on my wet face. Even so, it couldn't dispel the hot flush of shame that suddenly seized me, grabbing me by the throat and shaking me like a wet rag. He'd been in the house, cornered, and I'd run. I'd let him go.

A pair of headlights in my rearview mirror reminded me that I was back in the sheriff's territory, and the fear clutched me again and did macramé with my stomach muscles, and I peeled off the blood-slick gloves, put Alice into gear, and drove home.

The cut to my forearm was deep but only a couple of inches long. The one to my shoulder, I saw in the bathroom mirror, was longer, but shallow. Both were clean and straight, testimony to the sharpness of the carpet cutter. There were scratches on my legs from Max's window. I washed the cuts with soap and warm water and patted them dry. Then, catching my own acrid smell, I got into the shower and tried to scrub the fear away. I scrubbed for a long time.

Naked and wet, I climbed onto the roof of the downstairs room and stood in the moonlight, letting the air dry me. My entire body hurt, cut in places, battered in others. Topanga Canyon smelled sharp and dusty. The moon was only a few degrees above the mountain that blocks my view of the sea, going down and taking the night with it, pulling the day in its wake. I focused on a solitary light in a house at the bottom of the canyon and willed myself into that room, a room with people sitting safely in it.

Being frightened is part of my job. Giving in to it isn't.

This was something new, I thought, as I opened the refrigerator and took out a beer. This was something new and unwelcome. I drank the beer in three long, continuous swallows and opened another, taking it to the couch. The bright marriage brochures winked at me from the table.

This had been Eleanor's living room once. She had found the little jerry-built cabin, one board thick in most places, when we first decided to live together. Until then we'd maintained separate apartments near UCLA, where we'd met. She'd been specializing in Oriental studies and I'd been postponing my entrance into the real world, accumulating one worthless degree after another until my name, with all the initials following it, began to look like a bad Scrabble hand. I didn't know what I was going to do with the degrees—English literature, drama, and comparative religion—but at least I understood how college worked. It was a place where you did something and you got something—a grade, a degree—in return. All anybody in the real world seemed to get was money, and I didn't really care about money.

I was surprised to find that my bottle of beer was empty. I didn't recall having finished it. My muscles felt a little looser as I stood to get another. Since I had to go all the way to the refrigerator, I grabbed two.

Several months after Eleanor and I met, someone threw one of Eleanor's friends, a diminutive Taiwanese pianist named Jennie Chu, off the roof of one of the dormitories. Eleanor kept saying that no one could have wanted to kill Jennie, and as it turned out, she was right: Jennie had been tossed by a cocaine dealer who couldn't tell Asians apart even when he wasn't fried. By way of helping Eleanor through her grieving process, I found him and gave him to the police, but not until I had broken both his elbows, snapping his arms over my knees like sticks of kindling. They'd broken surprisingly easily. Cocaine, they say, weakens the bones.

My reaction to breaking his arms had been complicated. It had taught me something about myself I hadn't known before, something I'd been keeping an eye on ever since. My reaction to solving Jennie's murder, though, was simplicity itself: I'd found something I wanted to do. And I'd done it, with some success, after Eleanor and I moved into the cabin in Topanga, and I'd kept doing it after she packed her bags and left.

Now I wondered whether I could still do it.

He'd sounded so *friendly*.

Knives have always terrified me. They're so much more personal than guns. A bullet punches a hole into you when it enters and punches another when it exits, and it messes up anything it can get to in between. Knives are generally less le-thal, but I'll take the dull, brutal blow of a bullet over the sharp edge slipping through the skin any time. Still, I'd faced knives before without . . .

He'd surprised me. The room had been dark and small, the carpet cutter had been curved. I'd seen what he'd done to Max.

I'd had the sheriffs to worry about. There were a million reasons.

Eleanor's curtains, the curtains she'd made, still hung on the windows. She'd chosen the couch and paid for it, dipping into one of those mysterious bank accounts Chinese always seem to have. The couch was a collection of odd-shaped lumps now, and there were bullet holes in it, courtesy of a Chinese gangster who'd tried to kill me in this very room. I'd been frightened then, but not terror-stricken, not paralyzed with fear as I'd been in Max's bedroom. Something had kicked in, as it always had before, adrenaline or fury or a sense of outraged dignity, and it had held me together until that particular dance was done. I hadn't fallen apart until afterward.

The bottle in my hand was empty. I threw it across the room, opening the cut in my shoulder. The bottle hit the wall, harmlessly, just as the chair had. I could throw things at walls, it seemed, all night long without doing any harm. I picked up the other bottle and drank, bleeding onto the leather of the couch.

I'd run away from Eleanor, as my mother had pointed out during several of our rare personal talks. After we'd been living together long enough to begin talking about marriage, I'd had an affair, and then another, meaningless and passionless. Mechanical. Stupid. She'd found out, as I supposed I meant her to, and forgiven me. Then I did it again, and she stopped forgiving me and started suggesting I get some counseling. Instead, I had another affair. That was when she packed. Now she lived in a small cottage in Venice, working on her third book and writing occasionally about the New Age for the *Los Angeles Times,* and I lived alone on my hilltop, venturing out from time to time to make a little money. To poke around in other people's untidy lives. To get into knife fights in dark rooms with people who scared me senseless.

The bottle was half-full this time, and it made a nice splash when it hit the wall, beer spewing forth in a foamy arc to soak the carpet. See, I *could* do some damage. I climbed to my feet again and went to the refrigerator and drank the three remaining bottles straight down, standing there and staring at the wall. Then I grabbed a paper towel and pressed it over the cut on my shoulder until the bleeding stopped, and then I hauled my aching body to bed.

10
SPECIAL DELIVERY

I SURFACED out of a bad dream and into the knowledge that someone was in the house.

The house has only three rooms on the upper level: the kitchen, the living room, and the bedroom. The bathroom door opens directly into the bedroom, and the little room downstairs, the one whose roof serves as the sun deck, can be entered only from outside. That's the whole house. The noise that had punched a hole in my nightmare had come from the kitchen.

Sunlight burned through the window: late morning. I inched my hand to the edge of the mattress and then beneath it until my fingers touched the handle of the nine-millimeter automatic I keep there. I pulled it out and hid my hand under the covers and let my eyes close most of the way, looking at the door through the rainbows the sunlight made against my eyelashes.

The living-room floor creaked and something clinked, like a couple of bottles being knocked together. Then a sharper sound, from the kitchen again, metallic this time. Under the covers, I snapped the automatic open and then shut again, forcing a bullet into the chamber. It was deafening.

The bedroom doorway darkened and Eleanor Chan stood there, a coffee mug in each hand. I kept my lids down and enjoyed the sense of looking at her when she didn't know she was being observed, feeling the now-familiar knot in my abdominal muscles dissolve. She wore a pair of red UCLA gym shorts, an oversized gray T-shirt with dalmatians on it, and a pair of white knee-socks folded to midcalf. No shoes: Eleanor doesn't believe shoes belong in the house. Her black hair was pulled back against the heat, held on top of her head with an elastic band strung through two little red plastic balls that matched her gym shorts. On anyone else it would have been too cute. Dark wisps of hair fell around her high cheekbones, and she lowered her head impatiently and blew them away.

"You're a mess," she said.

I opened my eyes. "You've known that for years."

"You look like you walked into a windmill. The shoulder probably needs stitches, and the arm looks like it's infected."

"You saw my arm?" My arm was under the covers.

She regarded me from head to foot. "I saw everything. You were in a coma."

"So much for vigilance," I said. I reached over and put the gun back under the mattress. "Is one of those for me?"

She sat on the edge of the bed and I admired a smooth length of thigh. There's something unwholesomely interesting about knee socks. Her lips pursed in disapproval. "If you think you can manage it after all that beer."

"I only drank part of it. I poured the rest on the living-room floor."

"So I saw," she said, holding out one of the cups. "It's a novel way to cut down."

"Can you hang on to that for a minute? Sitting up is going to demand most of my attention." I put my hands flat on the mattress beside me and heaved myself upward, feeling the muscles in my legs and stomach form a union and wave little neural signs in protest. "Jesus," I said, staring at my cut arm. It was bright red.

"It's Mercurochrome, you dolt," Eleanor said. "I put some on your shoulder, too."

"And I slept through it?"

"That's not all you slept through," she said.

This did not sound good. "What else?"

"You'll find out." I took the coffee. "I don't suppose you're going to tell me what happened."

"I don't suppose I am."

She raised her eyebrows and sipped her coffee. "Why should today be different?"

Normally I love Eleanor's coffee, but the smell of it made my stomach heave rebelliously, and I turned it into a cough and blew on the cup.

"Told you so," she said with some satisfaction. "You're not as young as you used to be."

I closed my eyes. "People keep saying that."

She traced the cut on my shoulder with a light finger. "Maybe you should listen. There was a time, and I remember it more vividly than I'd like to, when you could go out and get minced and then come home and drink a case of beer, and you'd still wake up as fresh as a daisy."

" 'Fresh as a daisy,' " I said admiringly. "I like that. Is that a New Age expression?"

"I *have* a New Age expression for you," she said, "but I'm a lady."

"And yet here you are in a man's bedroom."

"An invalid," she said, "and I'm on an errand of mercy."

"I was wondering about that." She didn't usually come over these days unless I called, and sometimes not even then.

"Why don't you get dressed?" she asked. "If you can. And we'll talk about it."

"Whenever you say 'we'll talk about it,' I begin to perspire."

She got up. "Well, perspire your way into the living room, and we'll have a chat."

I got more toothpaste on my chin than in my mouth, and I cut myself shaving, but other than that my ablutions were uneventful. The orange shirt I chose first clashed with my Mercurochrome, so I traded it for a loose robin's-egg blue number with long sleeves to cover the damage and a pair of white drawstring pants Eleanor had brought me from the solo trip to Bali her first book advance bought her. It was eleven o'clock and the air was hot enough to melt bacon fat.

Eleanor was sponging the back of the couch with a paper towel and muttering under her breath when I came into the living room. When she heard me she held up the paper towel accusingly. It was wadded and rust-brown with dried blood. "You need a full-time nurse," she said. "Or a mobile hospital following you around."

"Sorry," I said. "If I'd known you were coming I would have bled outdoors."

"You did." She folded the towel over to present a clean surface and swabbed at the couch again. "You're hell on furniture."

I sat where the couch was damp. It felt cool. "Is this our chat?"

She avoided my eyes. "Where's your coffee?"

"Why, Eleanor," I said. "If I didn't know you better, I'd say you were stalling."

"I made it, you can drink it." She went into the bedroom and came out with the mug in her hand and stood over me until I'd forced some down and made appreciative noises. "I want you to know," she said severely, "that I had nothing to do with anything your mother said."

"I never thought you did. Not your style."

"She called me a couple of days ago. Said she wanted some girl talk, said your father had been grumpy all week and she was bored."

"He's not much on girl talk even when he's cheerful." The second gulp of coffee tasted better.

"She has a right to worry about you, you know."

"My God, what she went through," I said, "giving me birth. Did you know I was born at three in the morning?"

"Of course I did. I've known that for years."

I moved my arm experimentally. My shoulder hurt like hell. "I don't know what time you were born."

She looked down at the front of her T-shirt as though the dalmatians were a surprise. "There's a lot you don't know." Her eyes came up to mine. "But you *do* know I'd never set anything up with your mother."

"She wants us to get married," I said, working the other arm. That shoulder hurt, too. "She says we'd have adorable children."

"We would. Another genetic possibility goes unfulfilled." She tugged at the bottom of the shirt, which was perfectly unwrinkled.

"We chose names once, remember?"

Eleanor picked up the wad of paper towels, which she'd dropped onto the table, and poked it experimentally with her forefinger. Water dripped from it. "We did a lot of things," she said shortly. "Some of them were silly."

"Some of them," I said, "were pretty wonderful." I reached up with the arm that hurt least and took her hand, paper towels and all. Her hand felt as if it had been in mine forever.

"I'm having a little problem," I said.

She ran her nails over the skin on the inside of my wrist. "That's evident."

"You said it, that thing about there having been a time when I could get run over or whatever, and not lose the crease in my pants."

She was watching me, looking past the tone and under the words. "Yes?"

"Well," I said. "I'm scared."

She put her fingers around my wrist and rotated my arm, bringing the long cut into view. "That's probably a sign of good sense."

"It's not just that. I mean, it *is* just that, but why? Why now?"

"Simeon, you've spent so much time looking at other people's lives that you've forgotten about your own. Not that you ever wanted to know anything about yourself. Ask yourself why, out of all the jobs in the world, you chose this one. I mean, talk about outward-directed. You bounce from one set of lives to another, putting together what's broken if you can, trying to change things. And you think *you* don't change. You're impervious to it, when everyone else can tell from a hundred yards away that you're not the same person you were five years ago, or even three. Somewhere along the way, the big penny dropped. You've figured out you're going to die."

"I always knew I was going to die."

"Knowing it in your big fat head is one thing. You know it now in the center of your chest. And you know what that means? It means that life isn't infinitely elastic, the way it was in your twenties. You can't go back for retakes. You can't *fix* it. You're making choices you're going to have to live with. And some of them, if you'll pardon the candor, have been pretty stupid."

"You and me," I said.

"That's one."

I took her hand from my wrist and held it between both of mine. It felt cool, smooth, familiar, right. "Okay," I said. "Let's talk about you and me."

The door to the roof opened and Wayde walked in, stark naked.

"For example," Eleanor said, withdrawing her hand.

"Yo, Simeon," Wayde said on her way to the kitchen. "Your girlfriend is way cool."

"I'm cool," Eleanor said, watching Wayde's rear end analytically. There were no visible flaws. "She and I have had a chat."

"Can I have some of this Evian?" Wayde called from the kitchen. "I feel like a french fry."

"Sure," Eleanor said, looking at me. "He'll never drink it. The alcohol content isn't high enough."

"Want some, Eleanor?"

"Thank you, dear." She batted her lashes at me. "Doesn't that sound maternal?"

"Do you still want kids?" I asked.

"Here we are." Wayde twinkled into the room with two glasses of water and handed one to Eleanor. She had honey-colored hair above and below, an exemplary set of the usual biological accessories, and a navel that looked like Michelangelo had carved it on a good day. Eleanor eyed her appreciatively, as though she'd had a hand in the design.

"If I looked like you, I wouldn't wear clothes either," she said. "Would you, Simeon?"

"If I looked like her, you wouldn't be here."

"You guys are great," Wayde said cheerfully. "I wish more old people were like you."

"That's so sweet of you," Eleanor said between her teeth.

"It's just the way I feel," Wayde said with a radiant smile. "Thanks for the wawa." She went back on the roof.

"Wawa," Eleanor said thoughtfully.

"Oh, I forgot—" Wayde said, standing in the doorway, and there was a knock at the front door.

"I'll get it," I said. "I'm dressed."

"Very tastefully, too," Eleanor murmured.

"Cool," Wayde agreed. Not way cool, though.

"For an old guy," I said, opening the door. Orlando stood there, offensively slender and disgustingly young and handsome in a lime-green tank top and a pair of baggies.

"On the way to the beach," he said. "Am I interrupting anything?"

"The aging process," I said. "Come on in. Have some of Eleanor's memorable coffee."

"Is Eleanor here? Great."

Eleanor gave him her fondest, whitest smile. "Hi, Orlando. Don't you look Californian."

"Oh, my God." That was Wayde. She stood in the doorway, staring at Orlando as though Apollo had risen from the carpet.

"And this is Wayde," I said, a host to my fingertips. "Her clothes are on loan to the children of Bosnia."

"Aren't you pretty," Orlando said.

"Some girls are," I said, watching Wayde with fascination. She was blushing.

"I'll just get dressed," she said, backing onto the roof.

"Get *dressed?*" I asked.

"Not for me, I hope," Orlando said. He turned to me. "Where have you been hiding? I called last night, but you weren't home."

"He was undergoing surgery," Eleanor said.

His brow furrowed. "Nothing serious, I hope."

"Having an arm removed," I said. "But I thought better of it." I pulled up my sleeve and showed him my orange forearm.

"I used to love the color of Mercurochrome," Orlando said. "I painted my whole body once, when I was around six. Sonia about killed me."

"Have you heard from them?" That was Eleanor, always first with the niceties.

"Actually, that's why I called. Where's the coffee?"

"Oh, boy," Eleanor said to me. "Invite the lad in, offer him coffee, and then stand there showing off your wounds."

"Hi, again," Wayde said from the doorway. She was still naked. She looked down at herself and then up at Orlando. "My dress is really ugly."

"It's hard to imagine a dress that would be an improvement," Orlando said gallantly.

"Gee," Wayde breathed.

"Black, right?" said the creaking old man, from the kitchen.

"Fine," Orlando said. "You've got a beautiful neck, you know?"

"Thanks," I said.

"My neck?" Wayde asked, blinking.

"You should wear something with a little scoop in front, something to accentuate the line of your neck. I'll bet it's twice as long as mine."

"Your neck," Wayde said shyly. "Your neck is swell."

"Don't lead her on, Orlando," I said, handing him one of my few matching cups and saucers.

"You doddering old poop," Eleanor said reprovingly.

"You lack essential information," I told her in a superior tone.

"I doubt things have changed that much," Eleanor said. "Sit, Orlando, don't wait for Simeon to invite you. Wayde, why don't you come all the way in? We can see more of you that way. What's the word from Hawaii?"

Orlando sat on the far end of the couch, haloed by the light through the window, and Wayde stood there and gaped. "You've got an attractive uvula, too," Eleanor said.

"Huh?"

"Close your mouth, dear. You look hungry that way."

"Sorry," Wayde said, sitting on the floor. Her belly didn't even wrinkle.

"Sonia called yesterday," Orlando said. "It's rained non-stop, and Al keeps hauling her out in it."

"To do what?" Eleanor asked.

"Visit cops," Orlando said. "The only thing Sonia's seen is the inside of the hotel room and the Honolulu police station. Al brought letters from a bunch of L.A. cops, and he's determined to meet everybody."

"Poor Sonia," Eleanor said sympathetically.

"No, she's enjoying it. She's as bad as Al, you know. She can't wait to get to Maui, meet a whole new bunch of cops."

"Who are we talking about?" Wayde asked.

"Orlando's sister is a, um, policeperson," Eleanor said. "Married to another policeperson."

"My parents hate cops," Wayde said. "They hate cops and politicians and the guys who own stores and everybody, and they've got these big LOVE signs all over the house."

"I talked to Al," Orlando said. "I told him about that sheriff, that Spurrier, and Al said to stay away from him."

"Who's Spurrier?" Eleanor asked alertly.

"I'll tell you later," I said.

"Al said he was a motherfucker," Orlando continued, the word sounding awkward in his mouth. "He's been brought up for disciplinary action a bunch of times for pounding on people, especially queers."

"*Orlando.*" Eleanor sounded shocked.

He looked from her to me. "You didn't tell her?"

Eleanor turned cool eyes to me. "Tell me what?"

"That I'm gay," Orlando said, a bit defiantly.

A long hiss escaped Wayde. Her mouth was open, and she leaned forward, gazing at Orlando with a look of pure loss. Then she felt our eyes on her and sat up. "Way cool," she said in a very small voice. I wanted to lean over and kiss the top of her head.

"When did you meet this Spurrier?" Eleanor asked, deciding for the moment to glide over Orlando's revelation.

"After the wedding," I said. "When was that, the day before yesterday?" It seemed like a week ago.

"I have to pee," Wayde announced brokenheartedly. She got up and left the room.

"And why are you being told to stay away from this man?" Eleanor demanded.

"He beat Simeon up," Orlando said.

"Is he the one you're afraid of?" she asked.

"One of them," I said.

"Orlando," she said, "why don't you and I go out on the roof and you can tell me what's going on. Mr. Strong-but-Silent here is saving it for the third act."

"Sure," Orlando said promptly, standing up. So much for male bonding.

"And you," she said to me, "can wash the cups and figure out what we're going to do about lunch."

"I thought I'd just eat some raw beef," I said, getting stiffly to my feet. "And ladyfingers for Orlando and you girls." I toted the coffee cups obediently into the kitchen and turned on the tap, getting the usual mysterious clanking noises before the water made its appearance. I was leaning against the sink, counting silently to twenty and waiting for the water to turn hot, when someone behind me said, "Knock, knock," and I jumped about three feet and came down facing the door.

It was open, and Ike Spurrier stood in it.

"Guilty conscience?" he asked. A uniform, considerably taller than he, stood behind him, peering in at me as though the cabin were the Snake House at the Zoo.

"What do you want?"

"In the neighborhood," Spurrier said, not bothering to make it sound true. He wore the same yellow tweed jacket, but today's polo shirt was a particularly unappetizing shade of orange that emphasized the colorlessness of his eyes. He leaned forward and gave the kitchen and living room an uninterested once-over. Then he licked the red lower lip. "Guess being a gay detective doesn't pay all that well, huh?"

"I'd ask you in," I said, "but I don't want to."

"That so," Spurrier said, coming through the door. "Well, don't bother. I'm already in. Wally," he said, "take a hike down the hill. Look around, see if there's another door."

The uniform didn't move, so Wally was presumably someone else. Spurrier put both hands in his jacket pockets and smiled at me, the red lip stretching unappealingly beneath the mustache. "Hot, isn't it?"

I could feel the edge of the sink pressed against my back, and I forced myself to step forward. "Do you have a warrant?"

"In this heat," he said, "I'm surprised to see you in a long-sleeved shirt. I had you figured for a T-shirt kind of guy."

I buttoned the cuff I'd opened when I showed Orlando my arm. "Did you."

"Sure. All you buff guys, that the word? Buff? Like to show off your biceps. All that work in the gym, looking good for the other buff guys. Figured you for a formfit T-shirt."

"How about that," I said.

He focused on the door to the deck. "Where's your boyfriend?"

"Who?"

"Got a lot of them, huh? I guess a buff guy like you would. Nordine. Where's Nordine?"

"I haven't got any idea."

"There's a room down the hill," a male voice said from behind Spurrier. "No one there."

"Well, he's somewhere," Spurrier said.

"I'm sure he is," I said. "But he's not here."

"I really need to talk to old Christy," Spurrier said confidingly. "This thing with Max—you remember Max."

I didn't say anything.

"You ought to turn that water off," Spurrier said. "There's a drought." I reached behind me and twisted the tap without turning my back to Spurrier. "Somebody was in old Max's house last night. Went right through the seals. Used a key, how about that? Bled all over the place, too."

"What do you want, Sergeant?"

"In the neighborhood," he said again. "Guy who bled like that must have got cut up pretty good. Maybe on the arms, what do you think? Well," he said, turning his head, "look who's here. Hey, Chiquito."

Orlando came into the living room, giving Spurrier several hundred volts of pure disdain. "Has he got a warrant?" he asked me.

"Everybody wants to know about warrants," Spurrier said. "You wouldn't know where Nordine is, would you, sweetie?"

Orlando let a beat pass before he answered. "I've never met him."

"And I thought it was a small world." Spurrier took a hand from his pocket and tugged on his lip. "Well, I've got something he might want to hear about, in case you ever do. Tell him old Max's index finger showed up in Boulder, Colorado, this morning."

For a long moment no one spoke. Spurrier looked at us expressionlessly. Then Orlando put a hand against the back of my rocking chair and said, "I beg your pardon."

"Special delivery." Spurrier looked from him to me watchfully. "In a nice little ice pack. Along with a bunch of disgusting letters about what kind of guy he loved best in the whole wide world and some pictures. Cute pictures, too. Him and Nordine."

"Sent to whom?" I asked.

"The newspaper." He gazed at us, apparently thinking of something else. "Also a note suggesting it might make a good story. HOMETOWN BOY MAKES BOYS or something. Guess old Max was still in the closet back in Boulder." Shaking his head, he came back to us and said, "Where you from?"

"Here," I said. "I was born where I'm standing."

Eleanor came through the door and headed for the kitchen,

passing in front of Spurrier with an incurious look. "What about lunch?" she asked me, opening the refrigerator.

"My, my," Spurrier said, aping surprise. "The fair sex."

"His finger," I said. "Why his finger?"

"You're supposed to be a detective," Spurrier said reprovingly. "So it could be printed, of course."

"What's this about a finger?" Eleanor asked, holding a bottle of Evian.

"Never you mind, little lady," Spurrier said. "Although I'm not quite sure what the hell you're doing here."

"Me do laundy," Eleanor said in a singsong voice. "Velly fast, velly good. Even that coat I can get crean. Who are you supposed to be?"

"So you see," Spurrier said to me, "I've got to talk to Nordine. And I figure you're the guy who can tell him so."

"This doesn't have anything to do with Christy," I said.

"Hell, I know that." Spurrier's eyes opened in mock surprise. "Oh, I haven't made myself clear. This more or less lets Nordine off the hook."

"You're a policeman," Eleanor said.

"Here to protect you, my dear."

"I'll take my chances with the crooks," Eleanor said. "Is your name Spurrier?"

"Why does it let Christy off the hook?" I asked.

"Because it's happened before," Spurrier said, speaking as he would to a very slow child. "Max isn't the first."

"Ah," I said. It was happening too fast for me.

"So if you see him—" Spurrier began, and then he stopped short and his jaw fell open. Wayde ambled out of the bathroom, naked as the dawn, across the living room and out onto the deck. "Jesus," Spurrier said to me when she was gone, "you'll jump anything, won't you?"

"Next time, Ike," I said, leaning close to him, "come alone."

His face went white. Both hands came up in front of him,

balled into fists, and Eleanor stepped between us, holding out the bottle of Evian. "Would you like some water?" she asked. "You look hot."

"You and I," Spurrier said over her shoulder to me, "will have to have another talk. Our last one was obviously too brief."

"Go away," Orlando said from the living room.

Spurrier stared at him but spoke to me. "Tell Nordine," he said, his voice thick and tight. "Tell him he can come out from under his rock."

"Cheer up, Ike," I said with a courage I didn't feel. "You'll get a chance to punch someone out yet."

He glared at me and then turned quickly, pushing with his fingers on the chest of the cop behind him, and they were gone.

"Okay, Simeon," Eleanor said flatly. "Tell us everything."

TWO
THE BLACK
WIDOW

MOST OF THE TIME I'M SO REMOVED FROM BELIEF
THAT I CONFUSE IT WITH HAVING AN OPINION.

—PATRICIA HAMPL
Virgin Time

11
KILLING THEM TWICE

NORBERT Schultz had teeth like a mouthful of yellow paint chips. He'd been steeping them in coffee and nicotine for thirty or forty years, and they'd finally achieved the rich and variable patina of long-buried bones. In his work as a psychiatrist, he bared them frequently on the mistaken assumption that a smile made him look friendly. What it made him look like was someone who gargled with urine.

He was showing them to me now, without even knowing he was doing it, letting me know how happy he was to see me. We'd met under difficult circumstances when he was under contract to the LAPD, lending his expertise in the case of a lad who found meaning in life by setting people on fire and had decided to target me. Schultz was back in private practice now, but he still had a pipeline to the Department, and I was taking advantage of it.

"Five of them," he said without consulting the bulky LAPD printout on the desk in front of him. We were in his office on the ninth floor of a peeling, half-deserted medical high rise at the corner of Pico and Bundy, south and west of West Hollywood. The office was done in the Jung Moderne style favored by psychiatrists everywhere: industrial furniture, a battered leather couch, and spiky seventies abstracts on the wall. Some of them seemed to be made of stretched and pasted yarn, a medium that, for me, at least, ranks right up there with tempera on black velvet.

Friday afternoon had rolled around at last, bringing the promise of a more than usually stifling weekend, and the office's unwashed windows offered a daunting view of traffic clogging both streets in all four directions. Dirty sunlight highlighted Schultz's really remarkable nose as he ran a finger down the page to check his memory and then glanced up at me. "This is between us, right?"

"Right." I'd assured him it was confidential four or five times when I'd called him the day before, as soon as I was sure Spurrier was gone, but Schultz was a cautious man.

He went on being cautious. "Who's your client?"

It was a good question. I'd turned down the five hundred dollars Christy had offered me to go talk to Max, and no one had mentioned money since. "I suppose you could say I'm working for the victim." Another freebie for Max.

He nodded automatically, glanced down at the list, and then heard what I'd said. His head stayed down but his eyes came back to me. "How's he going to pay you?"

"Think of it as pro bono. And don't worry about it. It doesn't have anything to do with keeping this talk confidential. Treat me like a patient."

"Might not be a bad idea," he said, keeping a lemon-yellow

forefinger in place on the page. "A little introspection might do you some good."

This was getting to be a familiar theme. "I'm not interesting enough to think about for any length of time."

"You have no idea," he said, giving me the teeth again. Fluorescent light gleamed on his skull. "You're a locked box, Simeon, and that's not healthy."

"Five, you said?" I asked, trying not to sound impatient.

Schultz looked disappointed. "Counting the man here, the new one. I'm assuming they were all killed by the same person." He drummed his fingers on the desk and then realized that the gesture had cost him his place. "Why aren't you married?" he asked, searching for it.

"Norbert," I said, "there's already a small caucus working on that issue. Is there any reason to think it might not be the same person?"

"Always a possibility," he said. "But there hasn't been much press on this guy, so a copycat isn't very likely."

"Why hasn't there been much press?"

He stabbed the paper with the yellow finger and made a grimace of distaste. "A good reason and a bad one. The bad one is that the press isn't much interested in what happens in the gay community. The good reason is that this clown *wants* press. And the kind of press he wants, most papers don't want to give."

"Tell me about it. I've had enough enigmatic this week to last me a year."

"Well, he's essentially trying to kill them twice."

"Norbert, are you getting metaphysical on me?"

He opened the desk drawer and took out a pack of Benson & Hedges to replace the empty he'd just tossed in the wastebasket and tapped it twice against the back of the hand splayed across the page. "Nah. It's perfectly obvious. First he kills them the conventional way, always by beating, followed by an amputation with something sharp—" He paused to pull at the cellophane with his teeth.

"A carpet cutter," I said.

His eyes came up, looking interested, and then he went cross-eyed as he lit up. "Could be. Sharp but not very long. That's indicative right there because it means he carries his tools with him, the mark of a real obsessive. Not that there's much doubt about that, considering the amount of effort he expends."

"You were telling me about that."

Schultz blew smoke at me without thinking about it, and then fanned it away apologetically. "He set the pattern with the first one," he said over a stream of smoke. The printout claimed his attention. "This is a little more than two years ago. Victim was in his fifties, a college teacher, living in Chicago. They all live in big cities, all come from smaller ones. All leading, as novelists used to like to say, double lives. At home, they're straight. In the city, they're openly gay."

"How many cities?"

"Three. Chicago, New Orleans, Los Angeles."

"You said there were five."

He showed me his lower teeth this time, the worst ones, drawing them over his upper lip. It made him look like a shrunken head. "We'll get to that. Anyway, he killed the guy, although that's an understatement. First he kicked him to death, and then he cut him open from groin to sternum. One swipe, clean as a razor." I thought of the sound the cutter had made as it slit the blankets, and something small and cold stirred in the pit of my stomach. "In fact, they thought it might *be* a razor at first."

"Not deep," I said.

"Not deep. Then he cut off the man's right hand." He eyed the cigarette, a gravity-defying tube of ash, and tilted it to the vertical. "Three days later, a reporter at the paper in the victim's hometown opened his mail and found the index finger, along with some letters and photographs that made it clear what kind of a life the victim had been living in Chicago, and a note suggesting that the newspaper might want to verify the victim's identity by printing the finger. Clever, huh? The letter went on to suggest that the folks back home might like to read all about it, see what kind of a pervert they'd sent into the world." He checked the cigarette, too late. "Yipes." Ash tumbled into his lap.

"If all he sends is the finger, why does he need the whole hand?"

He brushed at his crotch in a panicky way that, in a patient, would have engaged his full attention. "Pardon?"

"Surely it's easier just to cut off a finger. Why does he take the whole hand?"

Schultz transferred the cigarette to his left hand, holding it Russian-style between his thumb and forefinger. This was an affectation that had once irritated me deeply. "Maybe he's got a collection," he said. "That wouldn't be unusual. You'd be amazed at the things these lunatics keep. They don't clean out their freezers very often, either."

"What kind of a note?"

"The new kind, technological anonymity. A laser printer. No way in the world to trace it."

"He goes to a lot of effort, doesn't he? First the beating, or kicking, then the hand, then the letter and the finger—"

"And that's not all. He's a ball of energy. He gets inside these guys' houses, inside their lives, before he kills them. He finds out where they're from, learns that the people back home don't know they're gay. He's probably young, by the way. Not meaning to stereotype, but most of these guys aren't interested in older men."

"He's young," I said.

"So in a sense," Schultz said, sounding pleased with himself, "he kills them twice. First he kills them physically, in the big city, and then he sends their remains home and kills their memory there." A light high on the wall behind him went on, flickered, and went out. That was the second time.

"A bone polisher," I said.

He paused in the act of lighting a new cigarette off the stub of his old one. "Beg pardon?"

"In Chinese culture, in the old days, when someone died outside China without enough money for his body to be shipped home and buried in the soil of the Middle Kingdom, they'd bury him temporarily wherever he died. Later, when the family had earned enough money, he'd be exhumed and his bones cleaned up to be sent back to China. That was the bone polisher's job."

"But that was benign," Schultz said.

I got a little prickly. "It's just a metaphor. I'm not claiming perfection."

"We work in metaphors," Schultz said loftily, and I caught another glimpse of the man I hadn't liked. "We take them very seriously."

"I'm sorry as hell," I said, "poaching on the linguistic territory of the mental-health profession."

"Do I really sound like that?" He was dismayed.

"When you don't sound like a person."

"Have to watch that," he said. His eyes went to one of the yarn abstracts, a uniquely ugly affair in burnt sienna and Dijon mustard that might have been meant to suggest baby poop. "Actually, it's not bad. He's sending part of them home, isn't he? Burying their reputations." He thought about it. "Still, I don't suppose he's Chinese, is he?"

"Is being excessively literal also a trait of the mental-health profession?"

"Ha, ha, ha," Schultz said dutifully. It was his therapy laugh, mirthless as a moan. "The second one was in Chicago, too. An attorney this time, early sixties. He burgled the house, by the way, something he's done only twice since."

"Was it an isolated house?"

His eyes went to the paper. "Doesn't say. You mean, he wasn't worried about anyone having heard anything?"

"Just wondering. He burgled this one, and he didn't seem

to care if the whole world heard him." The light went on again, and this time Schultz caught me looking at it and waved a hand.

"That's Miss Trink," he said. "My six o'clock."

It was four-thirty. "She's early."

He started to glance at his watch and caught the coal of his cigarette on the underside of the metal desk. "She's always early," he said, looking down at the carpet. "It's part of her problem. Anxiety syndrome." He ground out the coal with a well-worn suede boot. The carpet around his desk was pockmarked with irregular black holes, and another little moonscape surrounded the chair positioned at the head of the leather couch.

"Anxiety syndrome?" I grinned at him. "Sounds like a catchall."

"Of course, it's a catchall," he snapped. "If I knew what was wrong with her, she'd be cured."

"Or perhaps it's a metaphor."

"Am I being helpful?" he asked in a threatening tone.

I sat up attentively. "Extremely. Two in Chicago, you said?"

"And two in New Orleans."

Christy had been in New Orleans. Spurrier hadn't mentioned New Orleans, but then he wouldn't; he'd been trying to persuade me to get Christy to contact him. "When was New Orleans?"

"Earlier this year. January and March."

Could be. But I knew the man in Max's house hadn't been Christy. Christy wasn't that strong. The light blinked on again.

"Excuse me," I said, yielding to an impulse. "Bathroom in the hall?"

"Three doors down." He was bent over the printout.

I went out into the waiting room. Miss Trink was a thin, heavily made-up woman dressed in a long brown skirt and a brown shawl on a day that was well into the nineties. She wore her burlap-colored hair in a ponytail, which she had greased until it stood straight up from the top of her head, like the flame on a candle or a convenient handle for the Rapture. The table in front of her chair was littered with newspapers, and she was busily cutting out a story with an X-Acto knife. Clippings were scattered on the floor in front of her and over the cushions of the couch. She didn't look up.

"I won't be long," I said.

"No hurry," she whispered to someone who was floating several feet above my head. Then she reached over and pushed a button on the table next to her.

I stood in the hall long enough to make my excuse plausible, and then went back in. She was working on a different story, and she leaned farther over it when the door opened, hiding her face from me. The erect ponytail quivered.

"That woman's nuts," I said to Schultz.

"I get a lot of them," he said. The light did its agitated little blink. He shook his head. "It's good for her to wait. Being early is a manipulation mechanism, and I'm teaching her they don't always work."

"You mean she isn't really eager to talk?"

"Oh, she's dying to talk. She keeps badgering me to give her two-hour sessions, but I ask you . . ."

"You have my sympathy," I said. "Why the newspaper clippings?"

"She's organizing the world," he said. "She cuts up the papers and then rearranges them into some order that suits her. Sometimes it's geographical, sometimes chronological, sometimes by topic, sometimes by whether they've got photos." He shook his head. "A really boring mania. To tell you the truth, I miss police work. At least the nuts were interesting."

"You think our guy is organizing the world?"

He leaned back in his chair and inhaled half the cigarette. "Most crazy people are," he said, giving himself a smoke shawl. "We just don't recognize the patterns they're trying to fit it into. This guy certainly isn't happy about the presence of a third sex.

And his assumption that it's deeply shameful is interesting. I wouldn't be surprised if he thought that being outed was worse than being killed."

"Is he gay?"

The eyebrows went up, making wrinkles like tiny rice terraces all the way to the top of his bald head. "He's not acting out." He listened to what he'd said and blinked twice. "I mean, murdering people certainly qualifies as acting out, but I'd be surprised if he engaged in physical homosexual acts. My guess is that he leads his victims on, learns as much as he can about them without giving them what they want, what he *thinks* they want. The murder is the consummation. Of course," he added apologetically, "this could all be bunk."

"Sounds good to me," I said.

"Whenever we hate something deeply," he said, "it's almost always something we recognize in ourselves. Remember, when you point at something, only one finger points away. The other three point back at you."

"Whoa," I said. "Can I use that?"

He grinned, a flash of cheddar yellow. "It's not original."

"What about a cop who beats up on gays?"

"You mean methodically? Singling them out? Without cause?"

"He's infamous for it."

"Oh, dear. He needs help. And he's not likely to look for it." The corners of his mouth went down, making him look like a man fighting stomach cramps. "LAPD?"

"Sheriff," I said.

He looked relieved. "Don't know much about them." The light flashed again, signaling Miss Trink's finger, or perhaps her ponytail, on the button. "Damn that woman," he said.

"The healing attitude."

"Feh. You've got to be tough to heal crazy people. I'll bet our boy is burning to talk. I'll bet he's keeping a diary."

"You think so?"

"He's on a crusade," Schultz said. "He's cleaning up the world, making it safe for the heterosexual middle class. He sees himself on the side of the angels."

I got up and walked across the office and removed the baby-poop yarn construction from the wall. "Who on earth does these things?" I asked. "And why?"

His face stiffened. "My wife."

I hadn't even known he was married. He had the sloppy fussiness that often descends on single men in middle age. "It's certainly an unusual medium."

"She works with children," he said severely. "Yarn therapy is a good way to get them to externalize. Gradually, she began to do it herself."

I replaced it on its nail. "It's very . . ." I began, and then hit a wall. I had absolutely no idea where to go.

"It's calming," he said.

"Does she need a lot of calming?"

"I mean for my patients. It calms my patients. Some of them look at it throughout the entire session."

"It suggests childhood," I said to mollify him. "Infancy, in fact."

"Well," he said approvingly. "There you are."

"The two killings in Chicago," I asked. "Were they consecutive?"

"Could you straighten the assemblage please? Up a bit on the right. I was wondering when you'd ask that. Yes, they were. So were the two in New Orleans. So you see the pattern."

"He's going to do it again here."

"In two to three weeks," he said. "If the pattern holds."

"Will it?"

"That's another reason I wish I were back working with the cops," Schultz said fretfully. "These patterns always hold."

12
ROBERT AND ALAN

"**A SERIAL** killer?" Christy Nordine asked. *"Max?"*

"It changes things," I said. We were in the living room of a small house just south of Santa Monica Boulevard, not far from Max's place. Robert and Alan, whose guest Christy was, had met me at the door. Robert, about fifty, had graying hair combed straight back and wore a blue linen leisure suit. A silver fish silhouette, the old Christian symbol, hung from a chain around his neck. Alan, ten or twelve years younger, favored Ivy League, complete to a little buckle at the back of his chinos, a fashion touch I hadn't seen in decades, and no evident religious affiliation. They'd set out a plate of crudités and an ice bucket full of bottled mineral water and withdrawn to the back of the house, looking domestic and worried.

"What does it change?" Nordine challenged, settling into a wooden captain's chair.

The captain's chair was of a piece with its surroundings, which might have been one of my mother's numerous living rooms. Cherrywood furniture, imitation Early American, gleamed on hooked rugs. Two English Toby mugs, gap-toothed, weather-beaten old sailors with a cheery alcoholic flush on their cheeks, grinned at each other from opposite ends of the wooden mantel. Between them was a small coven of black cats cut from paper, their backs arched in fear or fury, the first Halloween decorations I'd seen. A pinlight picked out what might have been a real Grandma Moses above the mantel, and a grandfather clock ticked slowly next to the front door. The smell of Lemon Pledge was everywhere. We could have been in Grand Rapids.

I gave the crudités a fish-eye. I'd come direct from Schultz's office, and I hadn't eaten in what seemed like weeks. "It makes it tougher. Before, I was looking for someone who might conceivably have been in Max's circle of acquaintances for some time, who might have left footprints all over the place. This is someone who floated in from nowhere and doesn't know anyone, and now he's going to float out again."

Nordine's mouth set into a straight line that put vertical creases in both cheeks. "He still killed Max," he said. Despite the strain he'd been under, he looked more rested than I'd ever seen him. Alan and Robert were taking good care of him.

I spread my hands. "It's a different kind of animal."

"If you're worried about money—"

"I'm not."

"—I've got a small pile of it."

"Glad to hear it, but that's not the point."

"Well, what is the point?"

"I'm reporting to you," I said. "That's part of my job."

He sat back as far as the chair would allow, and three or

four emotions staged an argument over possession of his face. Relief won. "You're not quitting?"

"I'm telling you that things have changed, that's all. So far, I've checked out the places Max went, talked to the people he knew. All routine. All of it aimed at finding a hypothetical somebody from this community who got next to Max, probably in view of several people, and then killed him. The premise I've been operating on, if you can call something this thin a premise, is that the murder was spontaneous. At some point in the relationship or whatever it was, the killer decided that he could get more out of Max dead than alive, and he killed him. Up to that point, he had no reason to be particularly secretive. But this guy—the guy we're dealing with now—intended to kill Max from the beginning. He didn't let a lot of people see him. And he's not going to hang around, going through the motions of a normal life, because he doesn't have a normal life, at least not in Los Angeles."

"You said he was going to kill someone else here."

"I said that he'd followed that pattern in the past."

" 'In a few weeks,' you said." Nordine's stubborn mode was becoming very familiar.

"If the pattern holds."

"Well, then," he said, as though everything was settled.

"It may not be in West Hollywood," I said.

"Of *course* it'll be in West Hollywood. Why would he go anywhere else?"

There were a dozen reasons he might go somewhere else, but I didn't think they'd hold Christy's attention, and I needed all of it. "I want you to go to the cops," I said.

That caught him by surprise. He opened his mouth and closed it. Then he swallowed. "You're joking."

"Take a lawyer. Take two, if you've got a pile of money somewhere. I know a reporter on the L.A. *Times* you can talk to before you go in. Hell, she'd probably go with you.

Even Spurrier isn't going to pound on you with the media watching."

He considered it and changed the subject slightly. "They're already watching."

"Come again?"

"I told you they would be. Haven't you seen the paper?"

"I don't get one."

"Hold on." He got up and went into the back of the house, and I heard Alan's inquiring voice before Christy reappeared with a folded copy of the *Times* in his hand.

MURDERED MAN WAS TV STAR read the headline. Bottom right corner of page one. Not bad for a gay murder; the *Times* is so conservative on some issues as to be fundamentalist.

A West Hollywood man who was murdered on Tuesday was a popular television star in the 1950s, the story began. *Max Grover, 77, who was brutally beaten to death in his home by an unknown assailant, starred in a top-rated series,* Tarnished Star, *under the name Rick Hawke.*

"They finally woke up," I said. Nothing about the mutilation, nothing yet about the serial angle.

"Well," Christy said, the soul of reason, "Max kept it pretty quiet."

"All the more cause for you to talk to a reporter before you go in."

Reason went out the window and truculence came in. "I'm not going in."

"Shush," I said. I'd seen a name toward the bottom of the story.

Grover's longtime agent, Ferris Hanks, told the Times *that Grover had lived quietly since abandoning his career toward the end of the fifties. "Max could have been a major star,"* Hanks said. *"He was a great talent. When he quit, he could have had his pick of the networks."*

"Ferris Hanks," I said.

"Oh, how Max loathed that man," Christy said. "Said he

was inverse proof that the good die young. Eighty-two—he *says*—and still doing mischief."

"Did you ever meet him?"

"*Meet* him? We wouldn't go near him."

"Before Max. I mean."

"Of course not. Hardly my circle."

"But Max talked about him."

"Like you'd talk about an operation you once had. And he called a couple of times."

"What about?"

"He never gave up. He wanted Max to go back to work, can you imagine?"

That took me by surprise. "I thought he hated Max."

"He was terrible to him for years. The old 'you'll never work in this town again' stuff, as though Max cared. And then, just like nothing had happened, there he was on the phone, offering work. I ask you."

"But Max said no."

"Max, work for Ferris Hanks? Of course not. An unbeliev- able man. Absolute sewage."

"So everyone says."

"And for once, everybody is right."

"I don't know," I said. "It seems to me that a community is usually right when it passes judgment. Look how people felt about Max."

"And how they feel about me," Christy said, using my least favorite of his repertoire of tones.

"People don't think badly of you," I said. "They just won- der when you're going to do something on your own."

It startled him. Everyone was being nice to him, and here I was, kicking him in the shins. "Like what?" he demanded. "How much time—"

"I know all about that," I said, "and you have no idea how much time you have. You could live for years. You're going to have money. What are you going to do, Christy?"

"How would I know? I haven't thought about it."

"Start by going to the cops."

"Why? Why should I do that?"

"Well, they're looking for you, for one thing. You can't hide with Robert and Alan forever. You get caught, they're going to be in trouble, too."

"I'll go somewhere else," he said.

"And you can't help me until you're free to move around."

"Help you?" He sounded skeptical. "You think I can help you?"

"Of course you can. I've needed to talk to you a dozen times in the past two days, and I didn't know where you were. And even now, now that I do know, I can't call you from home because the cops might be monitoring my phone. I need to get into things, like Max's safe-deposit box, that I don't have access to without you."

"What's in the safe-deposit?"

"I don't know," I said, "until I look."

"Don't you think the cops will look there?"

"Same answer."

He got up and did a circuit of the room. His clothes sagged on him, but it wasn't until he turned his back and I saw the buckle on his pants that I realized he was wearing Alan's. They made him look even thinner than he was. At the mantel he stopped and picked up one of the black cats. "I don't know," he said.

"Do it for Max."

The cat got folded into half and then into quarters. Christy wasn't looking at it; he seemed to be studying the face of the grandfather clock. "What kinds of questions did you have?" he asked at last.

"Marta Aguirre, for example. She's not around."

He shrugged. "So?"

"So why not?"

He tore the cat in half. "What does it matter?"

"Is she legal?"

"No. Her cousin is. That's where she lives, with her cousin. Max hired her because she wasn't legal. His way of helping out, as usual. And she spied on us. She *stole* from us."

Ah, Marta the thief. "What kinds of things?"

"Little stuff. A couple of Max's rings. A gold chain Max gave me. Stuff she could put in her pockets."

"Max knew?"

Christy rolled his eyes to the ceiling. "Max gave her a *raise*. Said she must not be earning enough."

"What days did she work?"

"Mondays and Thursdays."

"My, my," I said. "Mondays."

Christy paused in the act of ripping the cat into quarters and stared at me. "The day before—"

"Do you have her address?"

"No, but her cousin's listed. Elena Aguirre. In Reseda, in the Valley. That's where we had to call if we wanted her to come in on an off day." He looked down at the scraps of paper in his hands and searched the room for a place to put them.

"What does she look like?"

"I'm no good at describing people."

"You're very good, though, at identifying things you're not very good at."

"She's tiny," he barked. "No more than five feet, and she's got short gray hair cut at the ears like a helmet, and one shoulder higher than the other."

"Any tattoos?"

"How should I—" He stopped and worked his mouth into a tight little knot, and then he smiled that same sweet smile. "That was a joke," he said. He suddenly looked doubtful. "Wasn't it?"

"More or less. Are you going to go to the cops for me, Christy? For Max?"

"I don't know," he said again, stuffing the cat into his pocket, along with the remnants of the smile.

I gave up. "Are you going to stay here, then?"

"Maybe." He sounded all of sixteen.

"Then I need to talk to Alan and Robert," I said. "There are some things they should know."

He looked stung. "You think I'd keep anything from them?"

"I don't know what I think, Christy. You're not willing to do the one thing I need you to do."

"I haven't said no yet."

I got up and crossed the room and knocked on the door through which Alan and Robert had disappeared. The door opened into a den, furnished in Intensive Cosy: quilts and lap rugs flung themselves aggressively across overstuffed furniture. Potted plants flourished in terra-cotta containers. Robert was watching television, wearing earphones, and Alan was reading a detective novel with a startlingly lurid cover.

"Excuse me," I said, "but I need you in the living room."

"I'm here," Christy said sulkily from behind me.

"Robert?" I said, miming removing headphones. Robert pulled his off, looking faintly surprised.

"What is it?" Alan asked.

"The two of you are in danger," I said, "and I thought somebody should tell you so."

"We're not afraid of the police," Robert said.

"I'm not talking about the police."

Alan drew in the corners of his mouth, looking like a schoolteacher weighing the punishment for some poor kid's spitball. "What, then?"

"The guy who killed Max," I said. "He came back to the house, looking for something, and I don't think he found it. If I were in his shoes, I'd be worried that Christy has it."

"I don't have anything," Christy said, and then he said, "he came back to the *house*?"

I told them about my encounter two nights earlier. "Whatever he wanted, it was small," I said, "and he hadn't found it when I showed up or he wouldn't have tackled me. And I doubt he stuck around to look for it after I left."

"What was it?" Alan asked.

"Something he couldn't leave," I said. "Something that ties him to the murder."

"Well, I haven't got it," Christy said insistently.

"That doesn't really matter," I said. "What matters is that he probably thinks you do."

"Why wouldn't he think the cops found it?" Alan asked.

"He's thinking past that. If the cops found it, there's nothing he can do. If Christy has it, though, there *is* something he can do."

"You *believe*," Alan said.

"I saw Max," I said. "Christy saw Max. If there's even one chance in ten I'm right, it's something worth worrying about."

They all looked at each other. I listened to the grandfather clock ticking in the living room.

"Assuming that you're right," Alan said judiciously, "which I'm not sure I do, what should we do about it?"

"It's what Christy should do. I want him to go to the sheriff."

"What would that accomplish?"

"It would get him out of here, for one thing," I said. "They're pretty sure it's not Christy. They just want to question him. I'll get him a lawyer—"

"I'm a lawyer," Alan said. "I'm a damn good lawyer."

"Then tell him."

Alan looked at Robert. Robert looked past me, at Christy.

"I'll go," Christy said. "I'll go tomorrow."

The best way to get from West Hollywood to Reseda is to take Santa Monica Boulevard west, through Beverly Hills and Westwood, and pick up the San Diego Freeway north to the San Fernando Valley. At nine-thirty on Friday night the traffic on Santa Monica was too heavy to make me happy: All I wanted to do was cross Doheny, the western border of West Hollywood, and get out of the Sheriffs' territory.

I didn't make it.

The red lights came on behind me at Almont. I pulled over and took out my wallet before they even got out of the squad car. I didn't want to make any ambiguous movements.

Something punched Alice hard in the left rear fender, rocking the car, and Ike Spurrier leaned down and grinned through the driver's window.

"You got a bad taillight," he said. He was holding a tire iron in his left hand.

"I've been meaning to have it looked at," I said.

He tapped the iron against the door. "Procrastination is a terrible thing."

A uniformed deputy shone a flashlight through the passenger window. "Dangerous, too," I said.

"For want of a nail," Spurrier declaimed, "the shoe was lost."

"Have you been following me? Somehow this doesn't feel like a chance meeting."

"It's a conspicuous car," he said. "We have radios, you know."

"Boy," I said. "The technological edge."

"I'm going to have to ask you to get out of the car, sir," Spurrier said, backing away from the door. "Be careful of the oncoming traffic, now."

"We wouldn't want anything to happen to me."

He gave me his wet smile. "Not out here, anyway."

I climbed out of the car slowly, keeping my hands in plain sight. When I was standing on the road I laced my fingers together and put them on top of my head.

"Aren't we cautious?" Spurrier said.

"I haven't updated my life insurance."

"Come around the car. On the sidewalk, please." I did as I was told. "Now put your hands against the car, spread your legs, and lean forward, putting your weight on your hands."

"For a broken taillight?"

"We're cautious, too."

The deputy patted me down, knocking my knees apart with more force than was strictly necessary. "Nothing," he said.

"Just stay there," Spurrier said. He handed the tire iron to the deputy and leaned forward and unbuttoned my right cuff. "It's an interesting thing," he said conversationally. "We've been poking around in Max's house, and it looks like we had *two* intruders."

"That's a lot of intruders." The deputy was shining his flashlight onto the backseat of the car.

"They both came in through the back door. Left the key right there." He rolled the sleeve up and examined my arm, then rolled it down again and thoughtfully buttoned the cuff. "One of them left through the bedroom window. And I mean *through* it."

"Must have been in a hurry," I said.

"I'd say so." He moved behind me and came around on the left. "The other one apparently went out through the door he'd come in through. Left it wide open."

"Probably raised in a barn."

"Did your mother use to say that?" He unbuttoned my right cuff. "My mother used to say that."

"Your mother probably had cause."

"Now, now," he said, rolling the sleeve up. "Don't antagonize the forces of justice. Whoever they were, they seem to have had a disagreement. How'd you get this?" He ran his finger up the cut on my arm.

"Cutting brush," I said. "Fire clearance."

"Good citizen. Wish we had more like you." He gave a little tug at the cut, and a line of fire ran up my nerves all the way to my armpit.

"Sergeant," the deputy called.

"This is sure to be important," Spurrier said confidingly.

"Latex gloves," the deputy said, holding up the box from the backseat.

"That so," Spurrier said. "I'm sure you can explain this."

"Damn, Ike," I said. "They were going to be my Christmas present to you. I figured, the way you must go through them—"

I stopped because he'd dug his thumbs into the skin on either side of the cut and pulled it open. I began to bleed immediately, and Spurrier yanked his hands from my arm.

"I've had enough out of you," he said, examining his hands for my blood. "I think we'll finish this at the station."

I grabbed a deep breath, filling my lungs with exhaust. "Arrest me," I said.

"I'll arrest you when I—"

"I want the whole thing, Ike," I said. "I want you to radio in now, and then I want the booking and the printing and the phone call, the whole dog and pony show. And I'm going to say all that again, loud enough for your deputy to hear me, and if you don't radio me in, I'm going to turn and run, and you're going to have to catch me in front of all these people."

"Don't you trust me?" He sounded betrayed.

"Not much."

"Take him in, Sergeant?" the deputy asked.

"Just a second," Spurrier said. He leaned closer to me. "You're messing with the wrong guy, sonny."

"Ike," I said, gambling, "you will not *believe* how much I know about you."

One of his eyes got very much smaller than the other, and he regarded me out of it for a moment that was long enough to make my legs begin to shake. "Check the trunk,

Hal," he called. "Keys are in the ignition." When Hal was as far away as he was going to get, Spurrier pushed his big face within a few inches of mine. "Anything specific we should discuss?"

"Not with you. I want to tell someone who'll be surprised."

He straightened up and put his hands in his jacket pockets, gazing across the street and moving his lips as though he were running through possible things to say. One of the hands came out of the pocket with what looked like the same crushed package of cigarettes, and he shook one out and lit it.

"We're not getting along very well," he observed. "I may not have made myself clear, about Max's house, I mean. There was a fight there, did I tell you that? What that means, the way I figure it, is that one of the people there was on our side. How does that sound to you?"

"Like enlightened speculation," I said. "Can I straighten up?"

"Sure," he said, as though he was surprised to learn I was still leaning against the car. "So I figure that person, like I said, is on our side, and maybe he's got something to tell us."

"Maybe he does," I said. "You told me to stay away from the case, and that's what I've been doing."

"You're shitting me," Spurrier said mildly. "You picked up Max's dry cleaning."

"I picked up Christy's dry cleaning," I said. "Max's just happened to be in with it."

Spurrier gave it a moment's thought and decided to go for the misdemeanor rather than the felony. "Then you've been talking to Christy."

"It was a personal favor."

"You want to do him another one?"

"If I can."

"Tell him to come see us."

I looked at my feet, feeling a warm wave of relief. "I don't know, Ike," I said.

"He can bring a lawyer," Spurrier said grandly. "We know he didn't do it."

I brought my eyes up to his, trying to look like someone about to walk through fire. "I'll do it," I said. "I'll get him there tomorrow."

For a moment I thought he was going to laugh, but all he did was shake his head. Then he stepped back and fired his cigarette into the gutter.

"You bled on your car," he said.

13
WOLF PACK

WITH a stop at a Thrifty Drugs to pick up a bandage for my
arm and fifteen greasy but satisfying minutes at a Burger King,
it was well after ten by the time I got to Reseda. Kids with
nothing to do were cruising up and down the main streets, and
I wondered—not for the first time—how anybody can have
nothing to do with all the things that so obviously need doing.
In a phone booth at Reseda Boulevard and Sherman Way, I
looked up Elena Aguirre's address and dialed Wyl's number.

"Fan Fare," he answered.

"Wyl," I said, "you're at home."

"Force of habit." The words were a little fuzzy at the edges,
and I remembered that it was Wyl's custom to drink a Man-
hattan or two, or as many as he had in the house, after work.

"Have you got an *Academy Players' Directory?*"

"Silly question. I've a complete set, beginning with 1945." Wyl always got a little British after a couple of Manhattans, and since he now sounded like Prince Philip, I figured he'd had four or five.

"Do me a favor. Get a recent one and look in the agents' section. I want an address for Ferris Hanks."

"He's alive?" I let it pass, and Wyl came to his own rescue. "Awful, awful man," he said. "You know, the good die—"

"*You're* still alive," I pointed out.

There was a silence, and when he spoke he sounded affronted. "One needn't say everything one thinks of," he said snippily. "One does not need to be reminded of one's age."

"Sorry," I said. "Listen, Wyl, I'm in a phone booth."

"Oh, you *poor* boy." He sounded aghast. "I'll get right to it."

A moment later I had an address. "That's up near the bird streets," he said, "just off Sunset Plaza. There aren't any offices up there. He must be working from his house."

"Thanks, Wyl."

"Anytime," he said. "Well, cheerio." Make it six Manhattans.

Thirty years ago the Valley was mostly Anglo, with a few Hispanic pockets tucked in to supply a work force in the remnants of the orange groves and tomato farms that once stretched, fragrant and fruitful, across its broad floor. Now, in the flatlands north of Ventura Boulevard, most of the Anglos had followed the orchards into memory. The faces in the cars and on the sidewalks were brown, black, and occasionally yellow. The new cash crop seemed to be the minimall, motley collections of unrelated businesses shoveled into cramped, fanciful stucco structures with too few parking spaces. The donut shops and the nail parlors were run by Vietnamese, and most of the video stores offered *películas en español*. Two Latino kids leaned out of the window of a primo seventies Oldsmobile and whistled appreciatively at Alice. "Bitchen Buick," the driver called. Then, when the light changed, he laid rubber all over the street. Some things hadn't changed.

Elena Aguirre's house was one of a set of five on Hesperia Street, as identical as grapes in a bunch. The contractor had attempted to disguise the limitations of his imagination by photocopying the same blueprint five times, throwing the copies into the air, and then building the houses however the plans landed. Some sported their front doors on the left and some on the right, suggesting quintuplets who parted their hair differently. Some faced the street and some sat sideways. They were painted a remarkable range of colors that extended from old mustard to new mustard. In the daylight, I thought, they'd look like Schultz's teeth.

Each house apparently served as the Mother Ship to three or four automobiles. The half-acre of pink primer on the fenders and doors offered a complement of catsup for all that mustard. I found a parking space opposite the address I'd copied from the phone booth and sat there, wondering what to do.

The scene with Spurrier played and replayed in my mind. He'd let me off easy; I didn't really think my threat of revelation had been anything but transparent. On the other hand, a man like Spurrier was likely to have a veritable convention of skeletons in his closet. And then there was Spurrier's closet itself— the one he was in, according to the man in The Zipper. Not likely to look for help, Schultz had said.

No one went in or out of Elena Aguirre's house. No lights were on.

Had it been Elena, or Marta herself who had hung up on me?

By now Marta knew about Max's death. I asked myself what I would do, if I were an illegal alien whose boss had been murdered, and I decided I'd do exactly what Marta was doing. I'd go to ground and stay there. But would I go to ground in my cousin's house?

I would if I didn't have anyplace else to go. Did Marta? For all I knew, she was back in San Salvador by now.

Why did I keep replaying the conversation with Spurrier? There was nothing remarkable about it. He'd wanted something from me that I was already prepared to give him, and when I finally gave it to him, he recognized it for what it was: a pawn waiting to be sacrificed. He'd almost laughed in my face. And I'd almost laughed back, and that was why I kept holding the encounter up to the light.

I hadn't been terrified. My mind hadn't overloaded and shut down, my stomach hadn't rebelled. I'd faced him down, both of us playing games and both of us seeing through the other's game, and I'd walked away from it with no more damage than a new bandage on my arm, a broken taillight, and a car that needed washing. I could have regarded myself as whole again, if it hadn't been for one thing.

It wasn't Spurrier who terrified me. It was the kid in the dark, the kid with the friendly voice and the carpet cutter.

Headlights swept the street, and a no-color Hyundai, as dented and puckered as a raisin, pulled into Elena Aguirre's driveway and a woman in blue jeans and a white T-shirt got out, lugging a pillowcase full of something soft and heavy: laundry. She was of medium height, and her dark hair reached mid-back. Elena, probably. She walked very briskly, back straight despite the weight of the load thrown over her shoulder, to the front door. All business, she dug through a ring of keys and did the necessary. Three locks, a lot of locks but not excessive for Reseda these days. She went into the house and pulled the door closed without so much as a glance around.

Wouldn't she look around if her cousin were hiding there? I decided she would and started the car. I'd pulled it out of the space and turned it around before I realized that no lights had gone on in the house.

So maybe she went to the back.

Maybe the electricity was off.

Maybe the Farm Boy was in there, waiting for her.

Shit. I backed into the space again and got out of the car.

It wasn't a wide street, but it seemed to take several minutes to cross. One small blessing: The builder had economized on windows, so I could edge around the side of the house without having to duck down more than once, as I passed a cheap, rectangular, aluminum-framed sliding affair that probably opened onto a dining room or a bedroom. Elena's car exhaled heat, creaking and popping behind me.

The backyard was dirt, with a few large rocks scattered around like a training set for an apprentice Zen gardener. A light gleamed through a square eighteen-inch window in the back door, and I crept toward it, bent as sharply as a man getting into a helicopter. Through the window I saw Elena Aguirre dumping men's clothing into a machine, singing in Spanish as she worked, a woman doing someone else's laundry. She didn't sort it. Maybe she was using cold water. Maybe she didn't care if the colors ran.

Even if Marta was in there, I didn't want to talk to her when her cousin was home. I went back to the car, walking straight this time, and headed back to West Hollywood.

"Whatchoo want?" said the voice through the little speaker. It was the voice of someone who'd earned an advanced degree in Urban Black. He'd spoken even before I rang the bell.

"Is Ferris Hanks there?" The gates across Hanks's driveway were black wrought iron, at least twelve feet tall, and must have weighed a thousand pounds apiece. They had a design of some kind in the center.

"Whoozzat?"

"Nobody he knows." My eyes interpreted the design in the center, rejected it, and reinterpreted it. It was *still* a spider.

"Fuck off," said the voice on the speaker.

"Say *please*, Henry," said a new voice. It was a dry, thin

voice, brittle enough to punch a finger through, but it had a lot of authority.

"Fuck off, please," said Henry, brandishing his social skills.

The spider had a red spot, shaped like a violin, on its abdomen. I wondered what the neighbors thought. "I'm here about Max Grover," I offered.

"It's a little late to talk about Max," the dry voice said. "Max is a dead issue." There was a pause, and I pictured him rubbing his hands, listening for my response. "*Heek heek heek,*" he finally said, a laugh of sorts, a laugh that needed to be taken outdoors and given a good shaking and hung on the line for a week.

"I only need a few minutes," I said. "I was a friend of his."

"One of Max's *friends?*" The voice had dismay in it. "I think not. We're not in the market for scruffy this evening. Leave at once."

"The hell I will."

"Well, you can't stay *there*. The Pinkerton Patrol will get you. And you can't climb the fence into the yard because my dogs will eat you alive. We haven't fed the dogs, have we, Henry?"

Henry rumbled a negative and then cleared his throat. "So fuck off," Henry said. "Please."

The fence, also wrought iron, was nowhere near as high as the gates. Just for the hell of it, I opened Alice's door quietly, got out, and kicked the fence. No ravening hounds barked at me. I got back into the car without closing the door.

"I'll see you," I said.

"In your dreams," said the dry voice.

The house sat on the curve of a narrow street, maybe a mile above Sunset, where the houses were half a city block apart. I coasted down to the next house, pulled partway onto a grass parking strip, and climbed out, my muscles no longer protesting each change of position. The city lay spread out below, a scattered cache of rhinestones cut off by the hard dark line of the Pacific.

Hanks's fence looked like it had been built to be climbed, a lattice of black iron that thoughtfully offered the would-be intruder both horizontals to step on and verticals to hold on to. When I got up there I found that the verticals reared two feet above the final horizontal at the top, demanding a delicate approach if a human male wanted to negotiate it and continue to sing any of the melodies on the bass clef. Hanging there and contemplating emasculation, I kicked the fence again, waiting for the whelps of the Hound of the Baskervilles to materialize beneath me, snarling and dripping foam. Mailmen face worse every day, I thought, dropping to the grass on the inside of the fence.

A line of oleanders marched in tight ranks parallel to the fence to mask the house. I pushed my way through them and found myself facing another row. Oleanders are noisy bushes, with flat dry leaves, but the dogs weren't waiting for me on the other side.

The lawn sloped downhill toward the house, a beautiful, rambling white twenties Mediterranean with a red tile roof and a round tower at either end. Hanks's gardeners had planted big generic bushes here and there to soften the house's lines, not that they needed softening, and the bushes looked like they might provide a convenient set of resting places as I worked my way toward the front door. I'd reached the third one when a bank of floodlights went on.

"Stay right there," Henry's voice boomed. "Move and I'll let them off the leash."

I froze. "I'm here," I said.

"Well, don't move your ass." Now I could hear panting. It was coming directly toward *my* bush, which suddenly looked very small. Too small to climb, at any rate.

"Oh, hell," said the dry voice. "Let them loose."

There was no getting to the fence. I stood there, paralyzed, as a series of clips was unfastened, and then the bush rustled and a cloud of Yorkshire terriers trotted around it, averaging about two pounds each, and gazed up at me, their tongues lolling. One of them bounded up and viciously sniffed my shoe.

Through the roaring in my ears I could hear the dry voice. It said, *"Heek heek heek."*

14
THE HALL OF THE MOUNTAIN KING

THE hardest part was reconciling the picture of Ferris Hanks I'd assembled in my imagination with the Ferris Hanks sitting across from me. I'd anticipated a wizened, exquisite Mandarin from Central Casting's criminal mastermind division: crippled perhaps, shaved bald as an egg, and wearing flowing robes or thigh-high boots and a black leather cape. What I'd gotten was a miniature Broderick Crawford. In a USC jogging suit.

Everything about Hanks's face was square. He had a nose like a thumb and a chin like a shoebox. His short dark hair, expertly clipped into varying lengths, was combed forward in Roman fashion, and the lower ridge of his skull, where it jutted out over the back of his neck, had a corner like a coffee table. The neck was powerful, roped with muscle, giving him the look of someone who habitually opened doors with his head. As short as it was thick, the neck emerged from shoulders as broad as an automobile bumper.

"Max was a fool," he said in his dry old-man voice. The voice was the oldest thing about him. "A good actor, but a fool."

We were in a living room almost long enough and almost cold enough for a game of ice hockey. Frigid air was being pumped energetically into the room through two vents, big enough to crawl through, high on the walls. It was a room my mother had definitely not furnished. Navajo rugs imposed dull-colored angular patterns over a gray slate floor, and tall hand-painted Japanese screens, profusely decorated with irises and camellias, concealed the corners. Crowds of men, women, and gods congregated festively on the walls, each crowd cut from a separate panel of heavy flat Thai teak. The furniture was low and massive, dark wood and burgundy leather, with the cushions tied to the wooden frames as though they'd attempted in the past to rearrange themselves while no one was looking. Against the longest of the walls stood a police lineup of full-size wooden cigar-store Indians. In the center of the lineup, looking like the one who dreaded stepping forward, was Henry. Henry had a gun in his hand and an ambivalent gleam in his eye.

"He did a lot of good," I said.

The Yorkshire terriers had scattered themselves over the burgundy leather couch on either side of Hanks, like living throw pillows. Hanks removed one from his lap and opened a profusely carved ivory box. He closed it again, looking disappointed. "He could have done more good by staying in front of the cameras," he said. "The damn fool."

I had a feeling this was territory Hanks had explored often. I also had the feeling Hanks thought a lot of people were damn fools.

Upon closer examination, it wasn't so much that Hanks didn't seem old; he just seemed a kind of young that did not, that never would, exist in nature. The skin drawn taut over the square face was the color of a glazed ham and the texture of a bat's wing. The short hair was a peculiar dark red that suggested a genetic link with the later Ronald Reagan. It all came together to create a sort of humanoid artifact, animatronic, perhaps, that required, and got, a great deal of skilled technical care.

He leaned forward, grunting with the effort, and pulled a brass box with a domed lid across the table. With thick, blunt fingers he pried at the lid without result. "What do you know about me?" he asked.

"You were his agent," I said. I was cold enough to shiver.

"Heek heek heek," he wheezed, bouncing slightly with each heek. He picked up the box, turned it upside down, and banged it against the edge of the coffee table. The lid popped off, clattering on the slate floor, and he kicked it under the table and peered into the box. One dog opened a curious eye. The others seemed used to it. "What else?"

"Nothing much," I lied. "What should I know?"

He'd lost interest in me. "Henry," he rasped, the back of his throat rattling like a box of rocks on the *H.* "Where are they?"

"Forget it, Ferris," Henry said.

Ferris Hanks raised both feet and stamped them on the floor together, causing a furry ripple among the Yorkies, and the dark face went a couple of shades darker. "Cut this shit," he said. "Go get them."

"I ain't leaving you here alone," Henry said stolidly.

"I know your counting skills aren't all they should be," Ferris Hanks said, "but I'm not alone."

"Fuck you, Ferris," Henry said, surprising me.

It didn't surprise Ferris. It seemed to calm him. "You're a fool, Henry," he said without force. Then, to me, "We've been together too long."

"At least you haven't started to look alike."

"Heek," he said. "Don't you think Henry's good-looking?"

"He's a veritable fever dream," I said.

"You hear that, Henry?" Hanks's eyes, long and heavy-lidded and a fraudulent deep-sea blue, came back to me. "And that's all you know about me? You mean, no one's maligning me these days?" He didn't sound pleased.

"I've heard your nickname, of course."

His thumb of a nose pointed down, like a disapproving Roman emperor, toward a broad, masculine mouth with a thin upper lip and a full, square lower one. The left corner went up, producing the closest thing I'd ever seen to the half-smile I keep reading about, and the left eye disappeared into a mass of leathery, batlike wrinkles. The right regarded me steadily and coldly enough to have belonged to someone else. "How do you think someone earns a nickname like that?"

The chair I was sitting in was big enough for me, Henry, and Henry's extended family, and it provided a lot of squirming room, which might have been why it had been offered to me. Hanks watched me expectantly. "I don't know," I said. "They called me Sluggo in school, and I never slugged anybody."

"You made that up," Hanks said petulantly.

I had. "Mr. Hanks, I'm sure you've had a fascinating life, crammed with really rotten stuff, but it's Max I'm interested in."

Hanks rummaged in the brass box, just in case something had materialized inside it while he wasn't paying attention. "You could pretend," he said.

"Stop fiddling, Ferris," Henry said. "They not in there."

He gave the box a thwack with his finger. "Did you hear why Max left me? He was Rick then. Rick Hawke."

"Sort of a silly name," I said, just to annoy him.

"I made that name up," Hanks said mildly. "I made up all their names in those days. They just trotted into the office, dozens of them every week, all as beautiful as a summer's day, looking to be stars. Truckdrivers, elevator operators, construction workers, men with real jobs. Now they're all *waiters*. 'Good evening, my name is Dwight, and I'll be your waiter until I'm discovered by a major studio.' " His voice had risen to a feathery whine. "I don't know how anyone can eat out these days," he said in a normal tone. "Every meal is a fucking audition."

"With a beefcake appetizer," I said.

"Jesus, it was fun," Hanks said. "All the studios wanted boys then. Girls were just scenery, an opportunity for the clothes designers to use a little color. I changed *that*. Remember Jimmy Dean's red jacket in *Rebel Without a Cause*? My influence. 'Put the color on the boys,' I said, 'they're the ones everybody's shelling out to see. If the girls want color, dump some on their hair, the silly bitches.' Just *busloads* of wannabes every month, pouring in from all over. And I owned the market." He reached up and twisted a lock of odd-red hair. "Owned the market."

"And what about Max?"

"Max, Max, Max," he said vehemently. One of the dogs looked up as though it had heard its name. "I'm much more interesting than Max. Not many people have lived their entire lives on their own terms and gotten away with it, boysie. It's a small club. I may be its oldest living member." The hand was still in his hair, and he yanked violently at the lock and then examined his fingers to see whether any had come out. He turned the hand to me and spread it open like a stage magician, showing me that it was empty. "Still, Max was special. Is it true what they're saying?"

I crossed my legs. "Depends on what they're saying."

"You needn't play it so close to the vest, you know. It wouldn't pain you to give a full answer once in a while. Unless you get paid by the word, *heek heek*. They're *saying* that some gay basher killed Max and cut off his hand and that he's some sort of lunatic who does this for jollies. Is that true?"

"Where'd you hear it?"

Hanks snapped his fingers with a sound like a gun going off, and pointed at me. Dogs jumped. "Stop that right now. You want, you give. Law of the jungle."

"You scarin' the wolf pack," Henry observed.

"It's true," I said.

His tongue came out and slid over the lower lip. "Did you see the body?"

I wasn't going to pay in that currency. "No."

"Hmmm." He regarded me dubiously. "Did the latest dreary young man?"

"He found Max, if that's what you mean."

"Probably wasted on him," Hanks said. "Max's boys were always so *hapless*. Although why he stole *that* one is really beyond me."

"Stole?"

"Snatched him away from that old poof with the Bette Davis eyes who runs the Bookstore of the Living Dead Celebrities or whatever it's called. On Hollywood Boulevard, which should tell you all you need to know."

Wyl had told me he'd pointed Christy to Max himself. "That's not the way I heard it."

"Well, I can't help that, can I? Consider the source, I always say. Who *was* your source?"

"Someone who knows all three of them."

"I suppose discretion is admirable," Hanks said, pushing two dogs aside so he could probe between the cushions of the couch. "But that doesn't make it good conversation."

"They gone, Ferris," Henry said. "They gone from behind the screen, too, so don't bother gettin' up."

"I don't know which of you I find less interesting," Hanks lamented to me. "You won't tell me anything, and Henry enjoys thwarting me. But whatever anyone told you, the transfer of that sullen lad from the antique dealer to the aging actor was not accomplished without a certain amount of melodrama."

"And who told you?" I asked.

"I really shouldn't call Max aging," Hanks said, ignoring the question. "He was *old*. Still, you know, he'd aged well. As well as anyone does." He looked through me, and I heard

Henry fidget against his wall. "He didn't quit acting because of me, you know."

I made a note to ask Wyl a couple of questions. "Why did he quit, then?"

"Max had *principles*," he said, making it sound like a disease. "He couldn't, what's the phrase, *live a lie*. As though we all don't in one way or another. Not Max, though, oh, no, not Max. It wasn't enough for him to have a TV show in the top five and pull down ten thousand a week, and that was *muchos dolores* in those days."

"*Dólares*," I said.

His eyebrows shot up as though something was chasing them. "Are you correcting me?"

"*Dólares*," I said again. "*Dolores* means pains."

"Henry?"

"The fuck would I know?"

"Well," Hanks said comfortably, "it was *all* a pain to Max. He had to be True To Himself. He wanted to—God's truth—he wanted to come out, as they say today." He sat back and watched me brightly, waiting for me to fall out of my chair. "In the nineteen *fifties*."

"And you wouldn't let him."

"Are you crazy? Rumors were already flying about my little stable. You're too young to remember *Confidential* magazine, but they were hot on our cute little tails. Most of my young men were discreet—two of them were even straight—but some of them had their nuts in the wringer. Parties got raided and there were all these boys in pajamas, or not in pajamas, depending on when the door got knocked in. All these studs with the superhero names I'd dreamed up for them and the oh-so-butch voices I'd taught them to use, hadn't I, sweetheart?" he asked one of the dogs, toying with its ear. "We did everything for them in those days. Actors knew they were cattle back then, not like now when they think they can elect *presidents* and run the Pentagon. We named them, taught them to walk—that was usually hilarious—gave them pasts, gave them *wives* when things got touchy, wiped their expensive new noses when they got sick. It was a big investment. Not something to be thrown away because a cop went through the wrong door or some damn fool wanted to be *true* to himself. Be true to *me*, I told him, be true to your *public*. Stop thinking about yourself all the time.''

"What did he say?''

"Said he wasn't thinking about himself, he was thinking about All Of Us, all us poor downtrodden queers locked in our closets. The closet's *good*, I told him. It gives us strength, gives us self-discipline. Gives us a *secret*. People with a secret are always more interesting than people who don't have one.''

"Do you really believe that?''

"Passionately. We were united then. We shared our problems, shared our jokes. The straight world was open to us, there for us to plunder, like King Solomon's mines or the Hall of the Mountain King. We were the Knights of Malta, a secret society, smarter and prettier and funnier than they were, and we had what they wanted, and they didn't know what it was or even why they wanted it. They had one little life each, and we had as many as we wanted. You can develop a lot of useful skills if you're leading a secret life, or three or four. God, it was a glorious time.''

"You were apparently outvoted.''

"Democracy is a terrible thing. The ordinary always wins. I was on the losing side. Max's bunch won, and look where it's gotten them. The Love That Dare Not Speak Its Name has become The Love That Cannot Shut Its Trap. Gays have become the one thing they never were: boring. Look at them, a bunch of bank tellers and dental assistants, holding hands on the sidewalks and *mooning* at each other. Joining neighborhood watch organizations. The fucking *Kiwanis*.'' He stopped to clear his throat, and it turned into a cough, deep and hacking, that bent him over the table until his face almost touched it. When he straightened up, he was the color of rare beef. "Henry," he said pleadingly.

"The drowning man," Henry said, ponderous as the Old Testament, "want his drink of water."

"Old age is vicious," Hanks said, wiping his eyes, "and I mean that literally. It strips away everything but our vices and then denies us those. If you're lucky, you'll die young."

No easy rejoinder sprang to my lips.

"It's disgusting," he said. "All I tried to do was get Max married, for his own good, to my perfectly nice secretary, and he hated me for the rest of his life. Quit the series, turned his back on all of us, went off to some filthy third-world country to get worms, and came back a cut-rate prophet, a walking Kmart of spiritual misinformation. Working his shabby little ministry for ego gratification, rescuing the dull, frumpy ones who weren't handsome enough or smart enough to qualify for the New Jerusalem, the bogus, bourgeois, inane empire of ennui with all its brave muscle-bound subjects. Oh, yes, in the new gay order, life is *free*, life is *open*, and all are welcome. As long as they're pretty and slim and *vapid* and . . ."

"Young," I suggested.

He sank back emptily on the couch, blinked, and smoothed the short hair down over his forehead. "That, too, of course. Not that age is at much of a premium in the heterosexual world, either."

"You called Max," I said. "Asked him to come back to work. Repeatedly."

His eyes got wary. "Someone's been talking out of turn."

"Why did you bother?"

"There were parts," he said shortly.

"And thousands of actors who could have played them. Why keep calling someone who'd turned his back on you, someone who was guaranteed to say no?"

Hanks's eyes flicked to Henry and then up to one of the

crowded Thai carvings. "Bought that at the wrong end of the market," he said. "I've always been better at dealing in people."

I didn't look at it. "Why Max?"

He watched the carving expectantly, as though he were waiting for the people to come to life and start dancing. "He was the one who got away."

I looked at him until the silence brought him back to me.

"Max was a good actor," he said, sounding defiant.

"You tried to destroy him."

He snorted, not a pleasant sound. "If I'd wanted to destroy him, I would have. Destruction is something I can do in my sleep. In a *coma*. Max destroyed himself."

"And you pursued him like a Fury."

"The Furies were always my favorites," he said. "Single-mindedness is such an admirable trait."

"And then, decades later, you tried to get him back."

"Self-interest," he said. "Economics, pure and simple."

I watched him until he looked away. "Max broke your heart."

"Hearts don't break," he said to the people in the carving. "You're old enough to know that. They shrink, they—they *corrode*—they atrophy with lack of use, but they don't break. 'Men have died, and worms have eaten them, but not for love.' That how it goes, Henry?"

"Thass how I recollect it."

"Henry is my literary adviser," Hanks said. "You may have been wondering what he was doing here."

"I hadn't."

"He likes to stand in one place for long periods of time. You've probably noticed that. He's not idle, though. He's working on a mental concordance of English lyric poetry. Aren't you, Henry."

"You say so, Ferris."

"I do say so," Hanks said. "I say it every chance I get."

"You loved Max," I said.

"Everybody loved Max," Hanks said, slapping the table with the flat of his hand. I'd heard a number of people say those words, but not with such intensity. "Max was one of those people other people throw love at. He accepted it like, like air, like confetti, like nothing. He didn't even know I loved him. He didn't *notice.* I turned my life inside out for Max. I got rid of clients who weren't his type, fixed it so other agents wouldn't take them on. I negotiated raises for him when he was already one of the three highest-paid actors in television. He didn't notice. He said, 'Really, Ferris? That's nice. Can we do anything about the scripts?' I got the best writers in town, writers who *hated* television. I blackmailed one of them to write scripts for Max, told him wouldn't it be awful if his wife found out about his little tootsie and started thinking community property. A writer everybody wanted, fucking *Brando* wanted him, and there it was in the trades that he was writing for *Tarnished Star.* Let me tell you something, boysie, one of the tricks of having power is that you don't throw it around. I was throwing it around like a drunk, like a novice, and all for Max. And what did it get me? *Gornischt* is what it got me. A lawsuit from the network when Max walked is what it got me. A nasty postcard from India is what it got me. Break my heart? Don't make me laugh."

"I haven't," I said.

He passed a hand over his forehead. "I don't remember the last time I laughed."

"Ferris," I said reprovingly, "you laughed when your dogs attacked me."

"Heek," he said, and both eyes disappeared. "You looked like you had wet your pants."

It was a smile, sort of. As much of one as I was likely to get. "I need your help," I said.

He got comfortable, a man in his milieu. "Of course you do. Why else would you have climbed my fence?"

"I want you to throw a wake for Max."

Whatever he'd expected, that wasn't it. "A wake? Whatever for?"

I'd expected a refusal, but not a question. "That's not how I work," I said. "I have ideas first and then figure out why I had them."

"How haphazard."

"I prefer to think of it as instinctive."

"I'm sure you do," he said. "What makes you think I'd consider such a thing?"

"We've already covered that. For Max."

"For years," he said, "I thought it was a question: 'Should old acquaintance be forgot?' My answer was always yes. As quickly as possible."

"But you didn't forget."

"Not for lack of trying. Lord, how I tried." He toyed with the brass box and then looked up. At Henry.

"Why not?" Henry said.

"An excellent question," Hanks said promptly, "and one that isn't asked often enough. I knew a prostitute once, a woman of almost inexhaustible willingness, and that was her credo. Anything anyone asked her to do, she replied, 'Why not?' Wound up owning half of North Hollywood. Ever wondered why they call it North Hollywood?"

"Because it's north of Hollywood."

"You lack poetry," Hanks said. "You should spend time with Henry." He fondled the ears of the nearest dog. "Why me? And don't give me sentimentalism."

"You can afford it," I said. "And it would amuse you."

He closed both eyes. "It might at that."

"You haven't laughed in years," I pointed out.

"I ain't never heard him laugh," Henry said solemnly.

Hanks still had his eyes closed, but the left corner of his mouth went up. "Halloween's around the corner."

"Great," I said. "A theme."

"I don't entertain at home," he said, opening his eyes.

"And I wouldn't ask you to. I want it in West Hollywood."

"The dreariest of venues."

"It's your chance," I said, "to show them how it should be done."

The right corner of his mouth went up, too. It made him look almost pleasant. "If I do it," he said, "I'll give them an evening they'll never forget."

"Anything you want, as long as it's legal."

"Where have you *been?* Everything's legal these days."

"You'll do it, then."

He lifted the paws of the dog nearest him and clapped them together lightly in applause. "I'll think about it. Call Henry at six tomorrow evening."

"You're not as bad as they say you are."

"No one's as bad as they say he is. I used to come pretty close, though." His eyes widened. "I thought you didn't know anything about me."

"I lied."

"We'll have lots of time to talk about me while we plan this thing." He waved the words away like smoke. "*If* I do it. It'll broaden your frame of reference." He picked up the ivory box and slammed it onto the tabletop. "Henry," he said, "it's midnight. I've practically promised this man a favor. *Now* can I have a fucking cigar?"

Henry stirred from his spot by the wall. "You got to say please," he said.

15

BACK FENCE

MY answering machine had kept itself busy in my absence. Eleanor had called to say she'd talked to Alan and Christy and that she'd be going to the station with them in the morning in her capacity as a reporter. My mother had checked in with a joke about an old man who found a frog that claimed to be a princess; all he had to do was kiss her to change her back again, with unspeakable delights, unendurably prolonged, as a fringe benefit. At ninety, the old man finally said, he'd just as soon have a talking frog. I wondered what Ferris Hanks would have said. Hammond had called from Maui. He and Sonia had met cops of many races, and did I know that Hawaiians ate paste? Three extremely hearty people in the marital line had called to offer me and the little missus a variety of things I'd never heard of and couldn't do without. Someone with the unlikely name of Ed Pfester—the *P* was silent, but he'd spelled it—had called, saying he was with *Back Fence* magazine, and I could call him back at anytime. He was on deadline, he said. In fact, he'd said it twice, both times he called.

Twelve forty-two A.M. qualified as "anytime," but I didn't feel an irresistible urge to talk to *Back Fence*. Think about *People*, printed badly and dumbed down to a roughly amphibian level, and you've got *Back Fence*. I could imagine the story they'd do on Max—*The Secret Life of an American Icon* or something—and I couldn't see any angle in helping them out.

There were a lot of things I couldn't see any angle in.

I'd brought Max's piece of *Nite Line* up the driveway, and I fetched a beer from the refrigerator and smoothed the clip out on the coffee table. Bearded Jack, at the dating service, had been surprised Max would carry something like that around, but it was all I had, and I'd been postponing working through the classifieds on the back of the page. Forty-three of them had been left whole by Max's scissors and another twelve had been cut through, leaving uninformative fragments.

Let's say Max met the Farm Boy through the classifieds. Let's say the Farm Boy worked his lethal scam from out of town, which made a certain amount of sense; he could probably subscribe to gay papers from all over the place, have them delivered to wherever he holed up between destructive forays into other men's lives.

A comparison of the out-of-town subscription lists of the major-city gay papers might have proved informative. It might also have proved informative to roll back time and watch while Max was assaulted, but I couldn't do that, either.

About a third of the ads provided phone numbers, all local. On a second look, several of them provided the *same* phone number, or numbers that differed only by a digit or two. The pros Jack had talked about, all claiming to be handsome, healthy, hankering, and hung. I crossed them out with a red marker, feeling decisive. There. A start.

Most of the others offered post-office boxes, and nineteen of them were out of town. I marked out the ones in L.A. and looked down at the page. Nineteen was too many by about fifteen. Okay, I thought, which ones would Max be likely to answer?

The parameters: troubled tone, low self-esteem, pleas for help. That meant I had to read the damn things. It was enough to make me get another beer.

Older "brother" needed, one said. *Whom can I turn to?* asked another, a little pedantically. More to the point, *Me: Young and inexperienced. You: Strong and caring.* Feeling young and inexperienced for the first time in years, I made a note of the P.O. box and the state. A little farther down, *Country mouse seeks city mouse.* Against the opposite margin, *Come and Get me.* At the top, *New life needed.* Next to that, *New and adventuresome*, right above *Mature Daddy wanted.*

The third beer went down more quickly than the first two. I was getting a fourth when the phone rang.

"Mr. Grist," Ed Pfester's voice said to the machine, "this is Ed Pfester again from *Back Fence.* I'm up against a heck of a deadline here. Please give me a ring whenever you get in." He gave the number again, as though I were a genie who could be prodded into action only by repeating the magic formula three times. I wrote it down out of habit.

Below Ed Pfester's number, this is what I had on my pad:

Older brother: Albuquerque, NM

A cry in the dark: Boise, ID

Country mouse: Kearney, NE

Me: young: Wheeling, WV

New life: Fresno, CA

Mature Daddy: Decatur, IL

Near Chicago, I thought. And then I thought, *So what?*

Come and Get: Colorado Springs, CO

New and: Provo, Utah

An atlas of sorts, an atlas of real or feigned small-town desperation. I was very happy I wasn't a closet gay in Provo, Utah, or anyplace else where the cops all went to church. Or, for that matter, in Ike Spurrier's territory.

Now what? Write eight letters? I knew the profile that might bring the Farm Boy through the mirror, carpet cutter in hand: older, prosperous, avuncular, roots in a smaller town. But the Farm Boy, according to Schultz's printouts, planned his joy-rides in pairs, two to a city. Keeping his travel expenses down, maybe. It seemed likely that he had both victims identified, had his correspondence or whatever it was well in progress by the time he packed his innocent expression and picked up his boarding pass.

How did he swing it once he got to his destination? Did he work them one at a time or simultaneously? Christy had said no one had been sleeping at Max's house, so he obviously slept elsewhere. In a hotel? At the home of the man in line to become Finger Number Two?

The penciled numbers on the margin of the page: *237/10/ 23/6:2.* Ten twenty-three was probably October 23, two days before Max was killed. What was 6:2? A Bible verse? What other numerical format demanded a colon?

Time, stupid. 6:2. Max being cryptic. 6:20.

That left me 237 on October 23 at 6:20, either A.M. or P.M. Two thirty-seven could have been an address, a hotel room, an office suite, a gym locker, a self-storage compartment, a numerical code of some kind. I was willing to bet it was a flight number.

Approximately ninety airlines fly into, and out of, Los Angeles International Airport, a total of more than eighteen hundred flights a day. The *Official Airlines Guide* lists all of them by city of origin, arranged alphabetically by destination and chronologically from earliest arrival to latest. It's a peculiarly infuriating publication, printed in a type that gets smaller every year, and I buy a new one every three months, on the off chance that I'll be presented with a reason to squint at it.

The twenty-third was a Sunday, so I could eliminate all the 6:20 flights numbered 237 with the notation "X7," meaning *except Sunday*. That would have been helpful if there had been any. There weren't. A beer and a half later, with my eyes watering, I'd learned that there weren't any flights from *anywhere* that had landed at LAX at 6:20 A.M. or P.M. on Sunday the twenty-third. Two veritable holes in the schedule of one of the world's busiest airports.

So maybe it was an address, after all. Or someone's waist size for that matter. Maybe Max had been murdered by someone with a 237-inch waist.

The phone rang, and I was exasperated enough to pick it up.

"Boy," said Ed Pfester, "am I happy to get you."

I wasn't happy. "Do you know what time it is?"

"Really, really late," Ed Pfester said cheerfully. "Did I explain that I'm on deadline?"

"Over and over again."

"And that I'm doing a piece for—"

"*Back Fence*," I said. "And I don't want to talk to you."

"You don't?" He seemed unable to believe it.

"I don't like *Back Fence*," I said. "It's written for people who put most of their mental effort into growing their fingernails."

"That's pretty strong," he said. "But, listen, this is important to me. It's sort of my big break."

"I don't really—"

"Oh, come on. Please? I only need a couple of minutes. Help the kid out."

Burbank, I suddenly thought. I may have slapped my fore-head.

"Ed," I said, "I'll give you ten minutes. Call me back in five."

"Promise?"

"Just dial the number." I hung up and went back to the small print.

One plane into Burbank Airport at 6:20 P.M. on Sunday the twenty-third. Western Air from Denver's Stapleton Airport. Flight 237.

Not good. Stapleton is a hub, a stop-off point for half the air travelers in America. If you're coming to L.A. and you don't have a direct flight, chances are pretty good you're going to hike through Stapleton to change planes. Still, it eliminated Fresno, and probably Wheeling. A Wheeling-based one-stop was much more likely to touch down at O'Hare in Chicago.

That left six, down from forty-three. It cheered me enough to make me pick up the phone and dial.

"Scribbling Ed Pfester." God, he was happy.

"Ed," I said, "have you ever thought about changing your name?"

"Every day of my life," he said. "But it'd break my mother's heart."

"Something like Brick or Dirk," I said, with Ferris Hanks's stable of names in mind. "It'd get rid of the assonance, at least."

"Brick?" he said. "Brick Pfester?"

"You'd probably want to do something about the Pfester, too."

"I'll think about it. Does this count toward my ten minutes?"

"No, this is on me. How'd you get my name?"

"One of the other people I talked to. Are you going to let me get away with that?"

"No."

"I didn't think so. Well, it was a sheriff's deputy. I'm going to be in big trouble if I use his name."

"Not Spurrier."

"Not. Is that good enough?"

The kid was hopeless. "I guess it'll have to be. What do you want to know?"

"Can I say you're investigating Mr. Hawke's death?"

"You can if you want to get sued."

"Boy," he said admiringly, "you don't have a problem with confrontation, do you? That's something I have to work on."

"Just practice," I said. There was something familiar about his voice.

"How well did you know him?"

"I met him once, for about an hour."

"That's all?" His dismay was palpable.

"That's it."

"And what did you think of him?"

What *had* I thought of Max? "He was courtly. Sort of remote, but not in an unfriendly way. Intuitive."

"Wait," he said. "I'm writing." I hung on for a moment. "Would you describe him as an inspiration to everyone who came into contact with him?"

"No."

"Oh," he said. "Well, how about someone who could teach us all something about life?"

"Where do you get this stuff? Norman Vincent Peale? *Reader's Digest?*"

"Not good, huh?" He didn't seem the least bit bothered. "How about in your own words?"

"Actually, I thought he was a little cracked."

"I can't use *that*," he said. "Ill of the dead, and all."

"Sorry."

"Hard news, then. I gather you actually saw the body."

"I don't want to talk about that."

"Terrible, huh?"

"Worse than terrible. The work of a subhuman."

There was another pause. "Writing," he said, after a moment. "Subhuman, you said?"

"Ed," I said, "why don't you buy a tape recorder?"

"Do you know what they pay me? I'm lucky to have a phone. Hey, listen, I'm hearing the killer may have left something at the scene."

A little breeze sprang into life behind me and blew directly onto the back of my neck. "You're hearing that, are you?"

"This could be a real scoop," he said. "You know what a scoop is?"

"I've heard the term," I said, getting to my feet.

"So did he?" he asked, and I knew where I'd heard his voice before.

I looked around the room, a deeply familiar room with Eleanor imprinted on it, and wondered whether I should go down the hill, get into the car, and drive somewhere very far away. "What's this phone number?" I asked.

A beat. "My apartment. Where else would I be at this hour?"

"Right," I said. Then I drew a long breath and let it out silently. "This is off the record, Ed," I said. "The answer is yes."

"Off the record," Ed Pfester said.

"You've heard the term," I said.

"Well, sure," he said. "I may be green, but—aw, you're kidding me."

"I'm kidding you," I confirmed.

"So, off the record. Who has it? Whatever he left, I mean. So I can talk to him, I mean."

I was walking now, dragging the long cord behind me. "I can't tell you that."

A brief silence. Then: "Can't tell me? Or don't know?"

"The former."

"You're not helping me much." He didn't sound so happy.

I looked at the moon through the door to the deck. Two

hundred forty thousand miles sounded about right. "It's not actually my purpose in life to help you, Ed."

"You're not going to tell me who—"

"I think I've made that clear."

He cleared his throat. "Do you suck dick?" he asked.

"With your mouth," I said.

"Faggot," Ed Pfester spat. "Stay out of dark rooms." He hung up.

"Who the fuck *is* this?" Hammond asked groggily on the other end of the line.

"Simeon. I need some help, Al."

"You know, pal, people sometimes sleep on their honeymoons."

"This is serious. I need access to the reverse directory."

"It'll leave tracks," he said. "They log all the requests these days."

"I can't help that." I told him what had happened.

"Call the Sheriffs," he said. He sounded wide awake. "Give it to them."

"I wouldn't give Ike Spurrier a catheter, big end first."

"Orlando told me about that. They're not all like Spurrier."

"Yeah, but Spurrier is."

He blew heavily into the phone. "Give me the number," he said. "I'll call you back."

I gave him Ed Pfester's number and got up and poured the rest of my beer into the sink. Then I went back to the *Official Airlines Guide* and checked out flights to Stapleton from Decatur, Provo, Kearney, Colorado Springs, Boise, and Albuquerque. Flights that might conceivably have connected to flight 237 landing at Burbank left daily from Kearney, Boise, and Decatur.

Down to three.

The prefix of the phone number Ed Pfester had given me was in West Hollywood, like everything else. He was at least forty-five minutes away, unless he'd used call forwarding, in which case he could be right down the hill.

I found the extra shells for the nine-millimeter at the bottom of my shirt drawer, wrapped in an ancient Disneyland T-shirt. I was throwing them into a nylon bag, along with some wrinkled clothes, when the phone rang.

"Thirteen twenty-eight Hayworth," Hammond said. "West Hollywood. It's an apartment house. Number seven."

"Thanks, Al."

"Don't do anything stupid," he said.

"Al," I said, "I already have."

16
APARTMENT
SEVEN

"**I WANT** to borrow Henry," I said, feeling exposed, unsafe, too big to miss. This was my week for pay phones. Late traffic hummed and whistled, burped and hissed along Sunset behind me.

"Have I missed a stage in our relationship?" Hanks demanded. "Did I sleep through something? I don't think we're on the kind of terms that would allow you to ring me up at three-thirty in the morning and request the loan of my literary adviser."

"Ferris," I said, "who else could I call at this hour?"

"That's a sad little question," he said. "There are *lots* of people I could call."

I closed my eyes and rested my forehead against the cold chromium of the phone. "I'll need him for an hour."

"Henry will have something to say about this. He has free will, you know."

"Tell him he might get to shoot someone."

"He'll like that," Hanks said. "Who?"

"The guy who killed Max."

Hanks sucked in his breath. "Is this going to put a crimp in our fête?"

"Quite possibly."

"Well," he said, sounding disappointed, "I suppose it's in a good cause."

"Ten minutes," I said. "I'll honk."

"Not in this neighborhood. He'll be out at the gate."

"Tell him this is probably going to be dangerous," I said.

"Of course it is. You must tell me all about it when it's over." He put his hand over the phone and said something. "Assuming you kill him, or catch him or something, we could still have the party, couldn't we? Make it a celebration."

"Sober up, Ferris," I said. "You sound almost enthusiastic."

"I've warmed to the idea," he said. "I was thinking in terms of a fountain of holy water. From Lourdes."

"If you've got any on hand," I said, "give some to Henry for me."

Henry had dressed for the occasion in black leather, looking like a cross between a killer cyborg and someone who dances behind Madonna. He got into the car without speaking and pulled out a small blue vial with a cork in it. "Direck from the Virgin," he said, pouring a thimbleful of water on me.

"I was joking," I said, pulling at the front of my wet shirt.

"Never joke about holy water with Ferris. He take this shit serious. How you think he stay so younglike?"

We were rolling down the hill. Despite the heat, I felt chilled where my shirt had been soaked. "I figured surgery had something to do with it."

Henry snickered. "Nobody cut ol' Ferris. He too scared about the blood supply."

"What about you?"

"I don't plan on bleeding."

"Hold that thought." I gave Henry a short version of my chat with Ed Pfester as I cut left on Sunset and right on La Cienega, one long downhill coast, both in terms of topography and real estate values. Below Sunset the world was running on something like normal time, and traffic was lighter. A thin layer of cloud had slid in, and the city's lights pressed up against it, turning the sky into a flat, reflective sheet of hammered metal.

Henry cleared his throat, making a noise like someone emptying a pool, rolled down the window, and spat. "You think he's going to be there?"

"If he wants to kill me, he is. But, no, I don't. I think he left the moment he hung up the phone. If I'd really thought there was any chance he'd hang around, I'd have called the cops."

"Well," Henry said, "at least you know you got something he wants."

"Even though I don't," I said. "Tell me about Ferris."

He gave me a sidelong glance. "You seen him."

"I've seen an old man in a big house. He's more than that."

"Ferris is something," Henry said approvingly. "Still at it, you know?"

"Still at what?" I asked cautiously.

A chuckle rumbled through the car. Henry was a lot calmer than I was. "Everything," he said, "but I was talking about business."

"Agenting?"

"Got all the guys he could ever want. Some of them working, too. He's not as big as he says he used to be, but they still take his phone calls." He opened the dash compartment idly and closed it again. "Sometimes. But he does okay, for a man who never made nothing in his life."

"What does that mean?"

"Agents," he said. "Agents don't *do* nothing. They're not actors, they're ten percent of actors. They're ten percent of writers, ten percent of directors. Add it all up, you got thirty percent. Other seventy percent is bullshit. Ferris is a man, you want someone to do something, he sends you someone and takes ten percent, fifteen if he can get it. They like to talk about packaging, *elements*, putting *deals* together. What's to put together? It's somebody else's idea, somebody else's script, somebody else's money. Except for that ten percent. Ol' Ferris, he takes it pretty easy."

"And you?"

"I take it pretty easy myself. It's a nice slow gig. I read a lot, walk the wolf pack, practice tai chi, help Ferris keep his schedule straight. Point a gun once in a while, when someone needs a look at a gun. People come over that wall a lot."

"It's not much of a wall." I was talking, I realized, to keep my breathing regular. My hands were slick on the wheel. *Stay out of dark rooms.*

"Ferris don't want much of a wall. He likes his trouble delivered regular. We get burglars, rough trade, sightseers—Ferris is famous in some circles, you know—people looking for something out of *Sunset Boulevard.* Expectin' some old H. Rider Haggard queen with four-inch fingernails in one of Nancy Reagan's castoffs. And we get the wishfuls who still think Ferris can dump stardust all over them. And sometimes he does."

"How'd he find you?"

"I found him," Henry said in a voice that suggested that the answer was complete. "Turn here."

Hayworth runs north and south at a slight grade, the kind of faintly dingy street that sings a siren's tune for the developers. Two bungalows had been razed on the east side of the street, leaving dark spaces like gaps in a memory. The vacant lots were overgrown behind chain link, crammed with a tangle of chaparral that looked wild enough to house coyotes. Two big scraggly tomcats bolted into the brush in exaggerated alarm as Alice's headlights swept over them. Cats take everything personally.

Thirteen twenty-eight bumped up against the lower of the weedy lots, a featureless two-story oblong with glitter shot into the stucco for that indispensable touch of glamour. Big faux-Oriental letters cut from plywood and sprayed gold told one and all that the building had a name: THE MIKADO.

The plywood eight at the end of the address had fallen sideways to make a slightly ominous infinity sign. Infinity spent at the Mikado seemed like it would last longer, somehow, than infinity anywhere else. An iron gate, wide enough to admit the Rockettes in formation, hung ajar in the building's center. Halloween decorations, violently colored plastic pumpkins and cats, dangled out of reach above the gate, and hibiscus blossoms littered the big bushes on either side, gawking open-throated at the night.

"Hustlers and screenwriters," Henry said appraisingly as we approached. "Screenwriters will live anywhere."

The gate's squeal had been given oil-free decades to develop a full, almost orchestral tone. When it stopped echoing in our ears, we found ourselves facing a parched courtyard, open to the sheet-metal sky. Green gravel simulated grass, and concrete paths cut straight lines through it, and the building rose dark and solid on all four sides. There was no opening at the far end. Dead center, a skeletal wooden structure that might once have suggested a pagoda to someone with a vivid imagination was collapsing in on itself in silhouette. Four sagging cacti, one at each corner of the structure, cried silently for water. The West Hollywood charm patrol, so ubiquitous elsewhere, evidently hadn't paid The Mikado a visit. It would be a dismal place to die.

There were twelve apartments downstairs and twelve up, and the entire enclosed area was visible from every single one of them. Their doors opened directly onto the parched geometry of the courtyard, each bordered by a single window about five feet wide. No cheerful lights called to the lonely traveler. Apartment seven was the door in the far corner of the lower level.

"Me first," Henry whispered. He had his leather jacket open and his hand inside it, brushing the dark skin of his abdomen. His stomach muscles announced themselves like an alluvial ripple pattern washed into stone.

"That's not polite," I said, stepping in front of him. "*I* invited *you*."

Henry wrapped long fingers around my arm. "He's not looking for me. I figure I'll go straight across, make a little noise, scuff a little gravel. You stay close to the walls, and when I go past the door you wait a minute and then kick it in."

My confidence, already low, waned further. "Kick it in?"

He raised a booted foot. "You know. Like on TV." His eyes went down to my feet, to my battered Reeboks. "Second thought," he said, "we both go around the side and *I* kick it in."

"Henry," I said, "the window's open."

Henry squinted across the courtyard. "In Los Angeles?"

Great. He was nearsighted, too. "Follow me."

He grabbed me again, harder this time, and hauled me around to face him. "I got Special Forces training," he said. "Do you?"

I pulled my arm free. "I'm what you might call self-trained."

"You gonna be what you might call dead, that guy still in there," he said.

"Goddamn it, Henry, I need a backup, not a replacement."

He brought his left hand up, fingers splayed wide, and rested it against the center of my chest, forcing me back three steps. It hadn't taken any visible effort. His right hand had his gun in it. "Ten feet," he said. "You stay behind me ten feet. I go through the window, you count to ten, and if you don't hear anything, come in. If I yell for help, come in right away. Otherwise, you're going in alone."

I was not going in alone. "After you," I said.

He nodded once, wheeled, and struck off straight across the courtyard, a man-shaped hole in the night. When he was ten feet in front of me I followed, feeling like one of Ferris's Yorkies. A very paranoid Yorkie. I took out my own gun and jacked a shell into the chamber.

"Shhhhh," Henry said.

The pagoda, or whatever it might once have been, loomed dolefully on our left and then receded behind us. I heard music, the muted thump of bass and drum, barely audible over the scuff of Henry's motorcycle boots. It grew louder as we approached number seven, floating onto the hot still night air through the open window.

At the last moment, Henry jogged left to stand directly beside the window and gestured to bring me beside him. "Start counting," he said, and then he stepped away from the wall, backed up two long paces, brought his elbows up, and dove headfirst through the window screen. At the count of two, I followed.

I landed on my elbows, getting a nice carpet burn, and rolled to the left, away from the door, until I hit a wall. I was pushing myself to my feet when the light went on, and Henry bloomed from the darkness with his pistol pointed straight at my middle.

"You count fast," he said.

The room was empty except for a low wooden coffee table with a telephone on it and a six-inch stack of newspapers pulled up next to the table, like a cushion. The edge of the table was fringed with long black scars as though cigarettes had burned themselves out on it. The smell of tobacco was heavy in the air.

A small kitchen glared white across a low counter. Next to it was a corridor. "Bedroom," Henry said, pointing to it.

Henry preceded me down the hallway, turning left to flick on the lights in the bathroom. I went on to the bedroom, found the light switch, and snapped it up.

The long white thing against the back wall was a bed of newspapers, maybe two inches thick and seven feet long, with an unopened copy of the Sunday *Times* drafted into service as a pillow. The shapeless olive thing crumpled at the foot of the newspaper bed was an army surplus blanket. The brown rectangle in the center of the room was another low wooden table, a twin to the one in the living room. The black thing in the center of the table was what was left of Max Grover's hand.

A turquoise ring gleamed at me as I approached. Clutched between two of the three remaining fingers was the stub of a filter cigarette.

I got down on hands and knees. The music came from a cheap boom box under the table: a cassette unspooled itself through the little window. The boom box was equipped with auto-reverse. It could have been playing for hours.

Four-twenty.

"The fuck is *that*?" Henry said from the doorway.

"I think it's Kool and the Gang," I said. "Did you touch anything?"

"The thing on the table," Henry said.

"Behold the hand of man," I said, "and dreadful are its works. I asked you whether you touched anything."

He was standing over the table looking down, his mouth screwed into a knot of muscle. "No."

"Give me some newspaper."

He grabbed a sheet from the bed and handed it to me, and I put it over the boom-box and picked the contraption up. Then I hauled it into the living room and opened the front door wide.

"Get ready to leave," I said. "We're going to move fast."

"I never been readier," Henry said at the door.

I cranked the boom box up full and positioned it in the center of the door. Stepping over it, I ran across the courtyard and through the gate with Henry right behind me. Kool and the Gang bounced off the walls behind us.

Henry was silent all the way back to Hanks's house. I dropped him at the gate, shepherded Alice down the hill to Sunset, and turned right. West, toward the freeway.

17
HESPERIA

BIRD'S flight down the freeway, actually free for once, eight lanes of blank concrete like a long sentence punctuated by blue-white lights and green-and-white signs; here and there the dependent clause of an off ramp. Left on the Ventura Freeway, premature morning traffic streaming south on the other side of the chain link fence with its desiccated, hallucinogenic laurels, and then off on Reseda Boulevard, gliding between looming old pepper trees and dark houses and the deathly glare of all-night markets.

My eyes burned like someone had put Tabasco in my eye-drops, and there was an empty, fluttery feeling in my gut. Drive-time disk jockeys, preternaturally alert guys who couldn't have passed for wits in a gathering of battery-powered appliances, made smutty jokes and played twenty-year-old music to ease the world into the gray disappointment of another day.

I'd driven this route only a few hours earlier, but it felt as distant as childhood.

By now some hustler or screenwriter, righteously steamed by the rhythms of Kool and the Gang, would have called the sheriffs. I hoped some alert deputy had awakened Spurrier from his dreams of shiny badges and broken jaws. Why should he get all the sleep?

The dawn was breaking pale and wet-looking, two fingers of vodka in the eastern sky, as I parked Alice around the corner and hiked the thorny lawns of Hesperia Street to Elena Aguirre's house. The nine-millimeter pressed against my thigh like twenty dollars in change, but my feet barely seemed to brush the ground and my head was anchored to my shoulders by the thinnest of strings. The world slid by like a baggage belt in an airport, and I was hardly moving at all. I ticked off the symptoms of exhaustion with an almost medical disinterest.

A light was on in the front window: The poor get up early. I drifted past Elena's dented car and went around to the back and sat on one of the big rocks. I was transparent, a cloud of gnats, something you could have read an eye chart through. The rock had a nice, regular, liquid motion. It was a cork, and we were afloat on an ocean of gelatin, and the ocean was thickening as the waves grew gentler and farther apart. We'd never get there at this rate. What we needed was a sail, or maybe a Mixmaster. I could hang it over the side and use it like an outboard.

I opened my eyes to a blare of light, a full brass section triple-tonguing brilliant baroque figures against my retina. The sun was a hand's breadth above the house across the street, and Elena's car was gone.

All the old aches punched the time clock, organized for action, as I stood up. Some of them went for my arms and others assailed my legs, but the really smart ones, the ones that had learned to use tools, picked up their Louisville Sluggers and took batting practice against my lower back. Trying to remember whether any of Joseph Campbell's heroes had back problems, I limped to the back door and tried the knob.

No go. The window at the side of the house was closed and locked, and the front door made it a matched set. Expecting nothing, I knocked and got what I'd expected. This was a situation that called for cunning and discretion. I went around to the back, picked up one of the smaller rocks, one about the size of my head, lugged it around to the side of the house, and lobbed it, shot-put style, through the window.

It sounded like the entire morning had been shattered. The noise sliced through my fatigue, galvanized me, maybe even frightened me. Eschewing Henry's highly personal head-first style, I found a place where I could put my hands without cutting them to ribbons and hoisted myself inside.

I had both feet on the carpet of a cramped little dining room when I realized that I was hearing a woman's voice. She babbled on, cheerful, confident-sounding, apparently unperturbed that an asteroid had just ventilated her dining room.

Television, I thought, and turned from the window to find myself looking down at a miniature human being, no more than twenty-four inches tall, with a large head and very small, white-clad feet. In my addled state it took me a good five seconds to summon up and discard three or four mutant possibilities and identify it as a child.

"Arounnaworld in thirty miniss," the child said loudly. "I'm Lyn Vaughn."

"*Shhhhh*," I said, forgetting that I'd essentially entered the house by coming directly through the wall. "For God's sake, be quiet."

"Awholeday's news—" the child began.

"Wait, wait, wait," I said. "We're playing a game. Look, look—" I picked up a saltshaker from the table and pointed it at the child. Salt poured out onto the floor. "This is the remote."

"Headlinnnnnnnne SPORSSS!" the child shrilled, raising both arms in a good approximation of a distance runner breaking the tape. It seemed to be a girl, but the evidence at that age is scant, and I'm no judge.

"And when I push the remote like this," I said frantically, salting the floor some more, "the sound goes off and you can't talk. Okay, now, *off.*"

Both of the child's hands went over her mouth. Her hands looked like she spent the entire day licking them and then running them over the dirtiest, stickiest surfaces that the planet Dirty Sticky could offer her. She stood there, the discreet monkey, eyes wide and snapping with impatience, shifting from foot to foot in her eagerness to spread the latest word about Michael Jackson or the intifada.

"Okay, now," I said, lifting the saltshaker and bringing it partway down with every word. "What's—your—name?" I pointed it at her and punched its side with my thumb.

"Boutros Boutros-Ghali," she said. And opened her mouth wider, but I pushed my imaginary mute button and the hands went up again.

"Are you alone here, Boutros?" Push the button.

"Tee Wee," she said. "Da da DAHT-DA—" The *Headline News* theme was cut off by the magic saltshaker. Her grubby palm smacked into her lips.

"Only the TV? Nobody else?"

She pulled the hands away.

"Ah-aah," I said. "I didn't push the remote." I added salt to the rug. "Go."

"*No entiendo.*"

Uh-oh, I thought. *Español.* Another of the many languages I don't speak. "Well, me, too. Mute's on." I gave her a couple cc's of salt. "Stay close," I said. "I mean, *vámanos.* And *silencio*, okay?"

"Hollywood minnit," she said before gluing her hands in place.

The dining room barely provided space enough for me, Boutros, a small formica table, and four chrome and vinyl chairs. A rickety wicker bookcase, hip-high, housed a collection of paperbacks with Spanish titles and no fewer than three Spanish-English dictionaries. In a plain wooden frame above the bookcase a lachrymose Jesus, bleeding profusely from the head, opened his chest to reveal a remarkably red and improbably symmetrical heart.

I followed Boutros into a kitchen with an old Gaffers & Sattler gas four-burner, the kind Eleanor wanted to find, and a refrigerator that would barely have held my average week's worth of beer. Ropes of chiles hung from the walls, pinned in place with big flat thumbtacks. Jesus was in here, too, his chest intact this time, with rays of light streaming out from his white-clad form. The floor was worn linoleum, the corners of the tiles curling up here and there, clean enough to give birth on. Beyond the kitchen was an infinitesimal laundry room. The man's clothes Elena had been washing the previous night were neatly folded on top of the dryer. There was no dust or lint anywhere.

What in the world, I wondered, had the child gotten her hands into?

Lyn Vaughn, ensconced on the blue CNN set in Atlanta, smiled at me in a newsy, discreetly foxy fashion from the screen of the hulking television set in the living room. The television set has replaced the piano in modern homes as a surface on which to display pictures, and the space above Lyn Vaughn's talking head was cluttered with framed snapshots, uniformly self-possessed faces that presented variations on a genetic theme: the echo of an uptilted eye here, a broad *Indio* nose there. A family. Three sober-faced boys—teenagers—decked out in stiffly starched shirts, one girl of eight or ten wearing a white communion dress, Elena herself in a puritanically simple dark dress, and a woman with a short thatch of steel-gray hair who had to be Marta. Marta, the troll-aunt, tiny and bent, with something simmering, insistent, and compressed, in her eyes.

I picked the picture up and showed it to Boutros, whose hands had found their way into her mouth. She tore her eyes away from Lyn Vaughn and looked at it. *"Tía Marta,"* she said around nine grimy fingers.

Another picture, the largest of all, showed Elena, the boys, and the girl, considerably younger, standing in front of a greener, lusher, muddier world that had to be El Salvador. They were all looking past the camera, laughing at something. The boy in the center had thrown his arms comfortably over his brothers' shoulders.

No picture of the baby. No man to take it since she was born? There wasn't much of anything to suggest a man's presence. There wasn't, in fact, much of anything at all: a couch, two chairs, a low table. A closed door.

Through the door, a hallway, parallel to the street. Three bedrooms, one with three beds—the boys?—one with two—Elena and her older daughter?—and one, the tiniest of all, a penitential nun's cell with a bare brown linoleum floor, an iron-framed single bed, and a four-drawer dresser of unpainted, unfinished wood, the kind people buy cheap, meaning to paint it, and never do. Surrounded by a pink plastic frame on top of the dresser, Marta's face squinted apprehensively out at me, waiting for the next blow.

The mystery of the child's hands was solved. Aunt Marta's room apparently served as a trap for all the dirt that entered the house. There were dust rats under the bed, grit on the linoleum. It may be sexist stereotyping, but it seems to me that when a woman lets her space get seriously dirty, she's usually depressed.

In the top drawer, rolled up into a sock, I found eleven hundred dollars in twenties and fifties. A lot of money for a maid. The child gazed up at me solemnly as I unrolled the sock's mate and heard something jingle. Marta's cache: a ring, another, a gold chain, a—

Somebody moaned, a constricted little vocal shiver with no force behind it. I looked at Boutros, but she'd dropped to her fanny on the floor, where she was rolling dirt ropes on the linoleum.

My spine went stiff, and the pain in my back wrapped itself around my middle, saddled me, and dug in the spurs. I closed my fingers around the sock and replaced it silently. For insurance, I picked up the saltshaker, which I'd been toting around with me, and zapped the child. A dirt rope went into her mouth, but she kept quiet. Easing the saltshaker into my left hand, I pulled my gun out of my pocket, trying to keep my body between it and the child, and slid my feet toward the door. My shoes squealed on the linoleum. Boutros got up and slid along behind me. *Her* shoes squealed on the linoleum.

Okay, skip stealth. I sprang across the hall and into the boys' room, gun extended, and kicked the door back against the wall. The child squealed happily at the noise. No one behind the door, no one in the room, no one in the closet, no one in the little bathroom.

I kicked the door again as I hurtled back into the hallway and slammed my back against the wall. Pulling both hands from her mouth, the child clapped them together. She was having a great time. I took three long steps sideways, hugging the wall, and then whirled and kicked the open door of the largest room, the room I'd taken to be Elena's.

It banged against the wall and bounced shut behind me, but by then I was raking the clothes in the closet with my free hand, keeping the gun back, at waist level, pointed into the closet. The clothes swayed back and forth, hangers rattling. No one.

There were two beds, a queen-size one with a cerise coverlet in the center of the room and a smaller one, a child's bed, up against the wall to the right. Boutros squatted Asian-style, bottom touching the floor, next to the larger bed and put a dark brown handprint on something white protruding from beneath the bedspread. A shoe.

It was a small shoe, a white canvas sneaker. It had a foot in it. It was perfectly still, as still as the foot of a corpse.

I put the gun in my left, reached down, and took hold of the corpse's foot. Boutros scuttled backward, and the corpse said, *"Yaiii."*

"Mr. Max give me," Marta Aguirre said sullenly. She was even smaller than I'd expected, a shrunken, malformed woman who seemed to have been compressed unevenly by external pressure, collapsed inward like a tin can at the bottom of the Mariana Trench.

She was sitting on her hands on the queen-size bed, and I was perched on the smaller one, the child's bed, feeling oversize and overtired and stretched far too thin for any of this. Boutros, whose name turned out to be Tina, was in the living room, glued to the latest carnage from Bosnia-Herzegovina.

"Don't be ridiculous," I said. "You've already admitted you took the rings and the gold chain. Why would Max give you more than a thousand bucks?"

"For gold," she said.

It was what she'd said before. I put a hand behind me and rubbed at the small of my back. Peter Pain immediately whammed me a good one. "Gold for what?"

"Surprise."

"Well, you're going to have to spoil it," I said. She glowered at me, and I tried the direct approach. "What kind of a surprise? For whom?"

Her mouth shrunk at the corners like a poison kiss, giving her an expression of surpassing bitterness, the expression of something little and bent that lived in the dark under a bridge and frightened dogs. *"Maricón,"* she said venomously. "Fancy boy."

"You don't mean Christy," I ventured.

"New boy," she said. Her right shoulder was a good two inches higher than her left. It made her look like a beast of burden.

"Marta," I said, "did you ever see this new boy?"

She squinted darkly at me, assessing me and finding me wanting on some private scale. "No." The word dropped like a stone.

"So let's say you're telling the truth, just for fun. You were supposed to buy gold for Max's new boy?"

"Make," she said, packing a surprising amount of contempt into such a short word. *"Make* gold."

I closed my eyes and thought briefly about lying down. The bed was too short. "You were going to take Max's money," I said slowly, "and make gold for his new boy."

"Stupid," Marta Aguirre said. I was beginning to share Christy's feelings about her. "Uncle make. Uncle make gold."

"Your uncle," I said, picking my way through the sparsest of verbal thickets, "is a goldsmith?"

"Wha?" Marta Aguirre said.

Maybe the bed wasn't too short. "A jeweler."

"Sí. Jeweler." She nodded vigorously, in case *sí* was beyond my powers.

"What was he supposed to make?"

"Stupid," she said again. "Gimme." She reached out a stunted hand, and I gave her the sock that had held the rings and the necklace. She fished around in it and pulled something out: a pack of military dog tags. "Make gold," she said, explaining the obvious to an idiot. "Uncle make gold. For fancy boy."

Steel dog tags. The steel chain taken from around Max's neck. I got up, feeling stronger and more energetic than I had in days, and pulled Max's wad from my pocket. I dangled a fifty in front of her, and when she reached for it I relieved her of the dog tags and read them. They said:

McCARVEY, JD SGT
AR5144597082
TYPE AB
ROMAN CATHOLIC

I hung the chain around my neck. Then I gave Marta Aguirre the fifty.

"Fix the window," I said.

18
HARD DRIVE

IT looked okay to me.

YOU'RE INVITED!!!
TO A WAKE!!!!

FOR MAX GROVER
THE NIGHT BEFORE HALLOWEEN
PARAGON BALLROOM, 7:30 P.M.
TRY OUT YOUR COSTUME!!!! WIN PRIZES!!!!!!
GRAND PRIZE: COMPLETE G. I. JOE OUTFIT
(VERY ALDO RAY) WITH . . .
SOLID GOLD DOG TAGS!!!!!

"Nothing about the holy water?" Ferris Hanks's feelings were hurt.

"Let's make it a surprise," I said. In the Sunday-afternoon light streaming through the window of *Nite Line*, Ferris's face was as orange as a carrot. He'd chosen to meet the world in a sober gray business suit, conservative in cut, made out of elephant hide. His eyes were green today, to go with his tie, which was wide enough to serve as an apron for a sumo wrestler and covered in shamrocks. The knot was the size of a fist.

"You don't know this audience," Ferris said from above his knot. "This is just the audience for holy water." Henry stood behind him, soaking up daylight. His black T-shirt said HAVE WE MET? on the front and HAVE ME WET? on the back.

"How do we know it's real holy water?" asked Joel Farfman, *Nite Line*'s editor, ad salesman, head reporter, and circulation manager. Farfman, a compact man with weight lifter's shoulders and a toupee that appeared to be made out of recycled lint, had a journalist's professionally suspicious face, and at the mention of holy water he looked like someone who'd just been handed a Xeroxed hundred.

"Oh, *please*," Ferris said disdainfully. "*Nite Line* is suddenly worried about truth in advertising? Your classified pages would be *blank*."

"You've answered them, have you?" Farfman wasn't awed by Ferris Hanks.

Hanks started to say something, and Henry spoke up. "Looks fine," he said. Hanks closed his mouth.

"And you're sure," I said, "that you can get this into Monday's—tomorrow's—paper."

"Piece of cake," Farfman said. I noticed that he had a punctured pupil in his left eye, almost as wide as the iris. The damaged eye lagged slightly behind the good one when he shifted his gaze from Henry to me. "Ready-mix."

"I thought, with typography and everything—"

Farfman allowed himself a lofty smile, a smile that wouldn't have looked out of place on the face of a Druid high priest, the one who knew how eclipses worked. His eye made the smile slightly mysterious, as befits a keeper of secrets. "There's no such thing as type any more," he said. "We use soft fonts, graphics, really, composed on the computer, and then we send the layout over the wire to the hard drive on the computer at the printing house. They park it there, on their drive, until it's time to print, which in this case will be . . ." He looked at his watch. "Ninety minutes from now."

A little bell went off in my head. Not much of a bell, probably in the egg-timer class on the international bell scale, but it got my attention. I hadn't been hearing a lot of bells lately.

"I notice you don't question the 'solid gold' bit," Ferris said, still rankling.

"Gold I can check," Farfman said resolutely. "Holy water? It could be bottled Arrowhead for all we'll be able to tell."

Hanks took his knot in both hands, apparently warming up to strangling himself.

"There isn't room for the holy water, Ferris," I said soothingly. "How much will that be?"

Farfman held up a hand so inky that I suspected him of inking it on purpose. "Gratis. For Max."

"I'm paying for this," Ferris said severely. "I don't want to owe you any favors."

"I hope it keeps you awake nights," Farfman said.

"Who sleeps *nights*?" Hanks snapped.

Farfman wasn't having any. "What I hear, I'm surprised you can sleep at all."

"Hold it," I said. "Tell me about how it gets printed again."

"We compose it here," Farfman said, using his hands to show me where *here* was and then moving them to the phone, "and send it over the wire to the—" I interrupted his hands halfway to *there*. "Jesus," I said. I looked at the three of them looking at me. "You know, I'm really too stupid for this job."

Grizzly Jack was dubious. "On my hard drive?"

"Why not? He had the telephone hookup. He probably had a macro so he wouldn't even have to dial the number. What easier place to park stuff?"

"Without telling me?" There was betrayal in the tone. In the living room the phone boys whispered digital nothings over the wire.

"He was keeping secrets," I said.

His fingers tangled themselves up in the beard, found a knot, and broke it. He didn't even wince. "That's not like Max."

I searched for an explanation that *would* be like Max and came up with one. "He didn't want to hurt Christy."

This time the knot got dissolved in a gentle rolling motion between thumb and forefinger. "It would be an archive file," he said, "one that you can't access without a password." My spirits plunged. "Probably in the library. That's where we put the archives."

"But if you can't access it—"

His hands emerged from the beard and waved me off. "No, no, no. *You* can't access it. From outside. *I* can access anything." He led me through the hallway toward the computer room. "I have to be able to read it all," he said. "Do you know who the bulletin-board cops are? The fucking Secret *Service*, that's who. You'd think they'd have their hands full protecting the president, but no, they've got lots of time to sneak around on boards. All the time in the world. First they lurk—"

"Lurk?" We were in the bedroom.

"That's what we call people who just read the stuff and don't post anything, lurkers. There are lots of them, shy geeks afraid to write anything. So the computer cops lurk a while until they stub their toes on the adult part of the board and then they like to try a little entrapment. Some of the filthiest, most lurid stuff I've ever read was posted by the Secret Service, just seeing who'll answer. Wetware at its worst. They *love* gay boards."

He rolled his chair to the big desk, hit the keyboard three or four times, and watched the screen. "Oh, well, it keeps them off the streets," he said. "Shame we can't run over a couple of them with a local bus. Computer joke."

"Local bus," I said, mystified.

He made a disapproving clucking noise and shook his head at the clutter on the display. "The whole world is online today. This always happens before Halloween. Something about Halloween just brings them out of the woodwork. Let's just disconnect a couple of lines, speed things up, or we'll be here all day." He reached up and turned off five modems, killing their little red lights and stranding people all over the information highway.

"Can you put something online for me?" I asked, watching him. "An invitation to a wake for Max?"

"No problem. All levels?"

"What's that mean?"

He gave me a look that said *are you kidding?* and decided I wasn't. "All levels means anyone who logs on can read it. If you don't want that, we can restrict it to certain levels of membership."

"All levels," I said. "Wakes shouldn't be restrictive."

"Library," he announced, peering at the screen. "Let's go down a subdirectory, to the archives."

"Let's." I'd rarely felt so useless.

"Why, the little dickens," Jack said. "Look here."

I looked there. The screen held a list of subdirectories, and Jack's finger underlined one in a swift cutting motion. The type said MAXPVT.

"PVT?"

"Private. Not very subtle, is it?" I withheld comment. It had been subtle enough for me.

Jack brought up the contents of the MAXPVT subdirectory. It read:

```
LETTER. ONE
LETTER. TWO
LETTER. THR
```

"Three," I guessed.

He turned to me, his beard brushing the keyboard. "You sure you haven't done this before?"

"I'm okay with applications," I said defensively. "It's computers I don't understand. Can you bring the documents up?"

"I think I can manage that. Which one do you want to start with?"

"Three. It'll be the most recent."

"Three it is." He smacked the keyboard, sure-fingered as Arthur Rubinstein, and we were looking at this:

◇□✻▲□✻✻✻✽

★❀❙

☆❧✻❧ ☆◆●● ☼✻ ☼▼ ▼✻✻ ✻☼▼☼ ❱✻▼✻
☼✻●▲ □■ ✈☼■✻ ❑◆□ ◆■☼☼✻◆▲ ✻□✻ ▼☼▲✽
▼□□⊠❧

"Um," I said.

"He was being a very bad boy." Jack was back to ripping knots from his beard. "Just not like Max at all."

"Are they all like that?"

Ten keystrokes later we had an answer. They were. Max had apparently been corresponding with a geometrical figure.

"I'll fool around with these," Jack said. "It shouldn't take too long."

"Can you give me a copy? On disk?"

He slid a diskette into a slot. "Trade you," he said, "for the info on Max's wake."

My computer at home ate the disk.

It accepted it eagerly, like a drunk popping an aspirin, sent it whirling, and then burped. I pulled the diskette out, turned off the computer, slapped it on the side a couple of times, and reinserted the diskette. Same result. Pushing the envelope of my technological expertise, I pulled out the diskette again, slapped *it* a couple of times, and fed it to the computer again. Three was the charm; the machine accepted the diskette without gastric distress and sat there, waiting for me to do something with it.

Do what? I keyed in *type a: letter.thr* and hit the ENTER key. Greek, literally Greek, spooled by, followed by a self-satisfied little beep. I brought up WordPerfect and asked it to retrieve the document. After some grumbling about the letter being in the wrong format, the program put its shoulder to the wheel and delivered the same geometric scramble I'd seen at Jack's. Progress.

I knew how to use the phone, so I called Schultz at home. Without bothering to sound patient, he told me that he'd done all he could on a Sunday; he'd used his personal federal crime-busting connections to get the military working on the dog tags, but I knew how the military was. Some of them might like to take Sundays off. They might regard defending the country as a higher priority. We failed to identify the enemy against whom they might be defending it.

"Not that that will hamper them," Schultz said.

"We have met the enemy," I suggested, "and he is missing."

"A call to the police might speed them up."

"From me? I thought you were the one with clout."

"Get married," he advised soothingly. "Settle down."

"Norbert," I said, "have you been talking to my mother?"

He turned shrink on me. "Should I?"

Eleanor wasn't home yet, so she and Christy and Alan were presumably still at the West Hollywood Sheriff's station. My mother would be out in the courtyard of her apartment house, having cocktails with her cronies, a group of women she calls the cacklers. My father regards the telephone as a small and noisy piece of furniture and generally refuses to answer it. When my mother comes in, he usually says, "Phone rang," as if that were helpful information.

That left the computer.

From the layout of the document, it was a letter. That confirmed what its name, *Letter.thr*, might have led even a nonprofessional to suspect. The four short lines at the top suggested that Max might be the kind of old-fashioned correspondent who put an internal address even in private correspondence, and wouldn't that be nice?

Detective fiction just crawls with skilled cryptographers who can take one look at a slate of characters in Mayan knot writing or Linear B, snort once or twice in a superior fashion, and read it aloud. I suppose such people exist in real life, too, but they don't seem to get out much. Still, a code is a code. Max's letters had to be based on the alphabet, and the alphabet has its own rules of internal consistency. The one everyone always seizes on is the fact that *E* is the letter that gets the most use. Unless, of course, the writer of the code is intentionally avoiding words with an *E* in them, or is allergic to the letter *E*, or belongs to a religion that regards the letter *E* as the devil's work, or has a keyboard with a broken *E* key, or is writing in a language in which *E* is the least common letter, or can't spell and doesn't know about the silent E, or . . .

The phone broke in on this productive train of thought, although "broke in" might be putting it a trifle strongly. So might "thought." I practically flew across the room to answer it.

"Your Sergeant Spurrier is a piece of work," Eleanor said without preface. "Never again will I wonder where the concentration camp guards came from, or the Albanian secret police, or the men who poured the hemlock into Socrates' mouth."

"He drank it himself," I said.

"Well, if the Athenian cops were anything like Spurrier, it was the wisest course of action. He browbeat poor Christy until it was a wonder Christy had any brow left. Every question got asked thirty-two times, one for each tooth, like it was some sort of chewing rule. And he kept *smiling* at me and calling me 'little lady,' as though we were on the same side in some loathsome conspiracy."

"How'd Christy take it?"

"He'll survive. He tires so easily, though. If it hadn't been for Alan, I don't think he would have made it. Alan, as Wayde might say, is way cool. He treated Spurrier like something that had just crawled onto land and needed a good kick back into the drink."

"Where's Christy going to stay?"

"With Alan and his friend tonight. Tomorrow, he said he

might check into a hotel. I told him what you said about staying away from the house."

"He can go back tomorrow," I said. "Tomorrow's Monday, the day *Nite Line* will hit the streets—"

"What vivid language."

"—and our killer will know Christy doesn't have his damn tags."

"Our killer," she said dryly. "Spurrier made Christy look at pictures of Max."

"He's a gob of phlegm," I said. "Write about it."

"I can't. They're giving it to someone on the police beat. Thank you very much, now butt out. How does someone turn into Spurrier?"

"Bitterness," I said. "He's only got one sport coat."

"I'm serious."

"How do I know? Some cops get like that. Some people become cops because they're already like that. As Harry Golden once said about an anti-Semite, maybe his teeth hurt."

"Well, I'm going to shower him off."

"I tried that once," I said. "It took a lot of water. What are you doing after your shower?"

"I don't know. Get dirty, I guess."

"Want to have dinner?"

She paused. I pictured her curling the phone cord around her index finger, something she doesn't know she does. She's always wondering why the cord gets knots in it. "I'd considered it."

"With me."

"A girl lives clean for months," she said, "deferring worldly pleasures in the pure faith that saintly conduct will be rewarded, and the world does not disappoint."

"Is that a yes?"

"What language do you *think* in?" she asked. "Of course it's a yes."

"We can work on my English," I said.

"You have more pressing problems. Eight o'clock?"

"Eight's great, mate," I said.

"I've got to learn to hang up earlier," she said, hanging up.

The phone rang again immediately. "Listen to this," Jack said. Then he read me Max's letters. They were even better than I'd hoped.

"How did you do it?"

"Have you got Microsoft Word?"

"No. WordPerfect."

"Well," he said with leaden patience, "import the document."

"I've got it on my screen." I carried the phone to the computer and sat down.

"Okay, go into fonts. Wait, wait, highlight the document first. Do you know how to do that?"

"Yes, Jack," I said through my teeth, "I know how to do that."

"Got it?"

"Hold it. Okay."

"Go into fonts. Choose roman, choose anything. Nah, choose roman. That's all Max did, the old codger. He wrote his letter, printed it, mailed it, and then saved a file copy in a non-alphabetic font called Monotype Sorts. Talk about transparent codes."

We shared a hearty laugh over how transparent the code was. I picked roman from the menu, and when the menu box cleared, I was looking at Max Grover's last letter.

Mr. Phillip Crenshaw
P.O. Box 332
Kearney, NE 68849
Dear Phillip:

You're a brave young man and a sweet one. I'm enclosing the cash for your ticket to a new life. I only hope I can help you find your feet here in the big city.

It's not as bad as you've heard, especially if you have friends. I'm an old man, but I have a lifetime's worth of friends. I know they'll want to help you as much as I do. Godspeed,

Max

P.S. I'll be at the gate with bells on (and your uncle's dog tags, too).

"Think that's the guy?" Jack asked.

"I know it is," I said. Phillip Crenshaw. Kearney, Nebraska. Farm boy territory.

19
TYPHOON

"**DO** you honestly think he'll come?" Eleanor was wearing a scoop-necked sleeveless silk top the color of fresh salmon, an antique necklace of silver, marcasites, and jet, and four thin black bracelets that kept sliding up her arm like designer shackles. Those bracelets had prompted a number of perverse fantasies in the past, and from the way I kept drifting away from the topic, they hadn't lost their power.

"Will he dare *not* to come?" I asked. "Maybe. But look what he's done already. He risked his life to go back to the house to get the tags, and he went crazy when he couldn't find them. He called me at home and actually left his number on my machine."

"A number in an empty apartment."

"Still, there were other people around, tenants, the manager. The sheriffs have a description now. Whatever information is on the tags, it's more dangerous to him than a physical description. Max's letter says they belonged to his uncle, but of course the kid told him that, and I don't think we should put too much credence in anything the kid says. Whoever they belonged to, though, there's a connection, a big LOOK HERE sign that points right at him. He needs to get them back."

"You don't think they were his?"

"I don't think he's old enough to have been in the military. And I think they belong to someone he hates."

Eleanor had decided on Typhoon, a modishly upscale pan-Asian restaurant that occupied the old control tower of a private airport and drew an unnaturally good-looking, semicelebrity clientele. It had been crowded when we arrived, full of people who were certain they'd be better known tomorrow and had decided to pick at sashimi and Burmese chicken while they watched the planes glide in and waited for a segment on *Lifestyles of the Rich and Famous*. We didn't have a reservation, but the manager had taken one look at Eleanor and led us straight to the best table in the house, overlooking the runway and far enough away from the semifamous to allow conversation. Eleanor always gets tables like that. She thinks everybody does.

"If the tags are so dangerous, why would he fool around with them in the first place?" She was really tucking into a plateful of steamed vegetables, which the restaurant insisted on calling Buddha's Delight; she'd wolfed down two forkfuls in only fifteen minutes.

"Schultz says they're a totem of some sort."

"Schultz," she said, making what she probably thought was an ugly face. She hadn't liked him the first time they'd met, and he hadn't much opportunity since to exercise his dreadful charm on her.

"He knows his stuff, although I wish he'd speak English. He says they're 'imprinted objects.' "

She interrupted her feeding frenzy, suspending in midair a fork containing a single snow pea. "I know about imprinted objects. They're superreal, like objects in a dream, usually associated with a trauma of some kind. They attain a kind of ritualistic importance."

"You should be eating with Schultz," I said.

She batted her lashes at me. "He didn't ask me."

" 'Ritual' is the word he used. He also used 'fetish.' Those are the ones I can pronounce."

"Why do you enjoy acting stupid?"

I poked through the shredded remains of my Filipino Beef Strings or whatever it was, looking for something I could chew. "I'm good at it. We all like to do things we're good at."

"Fetishes enable some people sexually," she said. "I wonder if he means that these dog tags enable your kid from Nebraska to commit murder."

"They are," I said, paraphrasing Schultz, "essential accessories to the act."

"Dog tags are a kind of identification. They probably turn his victim into the person he really wants to kill."

I looked under the table for Schultz. "You know," I said, "you could make small amounts of money and work unreasonable hours assisting the police."

"And put up with people like Spurrier? Thanks anyway."

I stole a forkful of her vegetables. "You like Al and Sonia."

She watched her vegetables all the way to my mouth. "They're different."

"No," I said. "Spurrier's different."

Eleanor caught a man at a nearby table staring, and gave him a smile that made him drop his spoon into his soup. "What are you doing about Nebraska?"

"Nothing yet. Post office is closed on Sunday. I'll call tomorrow and see what I can find out. For all we know, though, he sets up shop in a new town every time he decides to go back into business."

"What a life. It's almost enough to make you feel sorry for him."

"Spend it on someone who deserves it," I said. "Are you going to finish those?"

"Give me your plate." I passed it to her, and she slid most of the vegetables onto it and handed it back. "You're not drinking," she observed.

"Only in secret."

"It wouldn't do you any harm to cut down."

"Right," I said. This was familiar territory.

"For heaven's sake. You should see yourself. Your face is all squinched shut. You look like you're chewing an aspirin."

"I've quit aspirin. It leads to Anacin, and eventually to Excedrin."

"Be that way," she said. I was good at stupid, but she was superlative at indifferent. I probably bore some of the responsibility for that.

I stabbed my fork into the center of the mound of vegetables and left it standing there. "After he scared the shit out of me," I said, "I got drunk, and it made things worse. I was half-drunk when he phoned me, and he scared me then, too. Somehow, getting drunk doesn't appeal to me."

"So you're inviting him to a party."

"With a million people around."

"All in costume."

"If it weren't for the costumes, I *know* he wouldn't come."

"Sort of *Catch-22*, isn't it? If people aren't costumed he won't come, but if they *are* costumed you won't know which one he is."

The restaurant was octagonal, windowed on all sides, and jammed. About a third of the tables were made up exclusively of men: couples, foursomes, one large and ecstatically raucous birthday party, complete with paper hats and noisemakers. The birthday boy was made up like a cat, and when he'd gotten up to go to the bathroom—something he did with a frequency that indicated a small bladder or large nostrils—I'd seen that he had a long black tail protruding from the seat of his trousers.

"Halloween," I said, making the connection.

"Wednesday night. And you ain't seen nothing yet," Eleanor said, following my gaze.

"There should be a lot of people there," I said idly. "Tuesday, I mean."

A small plane coasted in, its frail-looking wings seesawing up and down before it evened off and hit the blacktop. "You haven't said much about Ferris Hanks."

"He's orange and he's little and he keeps his house colder than a meat locker and he laughs like this." I gave her my version of Ferris's *heek* noise. "For someone who probably thinks of *Justine* as a training manual, he acts pretty normal. Los Angeles normal, I mean. Anywhere else, I'm sure, they'd put him in a jar in some medical museum."

"Does he seem evil?"

"I'm not sure I know what evil is any more."

"Horsefeathers." Eleanor rarely swore. "You knew it when you met it at Max's house."

"Because it was aimed at me. And because he was so damned joyful. If I'd been in his position, I would have stayed in that closet or wherever, or maybe crept up and cut my throat from behind. Instead, he spoke to me, gave me warning, and *then* tried to cut my throat."

"More fun that way?"

A chilly little ripple ran over the skin on my arms, and I rubbed at my sliced left forearm with my right hand. "Maybe. Maybe he wanted to incapacitate me and ask me some questions. I don't know."

"You weren't wearing the dog tags."

"There's that," I said. "But I know he meant to kill me. I can rationalize it all I want, but he was going to kill me in that room."

She tucked her hair behind her right ear. "Do you dream about it?"

"I'm not sure. I can't remember my dreams, but they've been pretty vile."

"You should try to process them," she said. "Write down everything you remember as soon as you wake up. There might be something in them you need to know about."

"I'll do that," I said. I had no intention of focusing on those dreams.

"Or phone me," she said. "Call me the minute you wake up, no matter what time, and we'll talk them through. Don't go back to sleep, just pick up the phone."

I reached over the table and tugged her hair back down so it fell over her cheek. "You're okay," I said.

"Careful," she said, sitting back. "We might start to chat again."

I started to say something, stopped, and started again.

"Look, it's a toll call," she said. "Why don't you just come home with me?"

My dream was right out of "The Masque of the Red Death." A castle somewhere, dwarves and nuns and executioners and comic-book superheroes, wet cobblestones and candles everywhere, candles the size of a man that shed an elusive light that made people shrink and grow with every flicker. A figure in scarlet with a face like torn paper and eyes like broken glass, who was Christy somehow, and somehow not, and a wall either being raised or falling down and horses stampeding through the crowd, leaving a heap of empty costumes crumpled on the floor behind them. I began to fling the costumes aside, looking for the people, or for something buried beneath them, and they flew into the air and came down with people in them—different people—and the people stood stock-still where they landed, staring at me, their faces cut and battered by the hooves. One of them had cobblestones pressed into the bloody Oedipus holes in his head where his eyes should have been, stones round and rough and black, and a dumb joke came to me in the dream: *Oedipus Rocks,* and Eleanor shook me awake.

"You were laughing," she said.

"Yeah?" I said, sitting up to get closer to the square of moonlight on the foot of the bed. "Well, it wasn't very funny."

"Tell it to me."

When I'd finished, I said, "And I don't want to hear any nonsense about the big candles."

"It seems pretty straightforward. It's an anxiety dream about the wake, about searching through costumes to find someone. And you're ambivalent about Christy."

"What about the horses?"

She put an index finger on the bridge of her nose and rubbed it slowly up and down. "They came from behind a wall. They had tremendous strength. They, ah, they dispelled illusion; when they trampled the people in costumes it turned out they weren't actually people at all, and then they were different people."

"And?"

"You made a joke in the dream, which is pretty unusual in itself. A pun, a reversal of meaning. I'd say you know something that you're not acknowledging. Something you've put behind a wall, and when you raise or lower the wall, some of the people in the landscape surrounding Max aren't going to be who you think they are." She passed both hands, cupped, through the moonlight as though she could scoop some up and drink it. "That's pretty literal, but it's the best I can do."

I put my arms around her. "You could soothe me," I said.

I woke at eleven in Eleanor's bright bedroom, feeling rested for the first time in days. A note had been neatly safety-pinned to the pillow beside me.

At the library until 2. Coffee's ready—just pour water into the thing at the top of the maker.

What are you going to wear to the party?

The coffee maker, an Insta-Brew, had been named by someone who apparently didn't own a watch. By the time the coffee was finally ready I'd showered with lime-scented soap and Japanese camellia shampoo—a combination of smells that brought more memories than there was room for in the shower stall—and slipped into my jeans from the previous evening, rancid with Typhoon's cooking oil, plus a clean T-shirt Eleanor had laid out at the foot of the bed. I padded barefoot into the bright little kitchen and poured a cup to the brim and carried it carefully into the living room, full of furniture I'd once lived with, and settled into a chair that knew me well.

I'd never been alone in Eleanor's house before, and it was a peculiar feeling, both familiar and new. Things I recognized from our time together stood out here and there: a vase, a small painting we'd bought in San Francisco, the lacquer and mother-of-pearl end tables her mother had hauled all the way from China. Most of the objects in the room, though, had come into Eleanor's life after we'd parted company. I had a sudden pang of—of what? loneliness? regret?—imagining her bringing these new things home, finding the right place for them. To a stranger they would have been indistinguishable from the things I'd bought her, the things we'd chosen together.

Next to the window on the opposite wall, framed in sober black, hung Eleanor's bachelor's and master's degrees. I didn't have the faintest idea where mine were, but Eleanor's were on display. For years she'd deprecated their value, the value of her own achievement, hanging the degrees on the wall only when her mother came to visit. Her mother, like most Chinese parents, was fierce about her children's education, and if the degrees weren't in full sight when she came for dinner she embarked on a long harangue in Cantonese. Five minutes after she left, the diplomas came down again.

At some point, though, Eleanor had apparently decided to leave them up, and I'd missed the change. One of hundreds I'd missed, probably, over the years. She'd pointed out during our interrupted chat that I'd changed and, with her usual tact, hadn't mentioned herself, but she wasn't preserved in amber, as much as I might like to think she was. She wasn't the woman who'd earned those degrees, any more than I was the puzzled kid with all the scholarly initials after his name who hadn't a clue what to do with his life. She'd undergone her own changes. So far, she still kept a place of some kind for me in her life, but there were no guarantees. She'd had relationships with other men, and I'd handled them in the stolid, approved American-male fashion, hiding both the pain I felt when they began and the relief that had flooded over me when they ended. There wasn't anything decisive I could do; I'd waived my rights in that area when I'd let her walk down my driveway on the last day we lived together. Let her go because marriage would disrupt my life.

And what was so swell about my life, anyway? I was moving in patterns that had once had meaning, had given me pleasure, but now they were just habits most of the time, like a role in a play that has been running for years. Show up, do the old stunts, collect the money or applause or thanks, go home. A week later I didn't know what I'd done on any particular day. I drank too much, I didn't talk enough. I was lonely. Like most people faced with the challenge of getting through a life, I'd developed a bag of tricks that took care of my needs on a few levels and left me unsatisfied on all the others. And when the time came to learn some new ones, I screamed and dug in my heels and hung on for dear life to all the things that didn't satisfy me.

So what was I protecting against all that love?

The answer presented itself with that peculiar clarity that unwelcome answers usually have. Nothing.

Schultz was right. I should see a shrink, if only to force me to focus on the walls I'd built in my head.

A wall lifting or being lowered, horses thundering through the space where it had been.

I realized I'd been looking at the bright square of a window for long minutes. When I refocused on the room, a dark square floated in front of me. Retinal memory, real-seeming but false, an image from the past persisting until the nerves recharged themselves, a neural version of the emotional images of people we carry until circumstances force us to realize that they've changed. Or that they're no longer there.

On the table in front of the couch were some familiar-looking brochures, full of bright colors and images of wedded bliss. My mother, the emotional guerrilla.

I went to the phone.

It took three tries before I got the right post office. Kearney was apparently riddled with post offices. The woman on the other end sounded thrilled to talk to me, like no one had called in years.

"I sent some money—a cashier's check, actually—to Phillip Crenshaw, two *l*'s in Phillip, care of box three thirty-two at your office. He never received it."

"Hmmm," she said happily. "Did you put a return address on the envelope?"

"Sure. As I say, there was money in it."

"Oh, dear. How long ago?"

"Little more than three weeks."

She made a *tsk-tsk* sound. "That's *far* too long. Something must have happened to it."

"That's what I thought."

"Sent from where?"

"Los Angeles," I said.

"Well, what can you expect?" she said, as though that explained everything. "Los *Angeles.*"

"I took it to the post office myself."

"I'll give it a check. Can you hold on?"

"Sure," I said, thinking, *This is a civil servant?*

"Don't go away," she said, laughing gaily.

"I'm glued to my chair," I said truthfully.

Five minutes later she was back. I heard her humming before she picked up the phone.

"Sent it here?" she asked.

I gave her the box number again.

"I just asked," she said, "because that's a forwarding box."

"To where?"

"That's what's so funny," she said. "Los Angeles."

20
MCCARVEY

WITH only two days to create the world between the time *Nite Line* came out and the wake for Max, Ferris Hanks had swung into a frenzy of activity. When I checked my answering machine from the comfort of Eleanor's living room, I found no fewer than six messages, each pitched at a higher level of urgency. At the conclusion of the sixth, Henry took the phone away from him, leaving him piping orders in the distance.

"Call the man," Henry said. "Else, I'm going to have to give him a cigar to calm him down." The next message was from Spurrier, demanding to know if I had anything to do with the ad in the paper. He left a home number, sounding significantly irritated. I called Joel Farfman instead.

"More than a hundred calls," he said. "And that's not

counting the ones from Hanks. In, what? Four hours? You're going to have some party."

"You going to be there?"

"Wouldn't miss it. I'm coming as the Lone Ranger."

"Think you'll be the only one?"

"I'll be the only one with a faithful Indian companion. Wait until you see Tonto. But keep your distance."

Everybody seemed to assume I was gay. "How hard would it be for you to dig out everything you've run on the guy who killed Max?"

A brief silence. "Not hard. That's what interns are for."

"Can you meet me at the Paragon Ballroom in a couple of hours with some photocopies?"

"What for?"

"I just need to get my bearings."

"Will you give me an interview?"

"This is a trade?"

"Call it that."

"Okay. But you can't use my name."

"Screw that to the wall and hang a picture on it," he said pleasantly. "Remember who, what, where, when? You're 'who.'"

Nite Line, after all, was a weekly. With any luck, this would all be over by the time the next edition came out. And if it wasn't, I'd probably be safe in jail. "Okay. But the *Times* is on this, too."

He laughed, a pinched, wheezy sound like a squeeze bottle being emptied. "The *Times,*" he said. "I can imagine their angle. 'The Gay Ripper' or something like that."

"I don't think he's gay."

"When did that ever stop them? By the way, Max is in the new *People.* There's no press agent like death."

"You could do me another favor," I said.

"Yeah?" The tone was noncommittal; like Ferris Hanks, Farfman saw favors as a form of currency.

"I want to know who placed a personal."

"No can do," he said promptly. "Everything they want you to know is in their ad."

"This has to do with Max."

"Oh." He barked something to someone else, covering the mouthpiece, and came back. "I don't think I want to hear this."

"Sorry. It looks like Max met his killer through your paper."

I heard a small squealing sound: Farfman sucking breath between his teeth. "You're sure?"

"As sure as I am of anything at this point."

"Ah, shit," he said. "I really hate . . ." He blew into the mouthpiece of the phone. "Balls," he said. "Read it to me."

I unfolded the torn page, which was beginning to fall apart along the fold lines, and read it to him. "Who placed it, when it was placed, how he paid. Anything else you can think of."

"Yeah, yeah." There was something new in his voice, an edge that hadn't been there before. "You got it. See you at the Paragon."

After all that unaccustomed sleep the second cup of coffee gave me a mild case of the jitters, so I poured the last chill inch or so into the sink and cleaned up. I actually dried the counter. The new Simeon, preparing for domesticity. Then I went out blinking into the flawless sunshine of Venice and drove home.

I avoided the driveway and came up to the house from the side, hiking through tangles of chaparral and surprising a toad the size of one of Ferris's Yorkies as I hoisted myself up onto the deck. The place was just as I'd left it. No Ed Pfester, or Phillip Crenshaw, or whatever his name was, waiting in the living room and slicing up my carpets for practice. No new messages on the machine. No word from Schultz. A wind had kicked up, and the house was creaking like someone was practicing dance steps on the roof. I set the new world record for changing my trousers and took Topanga into the hot Valley to avoid the beach traffic, heading for West Hollywood.

I'd hit the Monday lull, lunchtime over and all the folks who keep civilization plodding along back in their offices until six, and the traffic on the freeway slipped between the lane lines like it had been greased. I turned on the radio and got the midday disk jockeys. There must be something about sitting alone in a little room with a microphone for hours that is fatal to the soul. The only things that sounded live were the commercials, which were recorded, and the music, some of which was made by people who were dead.

The Paragon Ballroom was a building I'd passed dozens of times without ever noticing it, a two-story red brick barn, liberally enlivened by graffiti, that occupied half a city block on a treesy side street just south of Santa Monica Boulevard. The doorway was arched, double wide, and open, the windows above it blocked with dirty plywood. The hand-painted sign hanging crooked to the left of the door advised all and sundry that Hollywood's most glamorous venue was available for very special events or, on a more mundane level, as a rehearsal hall. Four cars were scattered, isolated and looking lonely, around the big parking lot.

Inside, the Paragon was one enormous room with a gleaming hardwood floor that must have been sixty years old, blistered and peeling floral wallpaper, and three sets of metal stairs leading to a catwalk that ran along the upper half of the building: a vantage point for the tangle-footed who wanted to watch the dancers. A bandstand, bare plywood set on metal risers, stood against the far wall. The place smelled as though the doors hadn't been opened in years, a clogged, generic odor of disuse, like damp newsprint or pressed flowers. Three carpenters wearing T-shirts, cutoffs, and bandannas, as though they'd been costumed by the contractor, purposefully banged hammers against the plywood of the stage, and a man with an apron full of tools stood on a rickety, wheeled metal tower in the center of the floor, hanging lights from the beams below the ceiling. The most glamorous venue in Hollywood it wasn't.

"The man hisself." It was Henry, dressed to spar with Sylvester Stallone in gold boxing trunks and a sky-blue sleeveless formfit T-shirt that made him look even blacker. He had a pen tucked into the hair above his ear. "Ferris been pulling his hair out with both hands."

"Anxiety's good for him. It raises the pulse rate."

"He thinks the fountain might oughta go over there," Henry said, pointing to the corner of the room directly right of the stage.

Ferris's holy water. "Up to him."

"And close off the gallery up there. Keep everybody down on the floor. Put a couple of our helpers on the catwalk to keep an eye on folks."

"How many helpers have we got?"

"Many as you want."

"Two should do it up there. No need to be conspicuous. Where is he?"

"I sent him home. He was driving everybody crazy. We moved the stage three times already."

"So walk me through it."

He wrapped a big hand around my arm, making me feel like a toddler, and towed me to the door. "People come in here, which I'm sure is no surprise. Two guys here, handing out tickets for the drawing and identifying everybody they can. Valet parking outside—Ferris wants to control the cars. Hell, Ferris wants to control everything. He was all upset this morning that daylight savings was over, wondering who he could call about it. He's trying to get the street turned one-way for the evening. Okay, they come into the room and head for the bar—"

"Where?"

"Left wall. It's got the plumbing outlets. Bar'll go in this afternoon. Four bartenders, white wine, five kinds of bubble water, fruit juice for the fanatics. Eight of Ferris's actors dressed like Roman slaves, whatever that means, moving around with trays of what Ferris calls finger foods, fried fingers or something.

There's a kitchen in the back, but it's pretty dire, just pounds of rat shit in the ovens. Food's being brought in already cooked from Hugo's Hankerings. We'll scrub down the counters, nuke 'em good and cover them with butcher paper, just use them to hold the food before it goes on the trays. Four people there, shoveling the stuff whenever the slaves run out. They going to be costumed like French maids."

"A touch of class."

"You say so. One monitor—good word, huh?—over by that door to keep an eye on the bathroom, like you wanted. Make sure everyone who goes in comes back out."

"That's twenty-one so far, not counting the parking attendants."

"They stay outside."

"You know all these people by sight?"

"Ferris does. Like I say, a lot of them are going to be his boys. Then there's the band, the Silverlake Flyers."

"Bar band?"

"Old hits." Henry grimaced. "Disco, Jay and the Americans, Barry Manilow. The neighbors got any taste, we're in trouble."

"Invite them."

He pulled a small pad of paper from the elastic waistband of his trunks, retrieved the pen, and made a note. "I'll photocopy the ad, put it under doors and stuff."

"You're good at this, Henry."

"What's to be good at? You and Ferris thought of everything already. I just run around and check shit off."

"Other exits?"

He lifted his chin in the direction of the door leading to the bathrooms. "Fire door back there. We'll have a walkie-talkie outside."

"That makes twenty-two, not counting the stage crew. Good thing Ferris is rich."

"Ho." Henry's voice was flat. "Also, scoff, scoff. He's promoting the food and all the drinks except the wine. The waiters are working for free. Ballroom cost six fifty, band goes for scale. He's got a source in Lourdes for the holy water. He says. Maybe a couple thou all together. Don't you know about rich folks? They *never* spend money."

"The dog tags."

"Yeah, well—" Henry leaned toward me. "They going to be plated. Ferris is really pissed at—" He looked past me, toward the door. "Speak of the devil."

"Henry," Joel Farfman said. "Simeon." He gazed darkly around the room. The eye with the punctured pupil lazily followed the good one. "To quote Bette Davis, 'What a dump.' "

"Little glitter," Henry said impassively, "some bunting, turn down the lights and fill it with people. Gonna look great."

"You have a genuinely fervid imagination," Farfman said. "Where's John Beresford Tipton?"

"Having his nap," Henry said. "He got up early this morning, maybe ten. Hard on an old man, specially when he don't go to sleep until nine."

"I should have half his energy," Farfman said. "You can't *believe* the number of times he's called today."

"You have no idea what I'd believe," Henry said. "I live with the man."

"And you seem so untouched." Farfman held up a manila folder and waved it in my direction. "Here's your stuff."

"I got things to do," Henry said tactfully. "Some of these water pipes as clogged as Ferris's arteries." He trudged away across the floor, pausing briefly to assess the work of the man hanging the lights, and disappeared through the door into the kitchen.

I took advantage of a lull in the hammering. "Why was Hanks calling?"

"Staying on top of things, *heek, heek,*" Farfman squeaked, sounding enough like Hanks to unnerve me. "I made the mistake of telling him, the first time he phoned, that we'd been getting calls all morning. Since then, it's been every twenty minutes. Who's called? How many? Do they sound excited? Should we have put his name in the ad? How many photographers are we going to send? Will they be in costume? I told him they'd be dressed as photographers, and it seemed to satisfy him. For about fifteen seconds. Should he pitch the television stations? What about radio? Has anyone called *People* or *Us* or *Back Fence*? He's asked about everything except movie rights."

"He's probably sold them already."

"And you probably think that's funny. I'm sure he's already cast himself. Maybe John Forsythe."

"Too old," I said. "Not tall enough."

"Hey, can we get through here?" Someone prodded me on the shoulder, and I turned to see four beefy individuals crowded into the doorway. Behind them was a massive mahogany bar half the size of my living room. It was shaped like Florida.

"Left wall," I said. Mr. Official. "Careful of the floor."

"I don't know who you are," said the man who had tapped me. He wore a leather butcher's apron and a tie-dyed T-shirt, and he was bigger than both members of a wrestling tag team, but his voice was a rusty squeak. "I'm Mickey Snell, and I manage this place."

"Well," I said, following Farfman toward the stage, "it's a swell floor."

"Built in 1937," Mickey Snell cheeped at my back. "All old oak from a nineteenth-century sailing ship. Of course, it was saturated with—"

"Hey, Mickey," one of the bruisers said. "Can we cut the history and move the fucking bar?" Mickey Snell didn't even draw a breath. He was telling the air how the salt had been leached out of the wood as the bruisers shoved the bar through the door, making an unsettling squealing noise on the swell floor.

Farfman's folder held seven articles on the murders. The one on top had been written after the killing of the third man, the first of the New Orleans victims. It was on fax paper, and when I glanced up at Farfman, he reached over and slid a finger over its slick surface. He'd been inking his hands again.

"I had New Orleans send it to me," he said. "They had three stories. The others are our own, out of *Nite Line.*"

The first clipping was a more or less perfunctory rundown, short on facts. A fifty-four-year-old college professor and unsuccessful city council candidate named Jefferson Hope had been beaten and sliced to death and his hand severed. Police were making inquiries. The community was grieving. All pretty much standard, except for the tone, which was an unjournalistic cross between bereaved and outraged.

Chapter Two: Jefferson Hope's index finger had been mailed to the newspaper in his home town of Preston, Virginia, and the coverage blossomed. The second story was four times as long as the first. The cops were suggesting a link to two similar murders in Chicago. The reporter had done some investigative work, trying to trace Hope's movements in the days preceding his death, but without much luck. Hope, normally a gregarious man, had apparently dropped out of circulation about a week before his body was discovered.

Over behind the bar Mickey Snell was squeaking away about the water pipes—solid copper, it appeared—when I turned to the third article. This one warranted a three-column headline. It detailed the death of another New Orleans man, an orthodontist named William Smythe. Smythe was *not* a gregarious man, and the first indication anyone had that something was wrong came in the form of a call to the New Orleans police from a reporter in Mentone, Illinois, who had had the misfortune to open the morning mail and discover a human finger and some Polaroids in which Smythe was clearly identifiable. The Polaroids, the story euphemized, were "of a highly personal nature."

"Look at the next-to-last graph," Farfman said in a tight voice.

This time, the reporter's efforts had paid off. He'd found a friend of Smythe's who had dropped by the house unannounced the day before the murder and had seen someone in the hallway behind Smythe when he answered the door. He'd only glimpsed him for a moment; he'd assumed that Smythe was busy, made his apologies, and left. Smythe's guest was described as a young man, probably in his late teens, very good-looking, with light blond hair.

"He's the one who bought the ad in *Nite Line*," Farfman said tightly. "In person. I took the order myself."

"When?"

"October eleventh. For two weeks."

"Only two?"

He nodded. The good eye darted down to the clipping while the other wandered down my chest. "That's unusual. Most people want it in for a month or two. Some of them keep it in for a year; they just call in changes in the wording every now and then to make it seem fresh."

"Did you help him write it?"

"He had it all figured out. I remembered him the moment you read me the ad. He looked like, I don't know, someone who isn't hip enough to wait for the *walk* sign, but he knew precisely what he wanted. He even knew how much it would cost. He had the exact amount, in cash, in an envelope. I said something like, 'Two weeks isn't very long,' and he said, 'It'll be long enough.' "

The ad had expired on the twenty-fifth. Max had met the plane on the twenty-sixth, if I could trust his penciled notes on the newspaper clipping. Cutting it close. As Farfman had said, the kid knew precisely what he wanted.

"Don't people have to fill out some kind of form or something? Don't you keep records?"

"Under the newspaper stories," Farfman said.

It was a standard ass protector from some legal mill: The advertiser represented that the information in his ad was accurate and accepted all liability for any damages that might arise from misrepresentation. The advertiser understood that the newspaper was not responsible for any consequences that might follow from his decision to place the advertisement, bla, bla, bla. At the bottom a series of blanks had been filled out in long-hand: "Name: Phillip Crenshaw. Age: 19 Address: Box 322, Kearney, Nebraska." A phone number.

"Have you dialed this number?"

"I left it for you." Farfman seemed embarrassed.

"And this is his handwriting?"

He swallowed and looked away from me, one eye at a time. "It's mine," he said, blushing furiously. "I wrote it out for him. His hand was bandaged."

"Smart boy."

Farfman looked like a man who'd just been sucker-punched by his best friend. "And he seemed like he'd just come from milking a cow. Talked about how he couldn't find his way around L.A., how he had to go back home that afternoon, how he hoped someone would answer the ad, give him a new life."

I searched his face for a trace of the cynicism I'd seen the previous afternoon. "That didn't sound like bullshit to you?"

The blush deepened, and he slipped his hand into the collar of his shirt and ran it over the back of his neck as though he were perspiring. "Now that I say it out loud, it's patently ridiculous. At the time, though—if he'd told me he was trying to escape from an evil stepmother, I'd have believed him. If he'd said he was the bastard son of Howard Hughes and Marilyn Monroe, I'd have believed him." He put the inky fingers over his lips and rubbed, leaving a dark smear from his nose to the tip of his chin. "He was the nicest kid I ever met in my life."

"That seems to be the general opinion. Listen, Joel, he's good at this. He let five men get a lot closer to him than you got, and no one seemed to think anything was wrong."

"And now there are going to be six," he said. He riffed the clips with his thumb. "Look. It happens in pairs."

"Maybe it won't this time," I said, sliding down from the stage. "Let's try this number."

The room was filling up with men. The electrician on the tower had been joined by an assistant who pushed the big metal tower down the length of the beams as new lights went up. Two slender guys with dangerous-looking staple guns were attaching blue cloth to the edge of the stage to hide the risers beneath it. Tables laden with half-open floral arrangements had been trundled in. Mickey Snell's crew had the bar in position and were doing exotic things to the copper water pipes while Mickey speculated aloud on why the threading on plumbing fixtures ran counterclockwise. Like a dowdy old tart, like some architectural Apple Annie, the Paragon Ballroom was being pinched and prodded into a semblance of glamour.

Without interrupting the flow of speculation, Mickey Snell pointed a wrench in the direction of a pay phone in the hall near the bathrooms, and Farfman handed me a fistful of quarters. People who live in West Hollywood, where parking a car is more expensive than buying a house, carry a lot of quarters.

A harried-sounding woman answered the phone. Several children practiced for the Olympic Screaming finals in the background. No, no Phillip Crenshaw lived there. No, this wasn't a new number, they'd had it for years. No, she didn't know anyone named Crenshaw in Kearney. She didn't know anyone who answered Phillip Crenshaw's description, although she wouldn't mind it if she did.

When I hung the phone up, it rang.

"Don't you ever go home?" Schultz asked sourly.

"As little as possible at the moment. How'd you get this number?"

"The phone book, under Paragon Ballroom. You should try it some time. J. D. McCarvey, remember?"

"What have you got?"

"McCarvey, Jason David. Vietnam veteran, enlisted at

eighteen in 1964. That'd make him forty-nine now, right? Honorably discharged in '72, so he did a few tours."

I snagged Henry, who was shadowboxing by, and grabbed his pen. "What else?"

"Here's the good part. He was wounded. I mean, that's not so good for him, but for us it's a bonanza. The VA has him living in Seattle, 1432 Wooster Drive, Seattle, Washington."

I wrote the address on the wall. "That's great, Norbert," I said. "Thanks."

"Hold on," Schultz said. "Don't you want his phone number?"

THREE
THE WAKE

I WENT TO A DANCE THE OTHER NIGHT

EVERYBODY WENT STAG

I SAID OVER AND OVER AND OVER AGAIN

THIS DANCE IS GONNA BE A DRAG.

—BOBBY DAY
"Over and Over"

21
LONG DISTANCE

"**YOU** need professional help from Schultz," Al Hammond said. "You're nuts, off the edge, missing in action." The connection from Hawaii sounded like a meteorite shower was slamming the satellite: brief, sharp-edged shards of clarity embedded in bursts of ragged static. My own voice was mimicked by a sort of mission-control echo that had the unfortunate effect of forcing me to listen to everything I was saying, but the NASA comparison ended there: Mission control usually knew what it was doing. "Maybe I should come home," Hammond said between head-on collisions.

"Maybe he should," Schultz said peevishly. We were using the speakerphone in his office, and he was leaning back in his reclining chair, nervously trying to tie his legs in a knot. Even though Schultz was the one who'd insisted we call Al, and even though it was his speakerphone, he didn't seem to have gotten the hang of it. He addressed all his remarks to me and waited for me to relay them to Hammond.

"You're on your honeymoon," I said, being dutiful. Actually, having Al on hand sounded pretty good.

"We've met all the cops," Hammond said. "It's raining so hard you can't find the beach. We're the only people in the hotel who aren't Japanese. Japanese are different when there are more of them than there are of you. They look at us like they're waiting for us to shoot somebody. We feel like Mr. and Mrs. Godzilla."

"Tell him what I said," Schultz prodded. He'd managed to get one foot through the armrest. If the chair went over, he was ticketed all the way down.

I felt as though I were playing pass it along. "Tell him yourself."

"I told him he could go to jail," Schultz shouted to Hammond, taking long distance literally. "I told him he was interfering in an investigation." He started using hand gestures for extra emphasis across all those wet miles. "I told him"—he pointed at me—"to call the Sheriffs"—he put his hand to his head, finger and thumb extended, to mime a telephone—"and give them the phone number."

The speakerphone emitted space noises, perhaps a solar flare or a distant planetary system being blasted into cinders, and as the photons and neutrinos receded Hammond's voice said, "—ass in jail."

"My opinion exactly," Schultz said, vindicated.

"If what you're afraid of is that McCarvey will tip the kid off after I call, forget it," I said to both of them. "The kid's not in Seattle. He's here. In Los Angeles. And if Schultz is right, Al, this McCarvey is someone he hates, someone he keeps killing. They're not going to be chatting with each other. Look, all I want is a name."

"And if you get it?" Suddenly it was like Hammond was in the room.

"I'll give it to the Sheriffs."

"Huh." Hammond was unconvinced. "Sonia thinks you should call them now."

"Thank Sonia for a constructive share."

"And Sonia thinks this party you're throwing is even dumber than not giving them the phone number."

"It's a wake," I said for the second time, "and if he doesn't come, so what? Max deserves a wake. He helped a lot of people."

Audio bric-a-brac of hisses and pops. "—you know it's a waste of time," Hammond said.

"Actually," Schultz said, "I don't think it is." This was the part that made him *really* nervous, because he might be wrong, and he hated being wrong. He was leaning back in the chair, rocking back and forth furiously.

"Is that Schultz?" Hammond asked.

"My expert," I said.

"I remember," Hammond said sourly. He didn't like Schultz any more than Eleanor did. "Ask him why—"

I rapped on the desk for attention. "Look, you guys, this is a *speakerphone.* Break the word up, analyze its components. *Speaker,* as in loudspeaker. *Phone,* as in telephone. You can talk to one another directly. You're both speaking English, you don't need an interpreter. Now, Al, do you have a question for Norbert?"

Hammond woofed. "Schultz, your name is *Norbert?*"

"At least it's a real name," Schultz bristled. This was clearly an issue he and his own analyst needed to spend some time on. " 'Al' sounds like something on the periodic table of elements."

"Hey," I said happily, "you guys are talking to each other."

"So tell me, Norbert," Hammond said, heavy on the name. "Why do you think the perp is going to show up for Simeon's party?"

"I didn't say he *would*." Schultz, like most scientists, seemed to feel that definite statements were a conversational throwback, one step up from a grunt. "I think he *might*."

"And why is that? Why do you think he *might*? He knows someone has his tags, he's gotta figure he's already being traced."

"You're assuming they lead to him," Schultz said.

"A phone call might tell us," I interjected, just to keep the issue alive.

"But that's not the *point*." I'd forgotten Schultz's perpetual assurance that he was the only one who understood the point of anything. "The tags are probably magical objects. Ritual objects. They're part of who he is. Look, you have a man here who's devoting his life to killing people. He doesn't *have* a life, in the way you and I do." He passed a palm over his forehead, snagging his cigarette in what remained of his hair. I could smell it all the way across the room, but he didn't seem to notice. "Everything normal, all the ordinary routines and attachments, are held in abeyance, everything is arranged to allow him to go out on his killing trips. We are what we do, to a much greater extent than most people imagine. Once he gets started, he's practically a robot. He does what's imprinted on his circuits. The tags are part of the circuitry, part of this rite that he performs whenever he can or whenever he feels he has to, whenever the conditions are right."

"The conditions," I said. It was the third or fourth time something had thumped its knuckles on the wall Eleanor had described. There was definitely something on the other side of that wall.

"Exactly." Once he'd gained momentum, Schultz wasn't easily derailed. "When the conditions are there, he almost *has* to act. Whoever he was to begin with, there's not much left of him now. He's a ball of energy that gathers itself in the dark until it's time to come out and explode. The same cycle, over and over again. Find someone appropriate. Flirt with him, mislead him, make him fall in love. Betray him. Stomp him, cut him, reveal his sexuality back home, where it matters most. Then it's back to the cupboard until the next time. He probably would have been caught months ago if the cops had been really interested, if the victims were straight."

"You're saying he's stupid," Hammond said, disregarding the slur on the police. "Stupid enough to show up at this—"

"Not stupid, not smart." Schultz sounded impatient. "Cats aren't particularly smart, but they're very good at being cats. Efficient, ruthless, streamlined. You can't teach a cat not to kill. You can teach it not to kill while you're *watching*, but when it's outside, the birds had better keep their eyes open. Like I said, this man probably doesn't have much left of himself except the killing. The tags are an inextricable part of the act. He's already risked his life to get them back. How often does the murderer really return to the scene of the crime?"

"It happens," Hammond said. Sonia said something interrogative, and Hammond said, "Killer return to the scene of the crime." I heard Sonia's voice again, and Hammond said grudgingly, "But not much."

"If we could hear him thinking," Schultz said, "I'm pretty sure we'd hear two voices: the voice of the original human being, urging caution and common sense, and the voice of, oh, I don't know, the cat, arguing every point. Something like, 'I'd better get out of here.'" He lowered his voice almost to a whisper. "*'But everyone will be wearing a costume.'* 'It's got to be a trap.' *'I'll have to cover my hair.'* 'Should I take a chance on an airplane, or take the bus?' *'I could dye it and leave it exposed.'* 'I'd never get my hands on the tags anyway.' *'I'll never know unless I go. If I don't go, I'll never see them again.'* 'I'll never get away with it.' *'Of course I will, I'll just be one more faggot in a costume.'* Sorry about the, um, terminology," Schultz said in his normal voice. "I'm projecting here."

"Short answer," Hammond said, "he'll be there."

Schultz tightened the knot in his legs, hiking his trousers

to expose a stretch of bony white calf with little ginger-colored hairs scattered irregularly over it, an unfortunate afterthought in the design. "He'll come," he said, rocking back in the chair. "He may take one look around and hop a cab to LAX, but he'll come."

"You *think*," Hammond said.

"Of course I think." Schultz, stranded by his enthusiasm, was blinking distress semaphores. "I don't have a pipeline to the man's soul."

"Wish I could be there." Hammond said something muffled to Sonia.

"Sheriff's territory, Al," I reminded him.

"Look who's talking," Hammond said. "I'd be unofficial, of course. I'm on my honeymoon."

"I'm sure you'll fit right in. You hardly look like a cop at all."

"Might be hard to explain," Hammond mused. "Me and the little woman—*ow*—me and Sonia, I mean, at a fruit's— sorry, a homosexual's—wake."

"I don't know. It might lead to some interesting invitations."

"Anyway," Hammond said, retreating, "we're in Hawaii."

"And having a wonderful time, from the sound of it."

"It's okay," Hammond said fondly. "I'm with my little love-turtle." Sonia squealed in protest.

"Oh, Al," I said, "that's so sweet. Wait'll I tell—"

"You tend to refer to your wife in diminutives," Schultz said, a faceful of liquid nitrogen. "That's interesting."

"What do you call yours?" Hammond snapped. " 'Boss'?"

"We're sort of straying here," I said. "I want to call Sergeant McCarvey."

"Hold on. Let me talk to Sonia." The two of them conferred as I watched Schultz try, without success, to get his foot out of the armrest. He was taking off his shoe when Hammond came back on the line.

"I didn't say this to you. No cop said this to you."

"Got it. You're in Hawaii."

"If this balls up the investigation, you're going to be un-employed, as in no license. Just don't turn it into a felony. Use your real name. Tell the truth as much as you can. Don't even hint that you're a police officer, or you'll be looking at Spurrier up real close. Better still, don't make the call."

"I'm doing it. They're my goddamn dog tags."

"Okay. A bonehead's a bonehead. But you got the rules, right?"

"Right. Thanks." Schultz had twisted his left foot into a position that would have startled a yogi. "What are you going to do now?"

"Me?" Hammond was all innocence. "I'm going to roll my little love-turtle on her back and see what happens. Hey, Nor-bert, you want to listen in? You might learn something."

"Whoops," Schultz said, grabbing the edge of the metal desk.

"He's busy," I said. "Have fun."

"Sonia, I can't *believe* this is legal," Hammond said. He hung up.

Schultz was balanced on one wheel, most of his left leg protruding through the armrest, as though he'd decided to slide out that way. I got him back to earth and helped him work his leg free while he sputtered and protested and hung on to the desk. The moment he had both feet on the ground, he lit up.

"Hard to see you two as friends," he said from the center of a cumulus cloud of smoke.

"What *do* you call your wife?" I asked.

"Evelyn," he said with dignity.

"Well, she's a lucky woman," I said. "Having a man who steers clear of diminutives and all."

"And you," he said with the air of a man used to having the last word, "steer clear of intimate relationships."

"You're right, I do. And I'm thinking about it. Should I use the speakerphone?"

He was putting his shoe back on, trying to see his foot through the fumes. "For what?"

"For McCarvey."

"I don't want to hear it," he said promptly.

"All brains and no guts." I punched the button on top of the speaker to shut it off, picked up the phone, and dialed.

The recording told me in a chipper tone that the number I had dialed had been changed. The new number followed, spliced together to create a mechanically musical effect, like Chinese spoken by an android. I wrote it on my palm with Schultz's ballpoint, which said PROPERTY OF ARLO'S HAPPY LIQUORS on the side.

"New number," I explained, holding up my hand. Schultz, radiating disapproval, closed his eyes and puffed away.

Four rings, then: "Hello?" It was a woman's voice, low, slow, and possibly drunk.

"Is Sergeant McCarvey there?"

A long pause. "Who is this?" She sounded like she'd been snakebit on the tongue.

Tell the truth. "My name is Simeon Grist. I'm in the office of Dr. Norbert Schultz, in Los Angeles." Schultz's eyes flew open but, hell, it was true.

"And you want to talk to Jace?"

"Well," I said, choosing words, "we know that Sergeant McCarvey was under VA care for a while. This is just an informational call."

The woman laughed. It sounded like her very first. "Fucking government," she said.

Spurrier, wearing his latex gloves, breathed down the back of my neck. "This isn't actually official government business—"

"My husband's dead. He's been dead two years and four

months. Typical." She laughed again, getting the knack, dark and loose and slurred. "You jackass," she said.

"I'm sorry. Was his death service-related?" At the word "death," Schultz got up and started to pace the room, trailing smoke like the little engine that could.

"Go to hell," Mrs. McCarvey said. "Fucking bureaucrats. Jace was murdered. Eight years he gave you clowns, and you don't even talk to each other."

"This is very embarrassing," I said. "Did they catch his, um, his murderer?" Schultz pushed the button on the speaker in time to hear her snort.

"Fat chance. Cops are no better than you are. Hey, wait a minute. You got anything to do with pensions?"

"Pensions?" Schultz waved his hand at me, trying for my attention.

"My pension. Jace's pension. You listening, or what? Can you help me get it? I've been down there more times 'n I can count. I've sent letters—"

"I'm sure," I said, looking at Schultz, "that if you've got all of Sergeant McCarvey's papers—" Schultz nodded encouragingly.

"Course I got 'em. Jesus. Who else would have them?"

I covered the mouthpiece and drew a breath. So did Schultz. "And his dog tags," I said. "They might want to see his dog tags."

Silence. No, not quite. I could hear her breathing, and a television made meaningless happy noise in the background.

"Mrs. McCarvey?" I said.

"Don't you dare come around here, Darryl," she said at last. "Don't you dare. I'll cut your fucking head off."

She hung up.

Schultz was staring at the speaker as though he expected Mrs. McCarvey to burst through it, knife in hand. "She thought you were *him*," he said.

"And," I said, "she knows who he is. Darryl."

Schultz straightened the speaker on the desk and dropped into his chair. "You're going to have to—"

"I know," I said. I picked up the phone and called Ike Spurrier.

That night I stopped at the Paragon Ballroom on the way home. The only work in progress was being done by a very old man with an electric floor polisher who was buffing the hardwood in long slow straight sweeps, like someone cutting furrows into garden soil. The old man wore a loose, drab gray workshirt and baggy checked trousers, and he was bent forward in a position that looked painfully permanent, his shoulders hunched forward, rounded as a drawn bow. He never took his eyes from the floor.

Mickey Snell, who apparently never went home and never stopped talking, followed several steps behind, downloading information about the grain of the wood and the hardwood pegs that held the floor in place. The old man ignored him, wrapped in a cone of concentration and the hum of his machine.

The bar was in place against the wall, dark wood gleaming. Brass spigots spouted from its surface. On the other side of the room stood a gaudy vertical arrangement of three large glass seashells above a white porcelain basin: Ferris's fountain for the holy water, dry for now, and surrounded by dozens of spiky orchid plants.

When I stepped further into the room, the bandstand sparkled. Foil stars had been pinned to the deep blue drape, and more stars, made out of cut glass and silver wire, hung overhead from lengths of nylon filament. Clouds of cotton blossomed above the stars. High above it all was a pale crescent moon of old-fashioned milk glass, lighted from within. Max's heaven.

With the hum of the old man's buffer and the squeak of

Mickey's voice for company, I walked through the building. The kitchen was, as Henry had promised, dire, but it was spacious and I couldn't see the food handlers having any problems, and the ovens were too small for anyone to hide in. The bathrooms had been scrubbed until some of the tiles had fallen out. A room beyond the bathrooms was locked, and I figured it had to be Mickey Snell's office. The rear door was made of iron and was bolted shut. It would be open for the wake, but we'd have a man outside.

The conversation with Spurrier had been loud and long, and neither he nor Schultz had been happy when I put it on the speaker to give myself a witness. I'd handed Spurrier Mrs. McCarvey's phone number and told him how the dog tags had led me to her, but I hadn't given him the news that Henry and I had been the ones who found the Farm Boy's apartment. He'd figure it out sooner or later anyway.

It had taken some doing, but I'd declined an invitation to the Sheriffs' substation to discuss matters further. If Spurrier wanted to talk to me in person, I told him, he could do it to-morrow night, at the wake. Like Hammond, Spurrier had dis-counted the possibility that the Farm Boy would show, but we agreed to some commonsense rules that would allow him to put himself and three men on the scene without attracting at-tention. Spurrier was too experienced a public servant to risk missing the action if anything actually happened.

I sat on the edge of the stage and watched the old man work as Mickey chattered. He looked like one of Millet's potato farmers, like someone who hadn't lifted his eyes from the ground in years. Still, I thought, he'd managed to get old. That was more than most of the Farm Boy's victims had done. Get-ting old may be no bargain, as my father never tired of saying, but all in all I thought I'd prefer it to the alternative.

I wouldn't mind getting old the way that Max had. I'd want company, though.

Staying on the unpolished part of the floor and dodging the ghosts of dancers from the thirties, I said goodnight and pointed Alice west on Santa Monica Boulevard for the long drive home. Twenty minutes later, at Twenty-sixth Street, persuading myself that all I was doing was avoiding a surprise visit from Spurrier, I turned left instead and went to Eleanor's.

22
CALLIGRAPHY

THE door opened four inches and snagged on the inside chain, and Robert peered out, looking grim. When he saw me his face cleared.

"It's your detective," he called over his shoulder. Then he closed the door and slipped the chain, and when it opened again I saw Alan a foot behind him. Alan had a gun in his hand. It looked heavy and incongruous.

"Hi to you, too," I said.

Alan glanced down at the gun and his mouth twisted wryly. "It's been quite a morning," he said. "Come in. Have some coffee?"

It was just past eleven, and the caffeine from Eleanor's special brew was still rampaging through my bloodstream. Too much coffee can elevate you unnaturally, scramble your judgment, create a kind of false euphoria. "Sure," I said.

"It's fresh." He stepped aside to make room for me. "God knows we need it."

Close up, I could see a swelling under Robert's left eye. Alan had a fat lower lip. "What happened?"

"Thugs," Alan said. "Swine. Swine run in herds, don't they?"

"I don't think swine run at all," Robert said. "I think that's the point of being swine."

"*These* swine drove," Alan said, tucking the gun into the belt holding up his Ivy League chinos. "Six of them, all scraped bald like medieval executioners. They got us outside the bank."

"The two of you?" I asked.

"And Christy," Robert said. He looked at Alan's face and shook his head, and his ponytail did a little hula. "I'll get the coffee."

"Christy's in the den," Alan said, turning away from the Early American living room as though to guide me.

"Did they hurt him?"

"They would have," Alan said. "We were in the parking lot when they came around the end of the row and drove toward us, as though they meant to run us over. You know, you see things like that in the movies, and the hero always jumps free at the last minute, but of course he knows it's coming, he's rehearsed it a hundred times and there are probably mattresses everywhere to catch him when he lands—" He broke off, listening to himself, and put three fingers over his mouth and then drew a deep breath. "Anyway, they stopped in time, and got out of the car. The driver was screaming, '*Look where you're going, faggot,*' and I saw that two of them had baseball bats in their hands."

"Jesus."

"Well Christy just jumped into the middle of them. He poked his fingers straight into one man's eyes and banged his head into another one's face, and then one of them lifted his bat and I got to him somehow and grabbed the end and kept pulling it around behind him, and he fell down. And then I had the bat, by the fat end, you know? and someone punched me and I hit him with the bat on the forehead and it started bleeding, and then all of a sudden the Sheriffs were there. Three of them, two men and a woman. One of them hit Robert, by mistake, I think."

Spurrier, never far from center stage in my imagination, pirouetted into the spotlight in his yellow tweed sport coat. "Had the Sheriffs been watching Christy?"

"No." He smiled and immediately regretted it. A knuckle touched the swollen lip. "They were staking out the bank. They had a tip it was going to be robbed."

"So this is it? Your lip and Robert's eye? No other damage?"

"Our confidence has a few wrinkles in it. On the other hand, our self-esteem is absolutely flowering. Six skinheads and three of us, and we walked away. Of course, they claimed we'd started it. Claimed I'd commented on their *haircuts*, if you can believe that."

"Did the deputies?"

"No. These guys have been around for a while. They beat up a friend of ours a week ago behind Pavilions, you know, the market on Santa Monica?"

"Are the clowns in jail?"

"If they're not out already. One phone call to Mommy or Thug Central and they'll skate."

"Are you still out here?" Robert asked, emerging from the kitchen with a tray full of coffee things. "Is there an invisible barrier blocking the door to the den?"

"Christy came out of this thing okay?" I asked again. "No trauma or anything?"

"Christy?" Alan sounded surprised. "Right now I'd say Christy is the least traumatized person I know."

"Simeon doesn't know about it," Robert said. A look passed between them.

I watched them look at each other. "Know about what?"

"We'll let Christy tell you," Robert said. "He could have told you hours ago if Alan hadn't lulled you to sleep in the hall."

Neither of them gave any indication of being ready to move. "Well, let's go give Christy his chance," I said.

"Take your coffee," Robert said, holding out the tray. "We'll be in the living room."

I chose a cup from Robert's tray, grabbed two sugar cookies to go with it, and then stood stymied in front of the closed door, coffee in one hand and cookies in the other. Alan reached around me and turned the knob, looking vindicated.

"What would people do without lawyers?" Robert asked behind me.

The den was still crowded with throw rugs, lap robes, pillows, and plants. In the middle of the clutter, behind a card table littered with Alan's yellow legal pads, Christy looked up at me. He had a pencil in one hand and another behind his ear, and he looked five years younger than he had when I'd seen him last.

"Simeon. Perfect," he said, standing. He caught his knees on the underside of the table and it began to tilt foward, the pads sliding over its surface toward me. I stood there, juggling coffee and cookies, but Christy leaned forward nimbly and caught the table in both hands. I'd never seen him move so fast.

"What do you think?" he asked, picking up one of the pads and holding it out. Penciled on the top page, in large, dark letters I read: TO THE MAX. He lifted the page and folded it back, and on the page underneath I saw the words, THE MAX GROVER FOUNDATION FOR RECLAIMING LIVES.

"Sounds great. What is it?"

He dropped the pad to the table and ran both hands through his hair, pressing down as though he was trying to keep the top of his head from floating away. "It's what I'm going to do. For Max, for everybody. You were dead right, you know. I haven't done anything that was really mine. I've sort of floated along behind other people, like, do you know what slipstreaming is?"

"Getting behind a truck or something," I said, "using its drag to pull you along. It's always sounded like a dangerous way to save gas."

"Well, that's what I've been doing. Telling myself I didn't have any gas, poor deprived little me, shortchanged at God's filling station. Get into someone's orbit, Max's for example—I'm mixing metaphors—and use their velocity, their life force to sort of slip through the world. Trailing behind them like icebreakers."

"Reflecting their light," I said, "as long as we're mixing metaphors."

"Sit down," he said, clearing papers from the couch. One of them was a stapled bundle on white bond covered from edge to edge with angular black handwriting. He laid it on the table and dropped the others to the floor with a thwack.

"Here's the idea," he said, plopping back down as I sat. "We'll institutionalize what Max did, but on a bigger scale. We'll get kids off the street, gay, straight, I don't care, and we'll put them up in apartments and fill their refrigerators with food, on one condition: They go to school. It can be college or night school or vocational school, whatever they want, but they have to keep going. If they drop out once, we arrange counseling. If they drop out twice, they get a warning. Third time, boot 'em, use the money on someone else."

"This is your idea?" I asked, sipping Robert's coffee.

"Of course not," he said. "It's Max's idea. Oh, I mean, the details are mine, and I thought of the name—do you like the name?" He looked away, suddenly uncertain.

"I think it's a great name."

"*Isn't* it?" He balled his hand into a fist and slugged me on the thigh, hard enough to leave a dent. "Old Max. All his life he did this, one kid at a time. Now we're going to be able to open it up. Ten, fifteen at a time. Get them warm, get them clean, get them educated, get them jobs. Then they become our . . . our examples. They can come in and talk to kids who think they're staring at a wall, they can show them there's a ladder over the wall. Maybe, as they begin to make money, they'll even kick some in, do you think they might?"

"You're giving back," I said. "Why wouldn't they?"

"I am, aren't I?" Christy's color was high. "God*damn*, I feel good."

"You look good, too."

His eyes went down to his shirt, and he straightened a button that was already straight. "So Alan says. Did you know that Alan's been HIV positive for eight *years?* He says it makes him use every minute like it's precious. Did you guys talk?"

"About you? No."

"He sounds like you, I thought maybe—'Do something for somebody,' he said, 'and you'll do something for yourself.' You know, I could just kick myself black and blue. I had Max right there, right in front of me, all that time, and I never figured it out. Max was the best-looking, happiest old man in the world. It wasn't anything magical, nothing he brought back from India or anything like that. He was just—he just knew why he was doing what he was doing. He knew it every minute of the day, and there I was, with not too much time left, just stumbling my way through it, furious half the time and fretting about poor little Christy and actually getting *jealous* whenever Max gave somebody a hand. What a *wuss*. All that time, I could have been helping him, I could have been—"

"You could have been Mother Teresa, too," I said. "You're not. Most of us aren't. Most of us are just like you. Or a lot worse."

"Well," he said, taking one of my sugar cookies, "you're not."

"Christy. I go to bed so I can get up. I get up so I can get tired enough to go to bed again. I drink too much so I can stop wondering what the hell I'm supposed to be doing between the times I'm in bed. You met me in detective mode, which is the only mode I'm even remotely effective in. If you followed me around in my private life, you'd be deeply disillusioned."

"You don't know yourself," he said.

I changed the subject. "Is Max's house worth enough to pay for all this?" I waved a hand over the table full of pads.

"Oh, my God," he said. The cookie snapped in half in his hand, sending up a sparkling geyser of sugar. "I haven't told you, have I?"

"You haven't."

"And they didn't? Of course they didn't. You wouldn't be asking if they had, would you. Max put money in the bank all the time he was in that show. When he quit, he had more than three hundred thousand dollars. He just left it there. From 1959 until now. It's more than two and a half million, now, and it's all mine. Add the three hundred fifty thousand dollars Alan says the house is worth, and even after taxes—"

"Hold it. How do you know all this?"

"The will," he said, blinking. "We got the will. That's why we were at the bank today."

"You went into the safe-deposit box."

"Sure. That's what I'm telling you. Alan did his lawyer thing—"

"Was anything else in it?"

"Nothing that matters. A bequest to his sister and some little stuff, family pictures and some old contracts from the show. If there'd been anything important, anything that might have told you anything, I would have called you. In fact, I *did* call you, twice, but you weren't—"

"No," I said. "I wasn't. May I see it?"

"Sure." He reached over and picked up the stapled document he'd taken from the couch. "Here."

I looked it over, feeling something heavy and hard growing in my gut. It was written with a calligraphy pen with bold, disciplined vertical strokes, semi-Spencerian, like an invitation to a White House dinner. The old-fashioned approach extended to the numbers; Max had crossed his sevens and supplied little horizontal bases for his ones to stand on.

"Is this his handwriting?"

"He was proud of it," Christy said. "Beautiful, isn't it?"

"What?" I hadn't heard a word.

"I said it's beautiful." He was looking at me as though I had a smear of jam on my face.

"It's gorgeous," I said, getting up.

"Where are you going? Are you okay?"

"I'm peachy," I said. "Keep working on the foundation, Christy. Max would have loved it."

He nodded and put out a hand for the will, still peering at me. "You're sure you're okay?"

"Too much coffee. I'll see you tonight." I stood there, irresolute, looking down at the will. "That's really great."

On the way out, I saw Alan and Robert sitting on the living-room couch. Alan was icing his lip. I waved to them and went outside and stood on the doorstep, wondering where to go. For the first time, I didn't think the Farm Boy would be at the wake.

23
PARAGON

IT was, in a sense, my party, but I felt like an outsider, the stranger at the christening, the bee at the picnic. For one thing, I was virtually the only one there who was alone. Spurrier and I, the stags at the wake.

The parking lot behind the Paragon Ballroom was half full even before the sun dropped below the low flat roofs to the west. The temperature had not dropped with it. At 6:50 it was almost ninety degrees, and the parking attendants were running themselves ragged as car after car disgorged its overheated cargo of perspiring nuns, supermacho cowboys, Latino vaqueros, conquistadors, geishas, languid vampires, underdressed Aztecs, Chinese Mandarins, African tribesmen, sailors, hanging victims, motorcycle cops, wizards, mermaids, mustachioed men wearing chiffon dresses, muscle boys in jock straps, and a man in a Marie

Antoinette ball gown topped off with a headpiece modeled on the New York skyline. With twinkling lights.

From my vantage point near the curb I had the impression that someone had skimmed the multicultural stew of Los Angeles and come up with everything that floated, the airiest and most buoyant bits, the postcard images that glitter like bits of mirror embedded in the dreary grouting of everyday life. In addition to folks in national costumes representing every major civilization since Abyssinia, we had three Carol Channings, two Judy Garlands, two Diana Rosses, two Carmen Mirandas, one postaccident Jayne Mansfield carrying her head under her arm, one Hispanic possessed by the soul of Maria Montez, an indeterminate number of Terminator clones, and a variety of superheros in skintight spandex in every color.

Hanks's flurry of calls, probably reinforced by the breathless story about Max in *People*—titled "A 'Tarnished Star' That Shone Bright"—had brought out the lights and the microphones of the press, and even a few rumpled paparazzi. The TV and radio crews worked the area around the door, blinding people with the bright lights called sun guns and sticking mikes into faces, while the paparazzi flocked to the arriving cars in the eternal hope that one of them contained Madonna or Richard Gere. So far they'd had to make do with a couple of second-tier television actors and one of Madonna's rumored ex-girlfriends, and the television reporters were showing sportsmanlike signs of settling for a human-interest story.

Our identification system, such as it was, was working smoothly. As the McGuire Sisters, say, or Robin Hood and his Merry Men pulled to the curb they were greeted by the parking attendants. The McGuires or whoever had to mill around on the sidewalk until they received their parking stubs, which gave our outside watchers time either to identify them by sight or to make a note of their costumes and add them to the list of those who were to be kept in view as much as possible. Some of these question marks were eliminated as they passed through the door, pausing to get their lottery ticket, or when they bellied up to the bar. Another watcher was stationed at the holy font —now bathed in a submarine blue light that did strange things to the colors of the orchids and pouring an endless cycle of H_2 Blessed O from Lourdes.

Hanks had been right. Virtually everyone made a stop at the font.

Spurrier's three young deputies were in uniform, drawing admiring glances. I'd bought three pairs of cheap mirrored shades at a Sav-On drugstore and insisted the cops put them on, partly for that over-the-top touch that turned their uniforms into costumes and partly to hide their eyes. Cops' eyes are unmistakable. Spurrier was dressed in his invariable sport coat, topped off by a rubber Big Bad Wolf mask. My pleasure at his embarrassment was tempered by the fact that I was costumed as Donald Duck. Eleanor had surprised me with the outfit, claiming she'd chosen it because it was nonthreatening. When I put it on, though, she'd literally fallen onto the bed laughing. By way of getting even, I kept it on and showed her what I thought Donald probably did to Daisy between shows.

I'd been discreet. I'd told only about ten people who the Big Bad Wolf was, and made each of them promise to tell no more than five others, and only people they knew well. I wanted Ike to have an evening he'd remember. He'd already been goosed twice. The gay community, I'd been assured, considered goosing outré, but an exception was being made in Ike Spurrier's case.

I'd just finished a tour of the perimeter when a chauffeured Rolls-Royce purred its way to the curb and Hanks himself got out, blinking in the glare of the television lights. In the midst of the leather cowboy outfits, plus a covey of sequined Supremes, he looked like a rock in a bowl of M&M's. He was dressed in a black suit, white shirt, and dark tie. Something bright gathered itself in the gloom inside the car behind him, and Henry emerged into the light wearing a boxy, shiny, blue silk shantung suit, black-rimmed spectacles, and a gray fright wig that streamed straight up, as though he were standing under a giant vacuum. He warranted a few flash bulbs.

"You, I get," I said to him. "Don King."

"I told him it was too obvious," Hanks said, checking the crowd. He waved to a tiny Chinese woman holding a microphone, whom I recognized from one of my rare brushes with local TV news.

"But what are you supposed to be? The undertaker?"

He gave me the half-smile. "*Much* more subtle than that." He looked down at the suit with satisfaction. "I'm Mike Ovitz." He made his *heek heek* noise, and the Chinese woman, dressed head to foot in a lipstick red that would have been eye-catching anywhere else, pushed her way through the crowd toward us.

"He wish," Henry said.

"Excuse me, Mr. Hanks," the Chinese woman said to Hanks, licking her lip gloss with a pointed tongue.

One of the Supremes elbowed her way up to Henry. "You're what?" she asked, "Buckwheat?"

"Ho," Henry said, a man with a secret.

The Supreme bridled. "I am *not*. I'm one of—"

"As in ho, ho, ho," Henry amended quickly. "Like a Santa laugh."

"Mr. Hanks," said the Chinese woman.

The Supreme stopped glaring. "That's okay then. I'm the tragic Supreme, the one who killed herself?" She studied his wig. "Honey, you standin' at attention all over. You must be glad to see me."

"What a tragic Supreme needs," Henry said, leaning over and brushing her face with the flying hair, "is a literary advisor."

"Henry," Hanks said sharply. "I'm not going to be abandoned at the dance, am I?"

"Oh, help." The Supreme took a step back. "You're with

Mr. Hanks? Honey, you could be bad for a girl's career. Mr. Hanks doesn't forget."

"Thirty years ago Mr. Hanks didn't forget," said Joel Farfman, coming through the door with Tonto in tow. Tonto was a beefy fifty, plain and graying, but the pride in Farfman's eyes when he looked at him was almost heartbreaking. "These days, Mr. Hanks is lucky to remember to swallow after he chews."

"Are you here?" Hanks asked haughtily. "I knew we should have sent invitations."

"Mr. Hanks, can we have a few words?" asked the Chinese reporter. To her cameraman, she said, "Get over to the curb, Burt—I mean, Charlie—that way you'll see the crowd behind me." She waved him back and gave her hair a preparatory fluff.

"I have to hand it to you, Ferris," Farfman said as Charlie backed over the edge of the curb and fell into oncoming traffic. "Bernadette's *pissoir* is really packing them in. If only they knew what they're dabbing on their foreheads."

"Goddamn it," the Chinese woman said bitterly as Charlie untangled his legs from the cables. "I knew I should have brought Burt."

"How we doing with the whozzat list?" Henry asked me.

"Only about twenty so far. Almost enough to keep an eye on. The font helps. Most of them lift their masks when they splash themselves with miracle juice."

Charlie was up and unscathed, eye pressed to his viewfinder, and the Chinese woman raised her microphone to permanently wet lips, assumed an expression of Deep Human Concern, and said, "This is Candy Toy in West Hollywood, where joy and sorrow go hand in hand tonight."

A battered pickup truck, going too fast, bumped a wheel over the curb and knocked Charlie about four feet sideways. We all jumped back, the Supremes squealed a chord, and Candy Toy said, "Shit." A banner on the side of the truck read BLACK AND BLUE IS BEAUTIFUL. The passenger door opened and Little

Bo Peep, pastorally resplendent in crinolines and shepherd's hook, got out and curtsied to us. Beneath the blond wig, with its Mary Pickford curls, was the face of the man at the table from The Zipper.

"Where's your sheep at?" Henry asked.

"Driving," Bo Peep said in his sweet breeze of a voice. "If I don't let him drive he won't let me shear him." He gave Charlie, who had skinned a knee, a look of concern.

The leather giant came around the truck wearing a woman's full-length sheepskin coat backward and black spike-heeled shoes on his hands and feet. When he reached Bo Peep he dropped to all fours and Bo Peep took hold of a leash dangling from the black patent-leather collar around the sheep's neck. The sheep looked up at me and his brow creased in perplexity.

"Thought you were straight," the sheep said.

It wasn't worth explaining. "I was visited by three spirits," I said.

"Where's Christy?" asked Bo Peep. "Oooo," he squealed in mock alarm, catching sight of Spurrier, who'd just come through the door. "The Big Bad Wolf. You better stay away from my little sheep, Mr. Wolfman."

"Christy's inside," I said, brushing past Spurrier, who was immediately swallowed up by a squealing nimbus of Supremes. "I'll go in with you."

Candy Toy grabbed Ferris Hanks by the arm, curled a baleful lip at Charlie, and said, "This is Candy Toy in West Hollywood, where joy and sorrow—"

Henry joined me as I followed Bo Peep and her sheep into the ballroom. "Looks okay, huh?" he asked.

"You couldn't have done better," I said. The ballroom was completely transformed. Pinlights picked out the bar and the stage, where a warm-up band called the Bottoms played slow country and western. The lead singer, a woman with a brush cut and penciled sideburns down her cheeks, was doing her third k. d. lang song in a row while people near the stage danced or just swayed back and forth, hugging. Costumed men had formed a circle around Bernadette's font, waiting patiently to anoint themselves.

Ferris's handsome Roman slaves, decked out in short white tunics with a Greek key motif and wearing brass bands on their ankles and upper arms, wove through the crowd with trays of rumaki, petit fours, and other appetizers that had apparently been on ice since the fifties and that made me wonder how long it had been since Ferris had been to a party. The door to the kitchen swung open every few seconds as a newly laden tray was borne into the room. The ballroom's primitive air conditioning was already showing signs of giving up for the evening, and the slaves were sweating with effort.

"They in for quite a night," Henry said. "You wouldn't think it, looking at all these little-bitty waists, but this crowd is murder on free food."

"I'm going to check the back," I said. Henry stayed with me as we passed the kitchen and went down the dark hallway to the exit. The door to Mickey Snell's office was open, and he was seated at his desk, blowing cigar smoke and directing a stream of squeaky chatter at one of Ferris's Roman slaves, who was spreading tan body makeup on one of the whitest legs I'd ever seen. Henry stopped halfway down the hall and took hold of a man coming out of the ladies' room.

"None of that," he said. "We got real women here."

"I am a real woman," the man said. He was dressed as Barbra Streisand, complete with three pounds of putty on his nose. "Real enough for you, any day. Who in the world is doing your hair?" Barbra made a peace offering of air kisses and swayed her way back to the ballroom while Henry fluffed up his wig.

I pushed the rear door open and came face to face with Batman. "Everything okay?" I asked.

"No problem," Batman said. "Nobody in the lot but the parking attendants. Okay if I smoke a joint?"

"Have you got marijuana in your utility belt?" Henry demanded, still working on his hair.

"You wouldn't *believe* what I've got in my utility belt," Batman said, patting a complicated system of pouches surrounding his washboard stomach. "I don't know how I'm going to get along without it. Maybe I'll keep it when I return the costume."

"No grass," Henry said sternly. "No poppers, no coke, no nothing. I'll bring you some white wine, but that's it."

"Nobody talks to Batman like that," Batman said. "Who are you supposed to be?"

"Never mind," Henry snapped. "Whoever I am, I can tell Batman to go climb a pole, and if Batman don't get his ass up that pole fast enough, then I give ol Batman a ticket home. You know what that means?"

"No money?" ventured Batman.

"You got it, Bat."

"Batman knows the value of a dollar," Batman said.

"One wine, coming up," Henry said. "You got your walkie-talkie?"

"In my utility—"

"Well, take it *out* of your utility belt, Bruce, how you gonna get to it if you need it? Geez," he said to me. "I always hated Batman. Even when I was a little kid. All you had to do was look at Robin, you knew the dude was in deep trouble."

"Get personal, why don't you," Batman said sullenly.

"I ain't even started," Henry said. "And don't trip on your cape."

"Testing, one, two—" someone squeaked over the P.A. system in the ballroom, and I went back up the hall, past Mickey Snell's office, empty now, and the rest rooms, to see what was going on.

The Bottoms were congregated at the back of the stage, unplugging their instruments and calling to friends in the crowd. Mickey Snell tapped a muscular thumb on the microphone, making a noise like someone doing a cannonball into a vat of tapioca. Someone yelled, "It's *on*, Mickey. Do something about the *air*."

"Testing," Mickey Snell said implacably. "This little piggy went to market—"

Two of the Seven Dwarfs, complete with little peaked cap and granny glasses, were patrolling the catwalks, looking down on the crowd. One of them made a thumbs-up sign at me, conveniently pointing me out to anyone who might be wondering who was in charge, and I looked behind me, pretending to think the signal was intended for somebody else. Henry was right there.

"Okay, Doc," he called. "You and Grumpy trade off with Dopey and Sleepy in half an hour."

The sun came out. Ferris, basking in a circle of light with Candy Toy, and with Charlie the cameraman limping in tow, walked past me, pausing to give a glad hand and an encouraging word to people who had no idea who he was. Toy held her microphone inches from his lips, catching every historic syllable for the benefit of the guys who would edit it out back at the station.

"When do the eulogies start?" Ferris asked me. I turned my back to Charlie's camera and brought both hands up behind me with one finger extended in an ancient insult. Charlie's lights died.

"You know damn well when they start," I said. "And keep me off camera. Where are the dog tags?"

"Right here," he said. He reached into his jacket and withdrew a long thin red velvet case, like something a bracelet might come in.

"Remember words?" I asked, pushing the case back into the recesses of his jacket. "Use them."

"Aren't we touchy," Hanks said. "Opening-night jitters," he explained to Candy Toy.

Candy Toy jumped a foot and let out a muffled little scream, and I saw the Big Bad Wolf glaring over her shoulder at me. "He *pinched* me," Candy Toy said to Charlie.

"Be glad he didn't eat you up," I said. "What is it, Wolfie?"

"In the back," Spurrier said. "Got something for you." The Big Bad Wolf's mask had lipstick all over it, and someone had stuffed his jacket pockets with flowers. Spurrier's eyes were narrow with rage.

"Don't take this wolf stuff too literally," I told him as we fought our way through the crowd. "Just remember that most of these girls aren't."

He stopped and turned, giving me a glimpse of the indignant little eyes through the slits in the rubber mask. "Getting chummy?" His fingers dug through my Donald Duck sailor shirt and found a nerve in my upper arm, and a barbed-wire worm crawled up my neck, in between layers of skin. "Don't," he said. "We're not buddies."

"Ike," I said, "how long do you usually go without someone telling you you're an asshole?"

He compressed the nerve again, and I reached out and grabbed his face through the mask, squeezing as hard as I could. The rubber mask pulled at the skin on his face, and he stepped back quickly, letting go of my arm. Tallulah Bankhead was staring at us, so I pinched the black bulbous nose of the mask and said, "Honk, honk." Tallulah laughed her famous laugh, honking back at us, and I pushed in front of Spurrier and led him to Mickey Snell's office.

"Alone at last." I closed the door, shutting out some seventies rock from the Silverlake Flyers, who had taken the microphone away from Snell by force. Spurrier pulled off the mask, showing me four angry welts on his cheeks.

"When this is over," he said, "You're going to want to move out of Topanga."

"You're not that big a deal," I said. "I know half the deputies up there, and they just want to do their jobs. You're an aberration, Ike, and good cops know it."

He planted his feet wide and brought up a hand, and for a moment I thought he was going to take a swing at me. Instead, the hand went inside his coat. "Just so you know. We're a long way from finished."

I sat in Mickey Snell's copious chair and looked down at the front of my Donald Duck suit. "Be still, my quacking heart."

"This is the guy," he said, pulling out a folded sheet of paper. He opened it and dropped it onto the desk, just out of reach. I leaned over and picked it up, removing my mask for a better view.

The kid looked no more than eighteen. He had shoulder-length blond hair, parted carelessly in the middle, and even in the fax I could see he was good-looking. Except for the length of his hair, he had the face of the soda jerk the girls mooned over in small towns in the fifties. The nose was straight and well-formed, the broad mouth was strong. The eyes were wide, friendly, and guileless.

"Darryl Wilder," Spurrier said. "Twenty-three. Ex- of Seattle. Living no one knows where for the last couple of years. McCarvey was his uncle."

So that, at least, was true. "And his victim?"

"The drunk little missus sure thinks so. Something funny there, though. She didn't want to talk about it, not even a little bit. Did a clam on me when I asked her why she thought he'd done it."

"Something sexual," I said.

Spurrier's mouth went wide and straight in distaste. "Usually is."

"Well," I said, "thanks for the information."

He picked up the paper and refolded it. "Don't get all creamy. I figure you're in charge of the Odd Squad, you oughta have it. This guy walks in here and walks out again, we're all going to look like dog food."

"There were no stats with the photo," I pointed out.

Spurrier pulled it out again and looked at it as though he hoped I was wrong. Then he went through the folding routine again. "He's a big kid. Six one or something, maybe two hundred. Lifts weights."

"Like eighty percent of the people out there," I said.

"We're looking for the hair," he said. "Real pale blond. Longer than in the picture."

I looked up at him. "How do you know that?"

"Fag bar," he said, looking satisfied. "Grover took him into a place called The Zipper. Couple of hinks saw him."

"They should really put you into community relations."

He gave me the wet smile. "Two years, I'm outta here. Got a little place up near Eureka, right on the river. No more hinks. Just fish."

I looked interested. "The *Russian* River?"

The smile faded. "Whatta you know about the Russian River?"

"Big gay destination," I lied. "The Raging Rafters, a club here in West Hollywood. They're building a chain of bed-and-breakfasts up there. Named after actors. They've already got the Rock Hudson and the Rudolf Valentino open."

He literally paled. "You're full of—"

"Next up is the Liberace," I said. "Right near Eureka."

"I'm going to kill somebody," he said.

I got off the desk and opened the door. "Stayin' Alive" pulsated down the hallway, sung in falsetto harmony. "Put on your mask, Ike," I said. "We wouldn't want anyone falling in love with you out there."

He yanked it over his head and shouldered past me. "I hope there's trouble tonight," he said.

"There won't be," I said, thinking about the writing on Max's will.

The trouble started at eight.

24
PARAGON (2)

CONSIDERING the way the evening ended, it's probably not surprising that my memories of the last hour or so are fragmented, hard-edged, and discontinuous, like an image reflected in pieces of a broken mirror.

Spurrier and I circling each other and the partygoers, Donald Duck and the Big Bad Wolf, solo and conspicuous, each of us waiting without much hope for the arrival of the third outsider, searching the crowd for the gleam of blond hair above broad shoulders. Seeing it too often, crossing that one, and then that one, off the list. Trying to keep them straight as the groups formed and broke up and reformed in the arching space of the Paragon.

A tap on the shoulder. Daisy wanted a dance with Donald.

Daisy was big enough to wear Donald around her neck. Donald declined.

Mickey Snell, hijacking the eulogies. At 7:50 he'd been planted center stage for more than fifteen minutes, clutching the mike in his left hand like a man who planned to take it with him into the next world and nattering on about Max, while people on the floor danced without music and chatted with each other.

Beyond Snell, at the back of the stage and at the edge of the light, stood Ferris Hanks in his dour black agent's suit. During Mickey's eternal speech he had gradually developed a bag of tics: fiddling with his tie, smoothing his shirt over his chest, tugging at the bottom edges of his coat, combing his hair forward with his fingers, licking his lips. Once in a while, apparently at random, he gave his odd half-smile. He was, I realized, nervous, the host who sees his long-awaited party held in thrall by a bore.

Doc and Grumpy were back on the catwalk. They'd switched shifts with Dopey and Sleepy, and returned to duty, and now they were lounging against the rail and looking as bored as dwarfs can look. There was no one in the Paragon who hadn't been stricken from the whozzat list. Spurrier had paused at the bar, where he was putting a significant dent in the white wine supply and using both elbows to support himself.

One of Spurrier's deputies was over in the corner, chatting with Tallulah Bankhead. Tallulah reached out a handkerchief and mopped perspiration from the deputy's brow.

". . . to thee, blithe spirit," Mickey Snell was saying in a high, plummy Old Vic voice, sort of John Gielgud on helium.

I was at Ferris's font, avoiding Daisy, when a wad of rumaki struck Mickey Snell in the forehead. He blinked heavily, wrapped his other hand around the microphone—enveloping it completely—dropped to one knee, and began to sing "Feelings." It occurred to me that Mickey Snell was very drunk.

Ferris Hanks had had enough. He stepped forward, waving

his hands for attention, and caught a stuffed grape leaf on his lapel. It made an interesting smear, like a snail's track, down the front of his jacket.

Suddenly Henry was on the stage. His wig had wilted. He interposed himself between the crowd and Ferris, lifted a fist, and dropped it casually onto the top of Mickey Snell's head. Mickey Snell looked up at Henry with mild curiosity and then fell forward, on top of the microphone. There was a razz of static, followed by a snap like the world's biggest rubber band giving way, and then silence. In the hum that followed, I started to work the room again.

Kitchen, full of guys in French maid's uniforms. Bathrooms, empty for once. Batman at the back door, working on another glass of wine. Me, pushing through the crowd, carrying an odd weight of despair, waiting for Darryl Wilder. The whole thing feeling dismayingly familiar, dismayingly old. Donald Duck on a quest. Not very brave and faintly ridiculous. Poking my way again into other people's lives, lives that looked—from the outside, at least—fuller and more complete than my own.

People kissing in the corner. The Supremes working on their Motown moves.

Someone staring at me. Spurrier's eyes, mad little lights through the holes in the wolf mask. I suddenly realized that Snell wasn't the only drunk at the party.

Back in the main room, Henry was still on the stage. "We're running late," he said, all business. He stepped aside and tucked the mike under his arm while he conferred with Ferris. I heard a bellow from the bar and saw Spurrier straighten galvanically, throwing off a glittering arc of white wine, and clutch his rear end. Candy Toy came toward me through the crowd, looking grimly satisfied.

The front door was still manned, although the soldiers on duty had their backs to the street and their eyes on the stage. On the sidewalk, I breathed in the cooling air and watched the traffic. People drove by on the errands that take up so much of life, unaware of Max, ignoring the fact that someone could walk into their homes with a carpet cutter and, with one short upward swipe, turn all their plans, all their errands, into a bad joke.

The parking lot was full of empty cars. It was nice to be where nothing was happening.

". . . these testimonials would have embarrassed Max," Ferris Hanks was saying when I went back in. "He would have wanted us to have a good time. I'm going to suggest that you all write out your farewells, and I'll buy a special supplement in *Nite Line* so my old friend Joel Farfman can print them, along with the pictures and stories from this party. A special supplement for Max. How does that sound?"

"Expensive," called his old friend Joel Farfman, who had an arm thrown around Tonto's shoulders.

"*Heek,*" Hanks said perfunctorily, gazing at Joel as though he were a bad oyster. "That Joel. Now, before we raffle off the evening's door prize, I'd like to turn the microphone over to Christopher Nordine, who has an announcement to make."

Zorro climbed the steps to the stage. Christopher looked great, slender and dashing in his black clothing. He was wearing a pencil-thin mustache beneath his mask, and it emphasized the strong curve of his jaw. I sagged against my post at Bernadette's font and searched the room for Spurrier. Not at the bar, which was something.

Blonde hair across the room.

"Most of you know me," Christy began. Then he stopped and looked up at the lights as though he'd lost his place. After the time it took him to draw three deep breaths he hooked his thumb under the black mask and pushed it up onto his forehead so the crowd could see his face. "You probably wonder what Max saw in me. Well, now that I've had a little time without him, a little time to think about it, so do I."

I worked my way toward the bright head of hair.

Noise from the door, a sudden loud voice.

"You're a good guy, Christy," someone called. There was a smattering of applause.

"I've been a sorry excuse for a human being," he said. "I've been a taker and a user."

"And a whiner," someone suggested, but not harshly, and Christy grinned and nodded.

The blonde hair belonged to Marilyn Monroe, in her *Seven Year Itch* white dress. I'd checked her three times already.

"And you know what?" Christy was visibly gaining confidence. "That's what Max saw in me. Room for improvement. *Miles* of room for improvement. Enough potential for improvement, considering where I started from, to make it worth his time. Max wanted to fix everybody's life."

A sudden ripple of movement from the direction of the street, jostling its way into the center of the room, and someone shouted again. I went up on tiptoe but couldn't see anything.

"Max left some money behind," Christy said, squinting through the lights toward the door. "More money than—well, enough money to fix a lot of lives. And I've figured out a way to use it that will keep Max's memory—"

A folding chair sailed over the heads of the crowd and smashed onto the floor of the stage. Christy jumped back at the same time that I jumped forward, toward the door.

I couldn't get there. People had turned their backs to the stage, trying to see what was happening, and they were being pushed backward into the room. I shoved my way through until I came up behind a kimono-clad geisha who must have weighed three hundred pounds.

"Sorry," I said. I put my hands on the small of his/her back and pushed, using her as an icebreaker, and we plowed through six or eight densely populated yards before the crowd suddenly gave way and she pitched forward, barely remaining upright, and collided with a very wide young man wearing a plaid shirt and oil-stained blue jeans who grabbed her by the shoulders, spun her around, and brutally threw her back into the crowd.

He had at least a dozen friends with him. Some of them had tire irons and some of them had baseball bats, and all of them had shaved heads and glum, glowering expressions. They were all white and all young, and all larger than I would have liked them to be, and they stood in the center of a wide circle of partygoers, scowling into the room and tapping their bats against the floor with a sound like the first drops of heavy rain.

None of them was Darryl Wilder.

The geisha had taken four people down with her when she smacked into the crowd, and as they got up I saw that one of them was the deputy who'd struck up an acquaintance with Tallulah. He stepped into the middle of the circle. His drugstore sunglasses had been knocked crooked, and he looked very young.

"You guys had better turn around and get out on the sidewalk," he said.

"Look here," said the wide one who had tossed the geisha. "It's officer Florence." He took two steps toward the deputy, who didn't move.

"I'm ordering you to disperse," the deputy began nervously, and the wide man swung his bat.

It caught the deputy on the side of the neck, and he went over like a tree, hit the crowd, and bounced back again. The bat struck him beneath the rib cage this time, folding him in half. He emitted a strangled grunt and sank to the floor.

"Home run," said one of the skinheads.

Three of them broke from the group and grabbed a nun, pulling her into the circle. Two of the three pinned the nun's arms while the third seized the cloth over her head and yanked it down, revealing a crew cut with a bald spot at the back of the head. Suddenly the nun—Sister Victima, I recalled —was a struggling middle-aged man in an absurdly ostentatious habit.

I turned to get back into the room so I could signal the Seven Dwarfs and get Spurrier's attention for his fallen deputy, but the crowd was too thick. I was pushed back into the circle, just in time to see one of the bashers, a pig-faced baldie with a Hitler mustache, bring a tire iron around with both hands against the nun's left arm. I could hear the bone break ten feet away.

"You leave that nun alone," said a familiar voice, and the tragic Supreme stepped out from the crowd, her sequins glistening in the light. "Y'all should be ashamed of yourself."

The wide man tapped his bat against the side of his leg, major-league style, and said, "Well, well. A boogie. Double points."

"Pretty little boogie, too," said the man who had swung the tire iron. He stepped up to the Supreme and put his hand flat against her crotch. "Nothin' here," he said, playing to his friends. "You cut it off?"

"Maybe she's a girl," said another, a man fat enough to sustain a tribe of cannibals through a long winter. "You a girl, sweetie?"

"You got to check that yourself," the Supreme said coyly. She hiked her dress and extended a long, shapely leg. The skinheads watched the dress inch higher. The Supreme wrapped carmine-tipped fingers around the arm of the man who had swung the tire iron and guided his free hand toward her crotch. At the last moment, she sidestepped, put a hand on his shoulder, and flipped him over her leg onto the floor.

"Motherfucker," she said, raising a high-heeled foot.

The wide skinhead lifted his baseball bat, but he hadn't gotten it any higher than his shoulder before three hundred pounds of geisha sailed into him, knocking him over the fallen deputy and into his friends. Someone shoved past me, and I saw Little Bo Peep going in low and planting a shoulder into the gut of the nearest of the intruders, who tried to back up, bumped into the man behind him, and got hoisted four feet from the floor and dropped on his back. Behind Bo Peep came her sheep, slashing at every shaved head in sight with the spike heels on his hands.

He landed one on the cheek of the pig-faced thug with the Hitler mustache, opening up a red slice from eye to chin. The wounded man stumbled back into his pals, who separated and let him fall and then converged on the attacking sheep.

They didn't get a chance to do him much harm. A nearby cowboy raised his branding iron and imprinted the old Rocking-D brand on one shaven scalp, and after him came the deluge: A gaily dressed mob of Rockettes, vampires, Roman centurions, football players, cheerleaders, vestal virgins, Boy Scouts, killer bees, multiple Carol Channings, and Liza Minnelli clones charged the intruders with a roar. The last thing I saw, as I forced my way back through the crowd, was the three-hundred-pound geisha, kimono flying, planting both heels dead center in a plaid chest.

Hanks was calling for order from the stage, patting the air soothingly above the heads of the crowd with his free hand while Henry tried to stay in front of him. I waved for Henry's attention and yelled for him to keep an eye on Christy, who was trying to climb down off the stage and get into the action. Henry reached down and scooped Christy up by the back of his shirt, like he was picking up a puppy, but Christy twisted around and knocked Henry's hand away. Henry dropped him, and Christy, Zorro's cape flying behind him, headed for the brawl.

Darryl Wilder hadn't come in the front door; if he was here, that left the back. I passed Mickey Snell's office, looked in long enough to see Mickey snoring on his desk, before I threw open the back door.

The door caught partway, and Batman looked in at me.

"Anybody come in back here?" I asked.

"Not yet," Batman said. I pushed the door further, struck an obstruction again, and looked down at a pair of bare feet. The screams behind me reached a crescendo.

"Simeon?" Batman asked.

"What is it?" I gestured at the feet. "Who's that?"

"I've got a message for you," Batman said, reaching into his utility belt and pulling out a small silver automatic. "From Max."

25
PARAGON (3)

THE gun was aimed at my abdomen, where a bullet would do harm anywhere it hit.

"You put your mask on crooked, Darryl," I said. "Your hair is showing."

Wilder reflexively put up his empty hand, stopped it at chest level, and grinned at me. His teeth were white and regular. The grin, even beneath the mask, was friendly. "Darryl?" he said. The grin got wider. "You got me confused with someone else."

"I doubt it. Mrs. McCarvey remembers you very vividly."

"Mrs. McCarvey," he said, shaking his head. "Old Auntie Sarah. She drinks, you know. Don't you think it's terrible when a woman can't control her drinking? Such a waste of potential."

"Did you kill him?" I asked, glancing down at Batman's feet.

"Not enough time," he said regretfully. "Those jugheads just couldn't wait to get inside. No finesse."

"Pleasure postponed," I said. "I guess you know all about that, Darryl."

The gun made a tiny circle. "So you know my name. So what? Names are easy. And I don't know much about pleasure of any kind. Take off your mask, and do it real slow."

I lifted my mask to the top of my head. Someone came out of the women's room behind me. I heard her sniffle as her heels clacked their way down the hallway, and then the sounds were swallowed up in a new burst of noise from the ballroom.

"Wondered what you looked like. That was cute, leaving through the window. Scared you, didn't I?"

The door opened out. There was no way I could get my hands on it and pull it closed without giving him time to perforate my insides. "You're crazy," I said. "Crazy people scare me."

"I *am* crazy," he said calmly. "It's smart of you to recognize that, Simeon. I hope you'll keep it in mind as we negotiate our way through our next fifteen minutes together. Have you got a boyfriend?"

"No," I said.

"Well, there's someone for everyone in this world, so there's certainly someone for you. Just be glad it isn't me."

Henry was up on the stage. Spurrier and his cops were probably in the middle of the fracas. The Seven Dwarfs were God only knew where. "Go away," I said. "I'll give you ten minutes to get clear."

He made a kissing noise, two times, fast. "Is that a promise? Like 'it won't hurt'? Or 'I won't come in your mouth'?" Darryl Wilder laughed. Then he stopped, like someone turning off a tap. "Back up," he said. "Just three paces. Stick your hands in the front of your pants and keep them there. Don't do anything stupid, okay? You probably won't believe this, but I'd really hate to hurt you."

I did as I was told. The pressure of my hands against my stomach was oddly comforting, as though they might slow the bullet. Wilder put his free hand against the door and pulled, shoving Batman's bare feet back across the asphalt. He stepped inside, forcing broad shoulders through the opening, and tugged the door closed. The gun was rock-steady.

"Bathrooms?" he asked, looking at the doors to my left. I nodded. "And that one?"

"Office."

"Is it empty?"

"It might as well be."

"In there, then. In a straight line, okay?" He shielded the gun under the black cape and followed me into Mickey Snell's office, closing the door behind him. It had a little latch on the inside, and he threw it into the locked position.

Snell snored stuporously on the desk. Wilder barely glanced at him. "I used to think all faggots were handsome, you know, men who took care of themselves and put a little effort into how they look. But those are just the ones you're aware of, right? The ones that put on a show. You see a fat bag of shit like this, you never think he might be a fruit."

"Was Jason McCarvey handsome?"

"Uncle Jason?" He gave it some thought, dividing his attention between me and the comatose Snell. "You know, I don't know. I grew up with the man. And he looked like my father, and I guess you never really know what your father looks like. He was a real skunk, though, Uncle Jason, I mean, although my father was no bargain either. No wonder poor Auntie Sarah drinks."

"Where'd you get the skinheads?"

"I was tagging along after Max's boyfriend when they showed up. I followed them to the jail and bailed them out. I thought it'd be fun to bring them to your party. Take all their IQs and add them up, and you've still got a centigrade temperature. Who's got my tags?"

"I don't know."

"Well, sure you do." He sat on a corner of the desk that Mickey Snell wasn't using, fished in one of the pouches of the utility belt, and extracted a package of Marlboros and a heavy military Zippo. He seemed to have all the time in the world. "Do you smoke?"

"No."

"Mind if I do?" He waited for an answer.

"Darryl," I said, "I wouldn't mind if you ate the lighter."

"I guess not." He shook a cigarette loose, placed it between his lips, and put the package back. Then he fired the Zippo and inhaled. "Uncle Jason's," he said, showing me the lighter before he dropped it into the pouch. "Who's got the tags?"

"I told you—"

He waggled the gun. "It's noisy out there. I could shoot you and no one would hear a thing, except for our fat friend here. Empty your pants pockets."

"There aren't any," I said. "Donald Duck doesn't carry stuff around."

"Donald Duck doesn't wear pants, so let's not pretend to be purists. Lift your shirt and turn around."

There didn't seem to be anything to do but obey. The air felt cold on my stomach and back.

When I was facing him again, he said, "Open the shirt at the neck. The first four buttons. Pull it open."

"You won't get out of here," I said, "unless you go out the back door now."

He put the gun against Mickey Snell's belly and pushed it in. "No one will hear a shot through all this fat," he said. "I could pull the trigger just for fun. Open the shirt, like I told you."

I showed him my neck and chest, and he sighed. "You're

making this difficult. Help the kid out, and I'll be out of here. No one will get hurt."

"Until the next time," I said.

He drummed the back of his heels against the desk, the first sign of impatience. "I'm finished. I thought there would be a mystery or something when they died, something special. I thought I would feel something. Just like I thought faggots were different. But they're not. They're just like everyone else. They live stupid, disgusting lives and they die messy. When they're dead, they're dead. Nothing to get excited about, nothing interesting there at all. Just another shitty life and a lot of blood and bones."

The noise outside was dying down. "You mean that?"

"What? That I'm finished? Sure I do. I want a life, a job, kids." He smiled at me. "I've got a girlfriend now. I can't go on with this. I get home, she asks me what I did today, and I'm supposed to say, 'I killed a queer'? I want to go back—back somewhere—and be a person." He turned his head toward the door as though he'd heard something and then brought it back around to me. "I don't want to be crazy anymore."

"And you're telling me you won't hurt anybody here if I help you get the tags."

"Nope. Honest Injun."

"I don't believe you."

"I'm surprised. People usually do. It doesn't matter, though. I could just shoot you here and go get them myself."

The thought had crossed my mind, too. "There's a room full of people in costume out there. You think I know which one's got them."

"And you're denying it. Is that smart?"

"I'm not sure who's got them," I said. "That's the truth. I know who's got the gold replicas, but I'm not sure who has the real ones."

"I used to like science in school," Darryl Wilder said, as

though we were trading youthful confidences. "Let's go out there and try a few hypotheses. We go up to likely people and you ask them for the tags. Sooner or later, one of them will give them to you, and I'm gone. Simple."

"What if somebody stumbles over Bruce Wayne back there?"

The heels again, bouncing against the side of the desk. "Then people will get hurt," he said. "The longer we sit here, the more likely that is. If I have to shoot somebody for that reason, you're going to blame yourself."

Spurrier and his cops, Henry and the Seven Dwarfs were out there. My options in here seemed to be limited to getting shot. "Let's go," I said.

"You're going to be good?"

"We'll get the tags, and then I'll walk you to the door."

"That's exactly what you'll do, or there are going to be a lot of dead drag queens at your party."

"I hear you." I went to the door and unlatched it. "I guess you want to be behind me."

"Wait," he said. "I didn't give you your message yet."

I leaned against the wall. "No. You didn't."

"Max said you should get married. That's hard to believe, one fruitcake telling another to tie the old knot, but that's what he said. It was just about the last thing he said. Said you're one of those people who need love too much to let it into their lives, whatever that means, but the time has come. God, he talked a lot."

The wall felt cool against my cheek. "Is that it?"

"No. He said the girl won't wait forever." He thumped the desk again. "That right? Is there really a girl?"

"Yes."

"And are you thinking about it? Tying the old knot?"

"I suppose so."

He laughed lightly, the laugh I'd heard when he was Ed

Pfester. "A little resistance there? Boy, do I know how you feel. I've got this weensy little problem with love, too. But I'm trying to get past it, just like you. It's a bitch, isn't it?"

"I figured you lived alone."

"Oh, I do. But it's time—you know, you can get trapped in a pattern, and you don't even know it's there. Did you ever look at your life and wonder where it came from? It's like, whoosh, suddenly there you are, and you don't even know why you're living *where* you're living. You know what I'm talking about. I can sense it."

"Don't try it, Darryl."

A beat. "Try what?"

"This is what you do, isn't it?"

"Skip it," he said harshly.

"You cozy right up to them, Young Mr. Vulnerable, with all the same problems *they* have. You're an early edition of them, aren't you? A chance to unmake the mistakes they made in their own lives."

"Let's get the hell out there," he said furiously.

"I've got to hand it to you. You're pretty good."

"The girlie," he said. "Just think about the precious little girlie. She's not going to want you to come home with your guts in your pockets." I heard him ease himself off the desk. "I'll be right next to you, close enough to pick the spot where it'll hurt longest before you die. And then, of course, a lot of other people will die, too."

"No one has to die."

"Put on your mask, Simeon. And don't tempt me."

He followed me through the door, but before he could come up beside me we practically collided with Spurrier. Spurrier had his Big Bad Wolf mask shoved back on his head and one hand over his mouth. He looked fevered and disoriented.

"Hey, Ike," I said.

Spurrier barely registered us. "Ooolp," he said, barreling

through the door to the men's room. I watched one of my hopes disappear.

"Cop?" Wilder asked. A cheer went up from the ballroom.

"Yes," I said helplessly. Spurrier vomited violently in the bathroom.

"Cops are like women. They shouldn't drink. Are all the cops dressed out of Disney?"

"No. It's a coincidence."

"How are they dressed?"

"As cops." The cheering rose and peaked. "Sounds like your friends are in trouble."

"Cretins," he said. "Keep moving."

He threw his left arm over my shoulder and we came out of the hallway and into the cavernous space of the Paragon Ballroom. Wilder stopped near Bernadette's font, and I stopped with him. Hanks, Christy, and Henry were on the stage, but the space in front of it was empty. Literally everyone else had their backs to us, focused on the doorway.

The crowd broke open, and one of the skinheads emerged, bleeding from the head and trying to break into a run. He covered less than a yard before he was tackled from behind by a guitar-toting mariachi and Joel Farfman's beefy Tonto, who dragged him back into the thick of the melee. He got kicked by a remarkable assortment of shoes before he vanished from sight.

There was nobody near us.

Wilder registered it a split second after I did and began to withdraw his arm from my shoulders, but I grabbed his wrist in both hands, pulled it down, and stuck out my hip. I lifted him from the floor as he tried frantically to free the gun from the cape, and brought him around my hip, and he was down, slamming his shoulder against the base of the font, and I raised my foot to kick his gun hand, but he rolled away from me and came up on one knee, the gun pointed at my middle again, and I stopped cold, involuntarily sucking in my midsection. I was aware of a movement on the stage behind him, and Darryl Wilder screwed up his mouth and spat at me, swiveled on his knees, raised the automatic with both hands, and shot Ferris Hanks twice.

Hanks staggered back across the stage as though he'd been kicked by a horse, blood gouting from his side and one of his thighs. He collided with the wall behind the stage and started to crumple. He hadn't even hit the floor before Henry pulled a gun from the boxy suit and emptied the chamber into Darryl Wilder, punching him back into the font, which collapsed around him with a tinkle of glass and a rush of water.

There was no miracle. Darryl Wilder died while my ears were still ringing.

26
GOOD FRIDAY

ON Friday, two days after the wake and eleven days after Max Grover was murdered, Christy flew to Boulder to take part in the farewell service Max had designed in his will. It had been delayed twice: first for the police autopsy, and then to give Max's sister a chance to regain her bearings. When she felt well enough, she called Christy personally and invited him to come.

Christy later told me that the sun had been shining when he landed in Boulder, although it was unseasonably cold. He hadn't been dressed warmly enough. He'd taken a cab to a small white clapboard house on the city's outskirts, huddling in the backseat and using the forty-minute ride to continue outlining his plans for Max's institute. Helen, Max's sister, had come to the curb to greet him. Already inside the house were four tiny women in their eighties and Max's lawyer, the same Mr. Jenks

I'd talked to on the phone. Mr. Jenks was the shortest person in the room.

There had been hot tea and home-baked seed cake and talk of Max. Tears were not encouraged. Max, in Helen's view, had been exactly who he'd wanted to be, and the service was a way for them all to pay tribute to a good man who'd managed to live a good life. When they left the house, Helen asked Christy to carry the urn containing Max's ashes. Outside, they saw that the sky had disappeared beneath a featureless ceiling of gray clouds.

With Mr. Jenks at the wheel of a van, the seven of them drove up the side of a mountain and over several miles of dirt track before stopping at a grove of trees—the property Max had left to Helen. A wind had kicked up, forcing Helen to raise her voice as she read Max's farewell. Christy wouldn't tell me what Max had written. When Helen was finished reading she took the urn from Christy and threw a handful of ashes into the air. Christy raised his eyes and saw them coming down, coming down everywhere, thick and fast and white, lost in a flurry of sudden snow.

The day that Christy was in Denver, Ferris Hanks went home from the hospital. At seven that evening I drove up Sunset Plaza Drive and through the open gate, parking Alice on the brick circular drive that arched in front of the house. I didn't ring the bell; the front door was ajar. Cold air streamed through it into the night.

Two of Ferris's Yorkies met me at the door, sniffing my ankles in a perfunctory, professional manner. The big living room was empty. I stood there for a moment, listening to nothing in particular and looking around. The people crowded into the teak carvings held their frozen dance steps. Heavy cobwebs, gray with dust, drooped above the thick open beams. I hadn't noticed them on my first visit.

To the left were two steps leading up to a dark dining room, dominated by a massive carved table at least fifteen feet long. Chairs of wood and leather were pushed back from it all along its length, as though the party had risen only moments before. I counted twenty of them. Dust coated the leather seats.

The Yorkies trotted along in front of me, anticipating my destination, as I crossed the living room and climbed the spiral stair to the second story. The stairs curved upward, hugging the walls of a circular tower, sliced by long thin windows, some of them thirty feet high. The city blinked and glittered below like broken glass.

The hallway leading to the bedrooms was arched; its white plaster walls were lighted every four or five feet by black iron sconces left over from the Spanish Inquisition. The Yorkies scampered through a partially open door, and I followed them into an enormous vault-ceilinged, white-carpeted bedroom.

"What a nice surprise," Ferris Hanks said with his back to me.

He lay on his side, dead center in the king-sized bed, facing a small black-and-white television set and surrounded by his little dogs. He looked very small. The blankets had been tented above his broken leg. The screen of the television set showed me the hall I had just come through.

"Japanese," Hanks said, still looking at the screen. "They're so clever, don't you think? That's what people say, anyway. Watch." The picture changed: the front door. Then the living room. Then the gate outside. "You didn't bring me flowers," he said, still facing the screen.

"No," I said. "I figured you might be allergic."

"You're going to have to come over here," he said. "I can't roll over without help, and Henry seems to have decided to take a turn in the evening air. Just when I wanted someone to read to me. Would you like to read to me?"

I picked up the two Yorkies and put them on the bed. The

other dogs scooted aside to make room. "I don't feel like reading," I said, "but I'll tell you a story."

"Am I going to like it?" I still hadn't come around to the side he was facing, but he made no effort to turn his head.

"You should," I said. "You wrote it."

"What's the fun in that?" he asked plaintively. "I know how it comes out."

"Well, you're going to hear it anyway," I said. "Let's start with a secondary character. Darryl Wilder was an interesting guy. He was nuts, but he was interesting. I wonder who he would have killed if his uncle hadn't put a move on him. Someone, that's for sure. Bus drivers, maybe, or Girl Scout troop leaders, or left-handed horticulturists. Somebody specific, and he would have created an elaborate, self-serving story that justified killing them, and he would have killed them ritually, the same way every time."

"I've never understood how anyone can do anything the same way every time," Hanks said. "It's so boring. So perhaps your thumbnail appraisal of what's his name isn't accurate. Perhaps he *wasn't* an interesting guy."

Hanks may have been bored, but the dogs were paying attention. Nine or ten pairs of black eyes followed my every movement. "He was careful, too. Wilder, I mean. Did his research, meticulous as a graduate student. Gay men of a certain age, successful, living in a big city but born in a small town. That was important to him—that they came from somewhere else, somewhere small, where lots of people knew them. It gave him the opportunity to take a revenge that went beyond killing them. It *had* to be important, because it was the most dangerous part of his act. He had to send the papers and the finger. Anything you mail has a postmark, or if it's Federal Express it has a waybill number. He left a description of himself every time he sent off one of his little packages."

"Compulsives," Hanks said dismissively. "I don't see how you can think he was interesting."

"It was there the whole time," I said. "From the moment Spurrier told me about Max's finger arriving in Boulder. Max didn't fit the profile. The other men were in the closet at home; that's why the packages were so destructive. But Max went out of his way to let the entire world know he was gay. He walked away from a career to do it. He walked away from *you* to do it."

"I wish I could see your face," Hanks said.

"Max never answered that ad. There were enough troubled kids on the sidewalk to keep him in the guardian angel business for the rest of his life. Max didn't even read *Nite Line*. Someone put a clipping from the paper into the pocket of one of Max's pairs of pants. He even wrote a flight number on it."

"Some people," Hanks said, "are too fucking clever for their own good."

"He didn't try to forge Max's handwriting. Just numbers, cryptic enough to make it look like Max didn't want anyone to know what they meant. But Max was a calligrapher. He wrote numbers in the old style. He crossed his sevens."

"That's not all he crossed," Hanks said.

"Darryl Wilder came to Los Angeles to kill you," I said. "You and someone else he never got around to. You're from Walpole, New Hampshire. On some bizarre level, you think you're still in the closet. You *like* the closet, Ferris. You told me so, remember?"

He tried to move, groaned, and abandoned it. "If you're going to stay over there, would you at least help me turn over? This might be a little more interesting if I could watch you as you tell it."

"Watch your TV. You're never going to walk through your house again, so you might as well take a final look."

"And I'm *not* allergic to flowers," he said.

"He read about you somewhere, or heard about you. You represented a new phase in his career. Somebody famous, a trophy kill. He probably came up to the gate one night—I'm sure you don't answer ads in *Nite Line* any more than Max did—and he probably told you he wanted to be an actor. Henry said that still happens from time to time. He hadn't counted on Henry, though. After a few days he made his move, and Henry stopped him. Is that right?"

"It seems I was wrong," Ferris said. "I don't know how this comes out."

"When Henry had taken care of Wilder, tied him up and stuffed him in a cupboard or one of your dungeons or something, you began to think about putting together a deal. That's what you do, remember? Henry said it best: 'Agents don't do anything. They get other people to do things. They're not actors, they're not writers, they're not killers. Other people do the work.' "

"Henry said that?" He sounded hurt.

"Henry persuaded Wilder to tell the two of you what he was up to. Henry can be very persuasive. So you proposed a three-point deal. Point one. You didn't call the police. Point two. You told Wilder about Max, probably making him out to be what he looked like from the outside, an old man who preyed on helpless young ones. Point three. You offered him something—money, or a movie career—to do his act on Max. A man even more famous than you are."

"Just to keep you talking until Henry gets back," Hanks said, "let's say I promised him fifty thousand dollars. Could I have a drink of water?"

"So he placed the ad in the paper, just like he always did —you probably wrote it, even though you knew Max would never see it—and you told him where he'd be likely to meet Max. And Darryl took it from there. He put the ad in Max's pocket—he *wanted* the credit for the kill—he used Max's computer to write some letters I found on a computer bulletin board, he even wrote letters to Max, which Max never read. You probably wrote the letters from Max, too."

"Your characters aren't consistent," Hanks said. "If Darryl was a compulsive, he would have to do things his way. The way he always did them. The act of writing to Max would have been important to him. That's the way he did it before, right? So let's say I arranged a meeting—just talking story here—and Darryl sort of got things going and then told Max he had to go back to, I think it was Nebraska, and he set himself up somewhere in L.A. and started writing letters to Max and sending them to a post office box for forwarding. And Max wrote back out of the inexhaustible goodness of his heart, asking Darryl to come back to Los Angeles so Max could help him do whatever Max thought he could help him do. If you really want me as the heavy, though, I might have drafted a few points for *Darryl's* letters. Setting the bait, you might say."

"And Max took the bait, and Darryl killed him, and—and what? You decided not to pay him?"

"If I'd offered him fifty thousand dollars," Hanks said, "I might have rethought it. That's a lot of money to pay someone who's doing something he enjoys."

"You're used to dealing with actors."

"If you're suggesting that I usually do business with people who don't kill for their jollies, I'll concede that."

"You thought you could get away with it. You must have figured he'd just disappear. After all, you had Henry to protect you, and you could put Darryl in jail. Or worse."

He didn't say anything. He seemed glued to the screen of the TV, but I could sense him straining to listen.

"But you didn't know about the dog tags. You didn't know he couldn't leave without them. All you knew was that he was still here, still in Los Angeles, and that made you nervous. Did he phone you?"

A deep sigh. "It's your story."

"Let's say you got nervous enough to decide to pay him. And when you found out about the tags, you decided you'd give them to him. At the wake. And all the time, you were acting like Max's misunderstood friend, paying for his farewell party."

He lifted a hand above the covers. "I said I'd pay for the wake before I learned anything about the tags."

"Hell, Ferris, the wake was a chance to pay Darryl anyway, if he showed up. Or kill him. Have Henry kill him, I mean. You tried that once, didn't you? Henry had orders to go into that apartment ahead of me. If he'd killed Wilder, would you have gone through with the wake? Or would you have begged off, saved a little money?"

"That's a low blow."

"I couldn't aim low enough to hit you."

The Yorkies were sensing Hanks's agitation now, getting up and changing their positions on the bed. One of them jumped down, raised a leg, and started licking itself nervously.

"Stop that, Dolly," Hanks commanded. "It's disgusting." He turned his neck, allowing me a view of his battered profile. His face was an unhealthy yellow, made more livid by the dark circles incised beneath his eyes. "And if I had done any of this feverish nonsense, *why* would I have done it? What did I have to gain? Have you taken it that far?"

Something moved behind me in the hallway. I kept my eyes on Hanks's face. "Max left you. Max was the only person who ever left you. You tried to destroy him in the press when he quit the show. Then, after years without contact, you started trying to reach him. Maybe you had a fantasy of forgiving him. You have to have a lot of power over someone to forgive them. And he stiffed you. No response. No power, Ferris. After all those years of waiting, after all you'd done for him, after you condescended to fall in love with him, you couldn't get Max Grover to pick up a telephone."

"You think this was about power?" His position had to be uncomfortable, but he held it, the muscular neck rigid with effort.

"I think *you're* about power, Ferris. I think it's what keeps your heart beating. Orchestra conductors live to be older than anyone. They say it's all that arm waving, but I think it's the naked exercise of power."

"Wait a minute." His broad mouth stretched into a taut straight line and he closed his eyes, and moved beneath the blankets. The mouth opened just wide enough to emit a moan. Veins popped into relief beneath the yellowish skin, and then his upper lip lifted in a grimace, revealing his teeth, and I saw why he'd perfected the half-smile. His teeth were as false as George Washington's. When he let his head fall back on the pillow, he was lying on his back. He opened his eyes and aimed them at me, as flat and opaque as buttons.

"Max sentenced me to death," he said. His forehead and upper lip gleamed with sweat. Behind him, on the television screen, someone moved in the hallway outside the door. "After Max, there was nobody else for me. For years I lived with it. I had no choice, so it became one of the things I had to learn to live with. One of many. You have no idea, at your age, some of the things we have to live with."

"Who's 'we'?"

"People," he snapped. "Men and women. Every year you learn to live with something else, some failing or limit- ation, some sickness, some sin. They hang around your neck like chains, like weights. But you go on. If you're strong, you go on."

He tried to shift his position slightly, displaying the plastic teeth again, and his head twisted impatiently, trying to pull his weakened body with it. He gave up and looked at me out of the corners of the long eyes. "It's bearable to be alone when you're young," he said. "When you're old, it's death. No one should be alone when he's old. Max *wouldn't return my calls.* I gave up. I'm old. I'm sick. I was ready to die. The chains were too heavy for me to carry any more. Then Darryl Wilder came through my gate."

"Killing Max kept you alive?"

"You can never question what keeps someone alive. You'll find that out sooner or later."

"It would have been better if you'd died," I said.

He gave me the familiar half smile. "As I'm sure you'll allow, that's a matter of perspective."

"They probably won't kill you for this," I said. "Not at your age."

"*Heek heek.* Excuse me for laughing in your face, but with your face, you're probably used to it. *Heek heek.* We've just been talking, that's all. You've been entertaining a sick man. You told me a story and I improvised a coda for it. It was a good story, too, except for the letters. But you can't prove anything, not anything at all."

"No," I said. "But he can."

I stepped aside and Henry came through the door.

Hanks's eyes widened briefly and then narrowed again. "Where have you been?"

"You sposed to say, '*Et tu, Brute,*'" Henry said.

Hanks lifted his head an imperious two inches. "Get rid of this man."

"No way, Ferris," Henry said. "I cut a deal."

"You ignorant jungle bunny," Hanks said. "No one can prove—"

"Maybe, maybe not. If they couldn't, I made a mistake. If they could, though, I got to think about old Henry."

"What about me?" Hanks demanded. "What about loyalty?"

"I don't know how to tell you this, Ferris," Henry said, "but you don't inspire much loyalty."

"I'll leave you two to chat," I said.

"What Henry tells them isn't worth anything," Hanks said to me, raising his voice. "He's trying to protect himself. No jury will believe him."

"You could be right," I said. "They'll believe you, though.

I'm wired, Ferris. Every word we said was recorded in a Sheriffs' van parked in the street. They'll be up any minute now. Oh, and let me give you a tip. The one with the awful sport coat is named Ike Spurrier. I wouldn't get too cute with him. Bye, Henry."

I passed Spurrier and three deputies in the living room. It seemed like a lot of force for one old man with two bullet holes in him. Spurrier brushed past me as though the room were too small for the two of us, which I suppose it was.

Sitting in the car, I lifted my arms to the steering wheel. They weighed eighty pounds apiece, and I let them drop to my lap. *Getting old,* I thought. Too old for the likes of Ferris Hanks, anyway.

Two more deputies came through the gate, toting a stretcher between them. I didn't want to see any more. I started Alice and turned her around, and the two of us put-putted down Sunset Plaza to Sunset and headed toward the Pacific. Alice wasn't young any more, either.

At the Pacific Coast Highway I sat at the light and looked out at the flat black expanse of the sea. When the person behind me hit his horn I turned right, to the north, toward home. Toward my house and my view and my life. Toward everything I'd built for myself, intentionally and accidentally. I'd built it the way some mollusks build their shells, picking up pieces of debris here and there on the seafloor, and fitting them together to create a suit of armor that's too rigid to be crushed, too spiky to be swallowed, and virtually impossible to shed. Collector shells, they're called. Some of them are beautiful.

At Topanga Canyon I pulled over to the side of the road and waited until the traffic had passed so I could make the U-turn that would take me south. Toward Eleanor. Maybe she'd let me in.